THE TIES THAT BIND

THE TIES THAT BIND

Anthea Fraser

**SEVERN
HOUSE**

First world edition published in Great Britain and the USA in 2021
by Severn House, an imprint of Canongate Books Ltd,
14 High Street, Edinburgh EH1 1TE.

Trade paperback edition first published in Great Britain and the USA in 2022
by Severn House, an imprint of Canongate Books Ltd.

severnhouse.com

British Library Cataloguing-in-Publication Data
A CIP catalogue record for this title is available from the British Library.

ISBN-13: 978-0-7278-5058-4 (cased)
ISBN-13: 978-1-78029-794-1 (trade paper)
ISBN-13: 978-1-4483-0533-9 (e-book)

All Severn House titles are printed on acid-free paper.

MIX
Paper from
responsible sources
FSC® C013056

Typeset by Palimpsest Book Production Ltd.,
Falkirk, Stirlingshire, Scotland.
Printed and bound in Great Britain by
TJ Books, Padstow, Cornwall.

CHARACTER LIST

Rose Linscott
Fleur Tempest, her daughter
Owen Tempest, Fleur's husband
Jess Tempest, their daughter
Cassie Tempest, their daughter
Verity Tempest, their daughter

Justin Linscott, Rose's son
Kathryn Linscott, his wife
Patrick Linscott, their son
Amy Linscott, their daughter

Henry Parsons, Rose's friend
Hilary Grant, Justin's girlfriend
Dr Roger Price, Jess's ex-boyfriend
Tasha Crombie, Patrick's girlfriend
Rachel Firth, Jess's friend

Jenny Barlow, a family friend
Ron Barlow, her husband
Freddie Barlow, their son
Gemma Barlow, their daughter

Tony and Lynn Dawson, Cassie's godparents
Sue (Cassie's godmother) and David Davenport
Stephen (Cassie's godfather) and Holly Penrose

Maggie Haig, Jess's flatmate
Maggie's friends: Sarah, Di, Dominic, Connor and Laurence

ONE

Having removed dead blooms from the flower vase, Rose Linscott paused, as she often did, to glance through the window at her back garden and, beyond it, the roof of her previous home. It had been a wise decision, she reflected, turning it over to Fleur and Owen. Until three years ago they'd been living in Kent and she'd regretted missing the major part of her granddaughters' childhoods. The eldest, Jessica, had already been in her late teens and Verity, the youngest, approaching hers.

Then, to her delighted surprise, Owen was appointed Deputy Head at St Catherine's College, and they were faced with finding a home in this area. She had rattled around in her house since Malcolm's death, so the obvious solution was to hand it over to them and find somewhere smaller for herself close by. Sandstone was always meant to be a family home and they'd been extremely grateful, both for the offer of the house and for the generously low price she'd asked for it. St Catherine's-on-Sea was an expensive place to live.

Admittedly, it had not been her intention to be *quite* so close; she'd been looking at property a little farther down the coast when this bungalow in the next road came on the market, its garden actually backing on to hers, and she'd been unable to resist. Ironically, the houses themselves were screened from each other by a stand of tall evergreens that Malcolm had planted years ago to safeguard their privacy. It had been Fleur who'd suggested inserting a gate between the two gardens, ensuring that it was high enough to retain that privacy and with a bolt on Rose's side. Though grateful for the thought, she'd elected not to use it till physically incapable of making her way by road – though she might claim the odd dispensation, such as for this evening. The longer route would prove challenging in her new shoes, and she was determined to wear them to Cassandra's eighteenth. Justin and his family were coming up from Taunton and Jessica would be back from Bristol, where, partly to escape the attentions of an ex-suitor, she'd moved two months ago. It would be good to have the whole family together, a rare enough occasion these days. And, of course – sting in the tail – Jenny Barlow and her husband would be there.

Rose clicked her tongue, abandoned her musings and carried the watering can back to the kitchen. Enough of this wool-gathering; she must wrap her present and check all the creases had dropped out of her new dress.

Jess Tempest walked rapidly over the sand, its ridges digging unnoticed into her bare feet as her mind skittered helplessly in search of a solution. What should she *do*? she asked herself for the hundredth time. Oh God, what *could* she do, without – incredible thought – putting herself in danger? *Why* had she gone back to the flat after work? Might someone have seen her, or were they confident she had, as expected, already left for home?

The obvious course was to phone the police, but what could she tell them? The entire incident seemed ludicrous even to herself, and any evidence that might have supported her story had been removed with startling efficiency. What was more, if by any remote chance the police did decide to investigate, it would be obvious to those involved who must have blown the whistle.

She came to a halt, gazing over the receding water, her sandals dangling from her hand. As always there was a strong breeze down here, lifting her hair and winding her thin skirt round her legs. She'd always loved this place, looking forward all year to summer holidays spent with her grandparents, and had been overjoyed when Dad's appoint-ment to the college led to their moving here. It had made her Bristol decision a difficult one, but the combination of eliminating the daily commute – which would be perilous in winter fogs – and removing herself from Roger's impor-tunities had won the day.

Even before today's horror, though, she'd been having

second thoughts about her living arrangements: Maggie wasn't the easiest of flatmates and her lifestyle was very different from Jess's own. She'd been looking on this weekend and the holiday that was to follow as a welcome break, possibly an opportunity to rethink her position, but now everything would be overshadowed by this gnawing fear. *Why* had she gone back? What did it matter if she'd forgotten her paperback? She could have bought another, for heaven's sake, and spared herself this agonizing predicament.

She drew a deep breath, thankful that at least she wouldn't be returning to Bristol for another two weeks. Tomorrow she and her friend Rachel were flying to Italy for a long-anticipated holiday and she'd have to rely on her news app to learn of any developments. Should anything emerge, it might at least indicate what, if any, action she should take.

Somewhere in the town a church clock chimed five. They'd be wondering where she was, and she still had to wash her hair before the party. No nearer a solution to her worries, Jess set off for home.

It was a warm June evening and the French windows were open to the garden, where most of the guests had drifted, glasses in hand, to stand in small groups exchanging news. Cassie, the centre of attention, looked lovely, Jenny Barlow thought fondly. Her dark hair was caught up on top of her head, pinned in place by a pink rose that, by either luck or design, exactly matched the fabric of her dress, and her cheeks were flushed with excitement. Eighteen! Jenny marvelled. Where had all those years gone?

She turned to share the thought with Ron but he'd disappeared, doubtless to refresh his drink, and, temporarily alone, she realized with a mild feeling of panic that apart from the Tempest family the only people she knew here were Lynn and Tony, whom at the moment she couldn't see and who anyway, as Cassie's godparents, were in a semi-official capacity. She had, of course, been introduced to everyone on arrival, but now couldn't put a name to any of them. She should have paid more attention but she'd been too flustered. Was that tall, thin woman Fleur's sister-in-law from Taunton or Cassie's other godmother, whom she'd not seen since the christening and who'd apparently been Fleur's bridesmaid? She recalled that for some reason Cassie also had two godfathers, so one of the men by the pond might be the other. But who was the young couple talking to Verity? Someone's offspring?

Everyone except herself, it seemed, was engaged in conversation, and her sudden dread of being conspicuous triggered one of her wretched flushes, which began to scald her neck and creep up her face. Oh God, where was Ron? Why didn't he come and rescue her?

Deliverance, however, arrived from another quarter. 'Can I top you up, Auntie Jen?'

She turned gratefully to see Jess beside her, a jug of Pimm's in her hand, and hastily recovered herself. 'Thanks, love.' She held out her glass and the evening sun struck prisms in the crystal. 'I hear you've flown the coop,' she went on, making an effort to appear at ease. 'I don't know Bristol; is it a good place to live?'

Jess's hand jerked, splashing some liquid on her dress, but, brushing aside Jenny's murmur of concern, she answered quickly, 'It is, yes, and much more convenient for work.' She smiled. 'And after being away at uni, it seemed odd to be living at home again.'

'I suppose it must have. Are you sharing?'

'Yes, with another girl.'

'A friend?'

'No, I just answered an ad in the paper. It's in a nice part of town and we get along OK.'

It didn't sound a ringing endorsement, but before Jenny could question her further Jess had moved on to refresh someone else's glass and a moment later her husband materialized at her side.

'Think we'll be eating soon?' he asked in a low voice. 'I'm famished!'

As if in answer, Fleur appeared in the doorway behind them and clapped her hands. 'Supper's ready in the dining room, if you'd like to come through and help yourselves.'

'A buffet!' Ron Barlow said disgustedly. 'Fine for people with six hands!'

Jenny laughed, and, confidence restored, tucked her hand under his arm as they followed the others inside.

The evening seemed to be going well, Owen Tempest thought with satisfaction as he retrieved the bottles of champagne from the fridge. This was in fact the first of two celebrations, for family, godparents and a few close friends. Tomorrow there'd be a disco for Cassie's contemporaries, a much less civilized affair, he suspected, to be held at the tennis club. No doubt it would provide a welcome break from the gruelling round of A-levels. The summer term was always fraught, since exams unfailingly coincided with attacks of hay fever, as well as any hot weather they were to be blessed with that year. And this was one of the hot ones.

Fleur came into the kitchen as he removed the last bottle. 'I was about to take the cake through, but should they have the champagne first?'

'We'll synchronize. Is Tony ready with his speech?'

'I hope so. Lynn said he hardly slept last night!'

'As a barrister he should be used to public speaking.' The Dawsons had been their next-door neighbours in Bromley and, though several years older than themselves, had become close friends. With no children of their own, they'd been delighted when asked to be Cassie's godparents.

Fleur was silent as she watched her husband fill the flutes lined up on a tray. 'Ma thinks Jess is looking pale,' she observed then.

Owen bit back a retort. The one downside of his appointment at St Cat's was that they'd moved into what he wryly thought of as his mother-in-law's territory, open to her frequently expressed and often unwelcome opinions. Yet, he upbraided himself, she'd been more than generous in housing them.

'Well, the Italian sun will soon cure that,' he replied, deliberately taking the remark at face value.

'Perhaps she's having second thoughts about splitting with Roger,' Fleur mused. 'They'd been together a long time.'

'And outgrown each other,' Owen replied briskly. 'Now, if you're ready with the cake, darling, we can make our joint entrance.'

'How's my favourite cousin?' Patrick Linscott enquired, carefully balancing the cake on his plate as he seated himself beside Jess on the staircase.

'Hi, Patrick.'

'I hear you've given that handsome young doctor his marching orders and left home?'

'True on both counts but not, as you imply, cause and effect.'

Patrick raised a sceptical eyebrow. 'Really?'

'Well, not entirely,' Jess conceded. 'Roger *was* being a bit of a pain, but, let's face it, I'm too old to be living at home like a schoolgirl. It was time I spread my wings.'

'And are you enjoying your independence?' He took a bite of cake, clearly expecting an affirmative, and turned to look at her when it didn't immediately come. Jess was staring reflectively into her wine glass. She and Patrick had always been close, exchanging childhood then teenage confidences, and she regarded him as the brother she'd never had. This was neither the time nor the place, but . . .

'Well?' he prompted. 'Not having second thoughts already?'

She straightened her shoulders and turned to face him. 'Patrick, suppose someone happened to see something they weren't supposed to, something really worrying, but which could have serious repercussions if they reported it. What should they do?'

'I trust this question is hypothetical?'

'Of course,' she answered steadily, holding his gaze.

'Can you be a bit more specific about the something worrying?'

She hesitated, her mouth suddenly dry. 'Involving someone . . . dying.'

'Whoa!' His teasing smile vanished and he reached for her hand. 'Jessie, what is this? You don't . . .?'

'Jess!' a voice called. 'Patrick! Where are you? Time for the family photo!'

Jess quickly freed her hand and stood up. 'Our presence is required,' she said, and ran down the remaining stairs and into the sitting room. Patrick sat staring after her for a moment before slowly coming to his feet and following her.

Ron Barlow glanced sideways at his wife as they joined the coast road.

'Well, that wasn't too bad, was it?'

Jenny smiled ruefully. 'Bad enough! Danielle in the lions' den!'

'Oh, come on! Granted it was a challenge having to face them en masse, but Fleur was fine this evening, wasn't she?'

'She tried, I'll grant her that, and it helped having Tony and Lynn there, but Mrs Linscott barely acknowledged me, the old battleaxe!'

'Then let her stew!' He drew a deep breath. 'And now we can put it behind us and enjoy the rest of our holiday, which we're both in need of.'

Since the Tempest family moved to Somerset three years ago, Jenny and Ron had spent their summer holidays at a resort just along the coast and had usually managed to see the family two or three times during their visit. Jenny still lamented the move; when they'd all lived in Bromley it had been easy to arrange seemingly accidental meetings, and the change in holiday plans had given rise to comments from their own children. It was many years since Freddie and Gemma had been on family holidays, but they still seemed to resent what they referred to as their parents' 'annual pilgrimage' to see the Tempests.

'It's not as if Fleur and Owen were close friends,' Gemma had flung at her. 'It's the girls you're so hell-bent on seeing, isn't it? Why, for God's sake? Aren't we enough for you?' The query had lodged in Jenny's memory, an ever-present hurt, and despite her guilty protestations the exchange hadn't improved her always difficult relationship with her daughter. But nor had it stopped the Somerset 'pilgrimage'.

'Love?' Ron broke into her musings. 'Snap out of it, OK? Granted Jess will be in Italy, but we might be able to fix something with Cassie and Verity.'

Jenny, her eyes suddenly wet, laid a hand over his on the steering wheel. 'You're very good to me,' she said humbly.

It was over. The guests had gone, the house was more or less restored to normal, and the girls had retired to their rooms to be reunited with their iPhones. Alone for the first time in hours, Fleur was suddenly swamped by the fear she'd kept buried, and immediately ruthlessly repressed it. She would *not* think about this now, nor would she say anything to Owen. Not tonight. If they started to discuss it, she'd have no chance of sleep.

Holding her mind in abeyance, she took a last look round the sitting room, retrieving a glass that had been half hidden by a chair. Lipstick round the rim, she noted, carrying it through to the kitchen. Who'd been sitting there? Oh yes, Holly, Stephen's new wife. She'd been a surprise, being considerably younger than he was. Fleur had barely spoken to her during the evening – or, in fact, to anyone at any length. Which was why, knowing this would be the case, Owen had suggested that any godparents staying on for the weekend should meet them for dinner tomorrow evening. Sadly, Sue and David had to return home for a family wedding, but the others had readily agreed.

Rinsing the glass under the tap, she recalled Owen's reaction to the news that his friend had remarried. 'Well, there's a turn-up for the books!' he'd commented. 'I just called Stephen to invite them to the party, only to be told he and Sally divorced last year, he's now married to someone else and his kids won't speak to him!'

'I don't blame them!' she'd replied. 'He didn't waste much time!'

'Exactly. Probably been a bit of nooky going on for a while.' Owen gave a short laugh. 'I must say I never thought old Stephen had it in him!'

'So is he bringing the new wife?'

'Yep. Pity, though; I liked Sally – she was at uni with us and they got married while we were still there. This new one's bound to feel out of her depth, not knowing anyone.'

'Not really; none of the couples know each other well, except the Dawsons and Barlows. She'll be fine.'

And the evening did seem to have gone well, Fleur, holding on to this distraction, reflected now. Even the usual awkwardness with Jenny had been glossed over. Cassie had looked gorgeous, Verity had for once refrained from taking centre stage, and Jess . . . After her mother's vaguely unsettling comment Fleur had studied her eldest daughter more closely, noting that she was indeed paler than usual, even slightly on edge. Still, Owen was probably right and she was just in need of a holiday.

The sound of the front door diverted her musings, signalling his return from escorting Rose home.

'Mamma safely delivered,' he reported. 'And before you ask, yes, I waited until the front door had closed behind her.'

'Thanks, darling. She seemed to enjoy herself.'

'And no doubt she'll enjoy even more reporting back to Henry, adding the odd cryptic comment.' Henry Parsons, an elderly widower, was Rose's friend and admirer, a fact that gave rise to scurrilous speculation among her granddaughters. 'Ready for a nightcap, now we can both relax?'

'That would be lovely,' she said gratefully, 'but first, I could do with a hug!'

'Happy to oblige!' he said, and as his arms came round her she held on to him, eyes tightly shut. Please God, she prayed incoherently, let everything be all right.

Upstairs, Verity, at fifteen the youngest of the sisters, lay on her bed next to the cat, who'd taken refuge there during the party, and switched on her phone.

'Hi!' she said. 'Peace at last!'

'Was it as bad as expected, or did you actually enjoy it?'

'What do you think? Cassie prancing around looking pleased with herself, and a houseful of relatives! To crown it all my aunt actually told me I'd grown! How old must you be before they stop saying that? God knows why I had to be there anyway – no one took much notice of me and it was only the thought of tomorrow that kept me going.'

The cat nudged her hand and she automatically began to stroke him.

'Well, the good news is that Paul's dad will let him have the car.'

'Oh, that's great, Lizzie! So we can try that new place in Weston!'

'Possibly not,' Lizzie cautioned. 'Matt says they're very hot on checking ages, but there's plenty of other places. Unless, of course' – a teasing note came into her voice – 'you'd rather change your mind and join Cassie at the tennis club?'

'You have to be joking! So what time are we meeting?'

'Well, since it's Saturday we were thinking of making a day of it – taking a picnic lunch to the beach and going on somewhere later.'

'Fab! Everyone here has something on – Mum and Dad are out for dinner and Jess is off to Italy. Have you spoken to Penny and Si?'

'Yes, they're up for it, and we can just about fit six in the car. Call for you about eleven? The boys are bringing cans of Coke, I'm taking sausages and Penny's providing sandwiches. Could you supply something?'

'No prob. I'll have a choice of leftovers from tonight. See you later.'

Verity clicked off her phone, scooped up the protesting cat and, opening her bedroom door, deposited him on the landing. 'Time for your evening prowl, Minty,' she said, ignoring his reproachful look as she closed the door and, in a much better frame of mind, went back to bed.

On his drive home Patrick's conversation with Jess on the staircase kept repeating itself in his head and he grew progressively more anxious. *Involving someone dying*, she'd said. And *serious repercussions*. What the hell had she meant? He'd known damn well the question wasn't hypothetical. What had she got herself mixed up in?

He'd made several attempts to speak to her during the remainder of the evening, but she'd adroitly managed to avoid him. Probably regretted mentioning it now, but he couldn't let it go. As a last resort he'd sent her a text as he was about to drive home, asking her to call him; she would, he knew, check her phone as soon as she was alone. He switched to hands-free and throughout the journey waited impatiently for her call, but his phone remained silent. And, he remembered with frustration, she was going on holiday first thing in the morning.

Then, as if that wasn't enough, there was Amy. She'd wanted a word with him about the parents, but the opportunity hadn't arisen. She'd looked worried, though, and he wondered fleetingly if whatever it was might explain why the old man had been a bit fractious in the office lately. God! he thought with a touch of grim humour; he could do with going off to Italy himself!

Unable to afford town prices when he bought his flat five years ago, Patrick had opted for a small development on the fringes of town. Several old houses had been converted into apartments and he'd been lucky enough to acquire the first floor of one of them, affording him larger rooms than modern houses could offer and a pleasant open outlook over a park. Furthermore it was only a ten-minute drive to the solicitors' office where both he and his father worked.

Caught up as he was with family concerns, it was with a sense of shock that, having run up the stairs to the flat, he saw a strip of light under his door. Tasha? he wondered with mounting excitement, and as he inserted his key and the door swung open, he was met with the unmistakable breath of her perfume.

'So you decided to come home after all!' she greeted him as he appeared in the sitting room doorway. 'I was going to give you till midnight, then call it a day and go home.' The clock on the mantel showed just after eleven thirty.

She was curled up on the sofa, a glass of what looked like brandy in her hand, and he went quickly to kiss her. 'What a pleasant surprise! Why didn't you let me know you were coming?'

'It was a spur of the moment thing. I was driving home, I was tired, and suddenly Exeter seemed a long way away. So I decided to break my journey.'

He smiled. 'Nothing to do with wanting to see me, then?'

'That was an added incentive,' she acknowledged.

'Can you stay for the weekend?'

'Provided I can make use of your washing machine; I've

been away three days. But where have you been till this hour on a Friday evening? Should I be jealous?'

'If only! But no, it was a family do up at St Cat's. A cousin's eighteenth.' He was pouring a drink for himself. 'Believe me, I need this! With the drive home ahead of me, I had to limit my alcoholic intake.'

He sat down beside her, marvelling as he always did at his luck, even though, to his chagrin, he could lay no claim to her. For Natasha Crombie was in a class of her own – high-powered, intelligent and very much her own woman. An Australian by birth, she worked for an international firm based in Exeter, and her proficiency in languages ensured that she spent at least half her life abroad.

Described by acquaintances as striking, her nose being too thin and her mouth too full for beauty, she had nonetheless an arresting quality about her that invariably made passing strangers afford her a second, almost startled, glance. Just below six foot, she had a mane of copper-red hair that she wore up for work and clear, slate-grey eyes that steadily held those of anyone to whom she was speaking – a habit many people, unaccustomed to such directness, found unnerving.

And Patrick Linscott, over whom girls had fought since he was sixteen, had fallen helplessly, totally and irrevocably in love with her, though he'd the sense not to let her see it.

'And what about you?' he asked, sipping his drink. 'Where have you been this time?'

She shrugged. 'Around the UK, mostly to places that aren't near airports, hence the car.'

'So you won't be dreaming in Spanish or Danish tonight?'

She laughed. 'Not tonight, no.' She bent forward, put her empty glass on the coffee table and, turning towards him, traced the line of his jaw with one finger. 'And talking of tonight . . .' she said softly.

Abandoning his own drink, Patrick pulled her into his arms. 'God, Tasha,' he said indistinctly, and at her instant and passionate response, all thoughts of Jess and Amy dissolved like mist in the noonday sun.

TWO

'I thought the others might have been staying here too,' Lynn Dawson remarked. She and Tony were breakfasting in the sunlit dining room of the Grange Hotel.

'Well, we knew Jenny and Ron wouldn't be,' Tony replied, reaching for the marmalade. 'They go to the same B&B every year. As for the rest, with so many hotels to choose from, it would be more of a wonder if they were.'

Lynn nodded absently. 'Incredible to think Cassie's eighteen. I've always felt responsible, you know, but it turned out for the best, didn't it?'

'Of course it did, love.' There was an uncomfortable pause, then Tony went on quickly, 'What did you think of our fellow godparents?'

Lynn sighed, allowing herself to be diverted. 'I liked David and Sue; it's a pity they won't be joining us this evening. A family wedding or something. I gather she was Fleur's bridesmaid. I never got round to speaking to the other godfather. What was his name?'

Tony grinned. 'The cradle-snatcher? Stephen. Nice chap, actually. He told me he and Owen were at university together.' He glanced at his wife's still pensive face. 'Well,' he said bracingly, 'if you've finished, let's go out and explore! On previous visits we've always been with the Tempests, but today we can just be a couple of tourists!'

Lynn laughed. 'Sit on the pier and eat ice cream?'

'That too, but there's a lot more to the town. I was looking at some of the brochures in the foyer.' He pulled a brightly coloured leaflet from his pocket. 'They have a heritage museum and art gallery for starters, and a leisure complex containing a three-screen cinema, library and theatre. And there's also a landscaped park in the centre of town that might be worth a look; it has a stream running through it and, believe it or not, a bandstand, where a brass band plays on Sundays during the season.'

Lynn laughed. 'They should co-opt you on to their tourist board!'

Tony ignored her. 'Added to which they've won several awards for the cleanest beach and the best kept promenade gardens.'

'If we took in all that, we'd be exhausted by the end of the day!' She flicked a glance at him. 'I note you omitted to mention the attractions of the smart shopping centre that contains several designer shops!'

Tony smiled. 'Plenty of shops in Bromley. We're at the seaside – let's make the most of it!'

The persistent ringing of his mobile eventually dragged Patrick from the depths of a heavy sleep and he fumbled blindly to retrieve it.

'At last!' said his sister's voice crossly. 'Where on earth were you? Down a coal mine?'

'In bed, as it happens,' he muttered.

'Patrick, it's ten o'clock!'

Beside him Tasha murmured a sleepy protest and pulled the pillow over her head.

'So what? It's the weekend, isn't it?'

'Well, are you *compos mentis* enough to have a lucid conversation? I wanted to speak to you last night but you were pretty elusive.'

He sighed, ran a hand over his face and dragged himself into a sitting position 'All right,' he said. 'Let's have it: what's wrong?'

'The parents, that's what!'

Patrick frowned as his mind began to clear. 'What about them?'

'They've hardly a civil word to say to each other at the moment. And – and Dad's moved into the guest room.'

'Oh God!' He came fully awake, and at his change of tone Tasha removed the pillow and looked at him questioningly. 'That sounds serious.'

'That's what I'm trying to tell you. I'm really worried, Patrick.'

'How long has this been going on?'

'I've no idea. They seemed OK when I was home at Easter.'

'Have they said anything? I mean, how did they explain being in separate bedrooms?'

Beside him, Tasha gave a low whistle.

'They didn't, and it wasn't something I could casually bring up. I did ask Mum jokingly if Dad's snoring had got worse, but she just gave a tight-lipped smile and changed the subject.'

Patrick said slowly, 'He's been pretty shirty at work lately, snapping everyone's head off. It's not like him, but it's happened before when a client was being difficult, so I assumed it was work-related.'

'When did that start?'

'Oh, it's been going on for a week or two. I asked if there was anything I could help him with, but he brushed it off.'

There was a brief silence, then Amy said, 'What can we do?'

'How long are you home for?'

'Only the weekend; I go back tomorrow evening.' She was in her third year at an art college in Gloucestershire. 'Could you pop round today?' she suggested. 'Say you want to collect a book from your old room or something?'

Patrick glanced down at Tasha. Damn, damn, damn! 'Well, actually . . .'

'And don't you dare say you have other plans! It's our parents we're talking about, and if we miss this chance to intervene, it might be too late.'

Her raised voice had reached Tasha, who touched his arm and nodded.

He sighed. 'OK,' he said ungraciously, 'but I won't be able to stay long.'

'Let's hope it won't *take* long,' Amy replied.

While the Dawsons sampled St Catherine's amenities and Patrick revised his plans, Rose was serving coffee to Henry Parsons.

'So!' he began, taking a biscuit. 'How did it go? Were you the belle of the ball?'

She smiled. 'Hardly! I was the eldest by several decades.'

'Nevertheless!'

'Stop flattering me, Henry! The "belle", as you put it, was

undoubtedly Cassandra. She looked enchanting and seemed to be enjoying herself enormously.'

Rose paused, took a sip of coffee, and added reflectively, 'Which is more than can be said for everyone.'

'Oh?' Henry sat back, prepared to enjoy a titbit. He was a small man with a neat, military-style moustache and a full head of silver hair. As always, he was immaculately turned out, from his bow-tie to his gleaming shoes. Such a credit to his late wife, Rose always thought.

'So, was there a mishap of some kind?' he prompted.

She shook her head. 'Not at all; it all went like clockwork, as I'd expect. This was altogether more subtle. Nothing I could put a finger on, but there were – undercurrents.'

'Sounds intriguing! Can you elucidate?'

'For one thing, Jessica and Patrick were huddled on the staircase with their heads together, looking decidedly secretive. I can't imagine what they were talking about.'

Henry's moustache twitched. 'How frustrating for you, my dear!'

'Then,' she continued, 'there was a strained atmosphere between my son and his wife – too pointedly polite to each other, if you know what I mean, and I wasn't the only one who noticed; their daughter Amy kept throwing them anxious glances. And on top of all that Verity was distinctly sulky for most of the evening, as though it was the last place she wanted to be.'

'Perhaps it was.'

'Then she should have known better than to show it,' her grandmother said severely.

Henry smiled. 'Not much escapes you, does it, Rose?'

'I'm observant, Henry, that's all.'

'As a hawk!' he agreed.

He gave a small sigh of contentment and, settling back in his chair, let his eyes wander through the open patio doors to the sunlit garden with its lush summer vegetation. 'Too hot to sit outside,' Rose had decreed, and he was more than happy to relax in her cool sitting room with its pale green upholstery and pink cushions, its set of framed prints and the maple side tables she'd brought with her from Sandstone.

Over the last couple of years this had become his second home. When his wife died ten years ago, and with only one son living in Canada, he'd sold the family home and moved into a small residential hotel. It suited him well; his suite was furnished with items from his old home and kept spotless by the hotel staff. He enjoyed three good meals a day, and if he wished for company he could go down to the lounge for a game of bridge, chess or Scrabble. He was also within walking distance of the golf club, where he spent many happy hours.

But though he got on well with his fellow residents, it was Rose's company he most enjoyed. Quite apart from the fact that she was an attractive woman, they seemed somehow to be of like mind. He admired her intelligence, her sense of purpose, and looked forward to this weekly coffee morning and the lunch he gave her at the hotel once a month. Apart from these regular engagements, from time to time they visited theatres and concerts and went on organized coach trips to places of interest. It was, he thought gratefully, a good life, even without Helen.

On Rose's part, the arrangement was equally agreeable. She enjoyed male company and missed the cut and thrust of the stimulating conversations she'd been used to with her husband. She also enjoyed their monthly lunches in the rather sedate atmosphere of the Rosemount Hotel, where the residents, however longstanding, addressed each other as 'Mr' and 'Mrs' with what now seemed old-fashioned courtesy.

Over time, several of them had started to join her and Henry for coffee in the lounge after lunch. One in particular, punctiliously addressed as 'Mrs Hill', had a daughter who lived in the town and was a source of local news that might otherwise not have come Rose's way. 'Daphne was telling me . . .' had become a promising opening to a sentence.

'And that lady you don't care for?' prompted Henry now. 'I presume she was at the party?'

Rose's lips tightened. 'Oh yes, she was there, bold as brass. I can't think why Fleur invited her. After all, it's not as if . . .'

'As if?'

But to his frustration Rose had clamped down. 'Tell me

what you've been doing since we last met,' she instructed
briskly.

Henry sighed, wishing fancifully that the all-knowing
Daphne were here to fill in the blanks. 'It was the Merriweathers'
Diamond Wedding on Wednesday,' he volunteered a little
reluctantly. 'Their son and daughter-in-law flew back from
Hong Kong for the occasion and we were treated to champagne
before dinner.'

The Merriweathers, Rose recalled, were one of the two
married couples living at the hotel. Of the remaining residents,
six were ladies, four widowed and two unmarried, leaving
Henry and a Mr Warren, to whom she'd barely spoken.

'Sixty years,' she said pensively. 'Malcolm and I managed
only forty-seven. How long were you married, Henry?'

'Forty-five, so you did marginally better than we did. But
they were happy years, Rose, as I believe yours were.'

'Yes, indeed, very happy.' She straightened her shoulders.
'Still, you were telling me about the Merriweathers. What line
is their son in, to be based in Hong Kong?'

And the conversation, having teetered on the brink of the
maudlin, was safely restored to normal.

For the first time he could remember, Patrick felt apprehensive
as he arrived at his former home, realizing to his slight surprise
that it was some time since he'd been there, despite living
only five miles away. He saw Dad at the office, of course, but
couldn't recall when he'd last had any meaningful conversation
with his mother.

'Only me!' he called with false cheerfulness, and Amy came
running down the stairs.

'Just in time for coffee!' she said brightly.

Kathryn Linscott emerged from the sitting room, offering
her cheek as her son bent to kiss her. 'What is it they say
about buses?'

Patrick grinned shamefacedly. 'Sorry I've not been for a
while.'

'So what brings you hotfoot today?'

'Well, to see you. We didn't get a chance to speak last night.'

'And?'

He grinned again. 'OK, and also to retrieve a couple of books from my room.'

'Well, you're here now, so come and be sociable first. Did you enjoy yourself last night? You and Jess seemed to be having a heart-to-heart. Was it about her breaking up with that doctor?'

Jess! Another thing to worry about! God, what was happening to his world?

'No, we were just catching up,' he said offhandedly, following her into the sitting room. It was empty and he came to a halt. 'Where's Dad?'

'Playing golf,' Kathryn replied.

A wasted journey, then. He'd have a word to say to Amy, dragging him away from Tasha for no reason. Yet might it be better to approach their parents separately? He studied his mother more closely and saw with a tug of the heart that she suddenly looked older – the skin more tightly drawn over her cheekbones and shadows under her eyes. Why hadn't he noticed that before?

'You look tired, Mum,' he said gently as Amy came in with the coffee.

Kathryn flashed him a look of – what? suspicion? – but answered calmly, 'Not surprising. I'm getting too old for late nights and it was well after midnight before we got to bed.'

He seized on the 'we'. 'I hear Dad's been banished to the guest room!' he said half-jokingly.

Kathryn raised her eyebrows. 'I'm surprised Amy thought that worth passing on,' she returned sharply. 'But since you mention it, it was a mutual decision; we were disturbing each other.'

'After all these years?'

'Is everything all right, Mum?' Amy asked tentatively, when she didn't reply.

Kathryn's hand tightened on her mug. 'What is this – an inquisition? Is this the real reason you called, Patrick?'

Amy bit her lip. 'It's just that we're worried about you both. You're always snapping at each other these days and you never used to.'

'On the contrary, we've always had minor disagreements

– what couple doesn't? I can't imagine why you're making such a fuss about it. Now, before I lose my temper, can we please change the subject?' She turned to Patrick. 'Has Amy told you about her latest project?'

And there, perforce, they had to leave it. But it was a somewhat chastened Patrick who returned to Tasha later that morning.

Fleur stood at the kitchen window gazing down the garden to where Owen was removing last night's fairy lights. The day was slowly passing, but in the lull between those festivities and the dinner still ahead of them, the fear she'd succeeded in burying had again raised its head.

This time yesterday, she thought ruefully, she'd been looking forward to the family gathering. Her brother Justin had rung to ask if there was anything she needed them to bring – which there was not – and Jess had already arrived and immediately taken herself off to the beach, claiming to have missed the sea air. All she'd had to worry about was whether the salmon would stretch to eighteen, but, as Owen had reminded her, there was also barbecued chicken, a whole ham and a goodly selection of salads, not to mention the desserts that were to follow. No one was likely to starve, and, satisfied all was ready, she'd gone up for a shower.

And discovered it, this small but undeniable lump in her left breast. Shock and disbelief were swiftly overtaken by panic, then fervent denial. It was only a gland, she kept assuring herself – it must be – but why did it have to appear now, of all times? It had taken all her willpower to play her part as hostess, and by bedtime, when she and Owen were at last alone, it had seemed too late to talk it through. She still hadn't told him, reasoning that it was better he remain in ignorance for the evening ahead.

Oh *God*! She closed her eyes, gripping the rim of the sink, and tried to reason with herself. No point in dwelling on it till she was in a position to do something, and she had all tomorrow before having to decide whether or not to book a doctor's appointment – by which time, of course, the lump might have disappeared.

She sighed. There was, she had to admit, another reason to

postpone meeting Dr Price: she'd not seen him since Jess broke off her relationship with his son. Should she mention it? Might he? Or should she be a coward, choose a day he wasn't in surgery, and arrange to see one of his partners?

She'd been staring sightlessly out of the window, but her eyes refocused as Owen began to make his way back towards the house and, catching sight of her, lifted his hand in a drinking gesture. She nodded and, grateful for the distraction, switched on the kettle.

Holly Penrose stared at her reflection in the dressing table mirror: heart-shaped face, short curly hair, wide brown eyes enlarged by horn-rimmed spectacles. She looked, she thought despairingly, about twelve.

Of course she'd known when she married Stephen, more than twenty years her senior, that eyebrows would be raised, and had anticipated the tight-lipped disapproval of her parents. The more hurtful consequences – such as his children refusing to speak to them – had come as a shock, though perhaps they shouldn't have, since she was after all a couple of years younger than his daughter.

This weekend, though less traumatic, was also proving difficult. She'd tried to excuse herself on the grounds that, since they hadn't broadcast their marriage, his friends would be expecting to see his ex-wife, but Stephen assured her only a few of their fellow guests had known Sally. Nonetheless, she was acutely aware that she looked more of an age with the daughter whose birthday they were celebrating than she did with her parents. And her ordeal wasn't over; tonight she'd have to face some of them again in the more intimate setting of a restaurant.

She slammed her hand on the dressing table. Damn it, she was twenty-five, had a first-class degree in modern languages and taught at a prestigious girls' school, where she'd learned to smile when parents mistook her for one of the pupils. She should certainly be able to hold her own among Stephen's friends. Her main fear was that in their company he might come to see her through their eyes.

*   *   *

Stephen, on the other hand, showering in the adjoining bathroom, was looking forward to the evening. He and Owen had
met only occasionally over the years, most notably when each
was best man at the other's wedding and, of course, at Cassie's
baptism, but there was a strong bond of friendship between
them and he'd been grateful last night for the ease with which
Owen had smoothed over what could have been awkward
introductions for Holly.

Fleur he'd met only a few times, though Sally had liked
her. He seemed to remember there'd been some difficulty over
their children, but whatever it was it must have resolved itself,
since they now had three attractive daughters and it was his
turn to experience problems with his offspring – problems, he
fully accepted, of his own making.

Soaping himself vigorously, he wondered again, as he had
increasingly over the eighteen months of this marriage, whether
he'd actually done Holly a disservice in marrying her. He still
wasn't sure how it had come about, since Sally, the mother
of his children and the centre of his world since university
days, remained the love of his life.

But at the time there'd been friction between them, and on
that fateful day she'd accused him of being pompous and self-
satisfied, expecting everyone to kowtow as they did at the
hospital, where he was senior thoracic surgeon. 'They might
think you're God, but I don't!' she'd said bitingly.

And because he'd known there was some truth in her words,
they'd rankled and he'd reacted angrily. He'd had a meeting
that evening, after which, since he was in no hurry to go home,
he'd joined the others for a late supper. And it was there he
had met Holly who, with a girlfriend, was at the next table.
Had he gone straight home, he didn't doubt that both he and
Sally would have apologized and quite possibly made love,
as often happened after a disagreement. Instead, he drank too
much and joined in the banter that developed between the two
tables, ending by inviting Holly to lunch the following day.

The next morning, though appalled by his indiscretion,
he'd felt duty-bound to honour it, while sincerely hoping
she would not. In vain, of course, but during the meal he'd
discovered she wasn't the naive girl he'd assumed – who, now

he'd fulfilled his obligation, he could thankfully forget – but an intelligent and astute young woman whose company he enjoyed. Furthermore, the admiration in her eyes as she quizzed him about his hospital work was a powerful antidote to Sally's wounding comments and, telling himself it could do no harm, he'd arranged to see her again.

It was on that second date – if it could be called that – that Stephen realized to his surprise that he found her attractive, at which point, if he'd had any sense at all, he should have gracefully withdrawn. But even though he procrastinated, he'd still had no intention of taking it further, simply enjoying the buzz and slight prick of danger that their meetings engendered.

It was the third date that sealed his fate. As he dropped Holly outside her block of flats she'd reached up to kiss his cheek, and his jerk of surprise resulted in the meeting of their mouths. The effect was electric and totally unexpected to both of them, but it was immediately clear that there was no going back. He had completely lost his head, and as a result his marriage as well.

Which brought him back full circle. He loved Holly – of course he did – even if not in the way he loved Sally. He'd made his bed (a singularly apposite cliché) and must now lie in it, and, more prosaically, bolster her confidence this evening, when she'd be faced with people she didn't know and with whom she'd nothing at all in common. He was well aware that the dress she'd chosen was too formal for the occasion, no doubt designed to make her look older and more sophisticated, but although his heart ached for her he was powerless to rectify that.

With a sigh, he stepped out of the shower and prepared for the evening.

The Montpellier restaurant in the centre of town was renowned for its fine dining, and tables, particularly on Saturday nights, needed to be booked well in advance.

Owen and Fleur, arriving intentionally ahead of the others, were greeted by the proprietor, Crispin Hynes.

'Mr and Mrs Tempest! Good to see you! We've reserved a

table as you requested, but I was wondering if you'd prefer to sit out in the courtyard, since it's such a lovely evening?'

Owen glanced through the open doors at the back of the restaurant to where several tables were already occupied. 'What do you think, darling?'

Fleur hesitated. 'I think I'd prefer to eat indoors. It'll get cool later, and there's always the problem of midges, and moths too once the candles are lit.'

'Of course, madam. I'll show you to your table, then.'

They followed him to a corner table by the window, and were just settling themselves when Fleur saw Lynn and Tony arrive and hesitate in the doorway. She raised a hand and they came to join them.

'What a lovely restaurant!' Lynn commented, seating herself opposite Fleur and looking about her. 'In fact, I must say we're very impressed with your town. We did a lightning tour of it today; Tony had his nose in a brochure and insisted on listing the features and history of everything we looked at!'

Fleur smiled. 'We certainly love it. As you know, I grew up here, and the thought of coming back softened the blow of leaving Bromley!'

Tony and Lynn both laughed. 'I bet it did!' Tony said.

A waiter appeared at Owen's elbow. 'Would you like to see the wine list, sir?'

'You can bring it, yes, though we're still waiting for a couple of friends.'

As he moved away, Tony said, 'And by the way, this is on us, so no unseemly arguing at the end of the meal!'

'Oh, now look—' Owen began, but Tony raised a hand.

'Stephen's completely in agreement; I had a word with him last night. You did us proud yesterday, now it's our turn to reciprocate.'

'But this was my suggestion, so we'd have a chance to talk! At least let us split it three ways—'

'Not negotiable,' Tony said.

Any further discussion was cut short by the arrival of Stephen and Holly. They too paused in the doorway, and as Owen stood to greet them, Fleur and Lynn exchanged raised eyebrows. For Holly's outfit was more suitable for a prestigious first night than a meal in a seaside restaurant. Her sleeveless dress was in dull gold satin, with a draped bodice that clung to her figure; she was carrying a gold clutch bag and wore high-heeled gold sandals. Stephen's hand under her elbow seemed to Fleur to offer support as much as guidance.

'Sorry we're a little late,' he said evenly. 'The first taxi we ordered didn't turn up.'

'We've only just arrived ourselves,' Tony said, pulling out a chair for Holly. He smiled at her. 'As you can't be expected to remember the names of everyone you met last night, I'm Tony and this is my wife Lynn, friends from Bromley.'

Holly smiled at him gratefully. 'And you're both Cassie's godparents, is that right?'

'Quite correct.'

The waiter who'd been hovering with a pile of menus now approached and these were handed round while Stephen and Tony, studying the wine list, consulted with Owen. Choices made and relayed, the waiter moved away and conversation resumed. Stephen made some comment to Lynn, who was seated on his left, and Fleur, not wanting Holly to feel left out, leaned towards her.

'I see you went for the sea bass. Good choice! They have an interesting way of serving it, and it's delicious!'

Holly smiled. 'I'm glad to hear it, because I was spoilt for choice! But that's the best part of eating out, isn't it, the chance to try new dishes. Actually, Stephen and I met in a restaurant.'

'Well, steak house!' Stephen amended wryly.

'He was at the next table,' Holly continued. She gave a little laugh. 'And to think, I very nearly didn't go! I didn't want to, but my flatmate finally persuaded me.'

'Why didn't you want to?' Lynn asked.

Holly's smile faded abruptly, and it was clear to Fleur that she was wishing she could take back her last remark. Lynn, however, who'd been retrieving a handkerchief from her bag, hadn't noticed. 'I mean, since you usually like going out for a meal?' she added into the growing silence.

Holly bit her lip, but everyone was now waiting for her

reply. 'I was feeling miserable,' she said in a low voice. 'My best friend had . . . just died of breast cancer.'

Fleur, in the act of lifting her glass, jerked and a red bead flowered on the tablecloth. Owen glanced at her briefly, but Holly was the centre of attention.

'Oh, my dear!' Lynn exclaimed, in her turn wishing she could retract her query. 'How terrible for you!'

Stephen leaned forward. 'Darling, I really don't think we need to go into that. This is supposed to be a celebration!'

Holly flung him an anguished glance. 'No, I'm so sorry. I didn't mean—'

To everyone's heartfelt relief a couple of waiters arrived with their first courses, and as they moved away conversation started up again, with Stephen asking Owen about St Catherine's College.

Lynn, quietly listening, wondered how someone as sensible and authoritative as Stephen appeared to be could have abandoned his longstanding wife for this . . . schoolgirl. She'd been surprised to learn of his divorce, but then she barely remembered him, let alone his first wife; she'd met them only once, at Cassie's christening nearly eighteen years ago.

Holly had remained subdued after her earlier slip, and as the meal progressed Fleur again tried to draw her into the conversation by asking if she worked at the hospital with her husband. Both she and Lynn were surprised to learn of the position she held at the widely acclaimed Highfield College. Obviously they'd underestimated the young woman they'd subconsciously dismissed as Stephen's child bride.

Holly herself, who'd become animated when talking about a job she clearly loved, asked what subjects Cassie was taking for A-levels, and was interested to hear they included French and Spanish. 'I wish I'd had a chance to speak to her,' she said, 'though she mightn't have welcomed discussing exams at her birthday party!' She took a sip of wine. 'Is she at your husband's school?'

'Yes, both she and Verity go to St Cat's,' Fleur replied. 'Jess didn't, though – she was nineteen when we moved here and already at university.'

'They're lovely girls, and all so different. To look at them, you'd never know they were sisters.'

Lynn, aware that the men were now listening, said quickly, 'Well, they all have their own interests, of course. Verity's the artistic one; even from a small child, I remember her being absorbed in drawing and painting. Takes after her mother!' She flashed a smile at Fleur, who was an illustrator of children's books.

But Holly was not to be diverted. 'What I meant was there's no family resemblance. At school, I can usually tell which girls are sisters, even if they have different colouring.'

Lynn had the sensation that everyone was holding their breath. Then, into the brief but somehow electric silence, Fleur said clearly, 'That's because Jess and Cassie are adopted. I thought Stephen would have told you.'

So that's what it was! Stephen cursed his sketchy memory. If only he'd pursued the thought earlier, he could have prevented what for some reason seemed to be a tense moment. Holly was looking both embarrassed and bewildered at the subtle change in atmosphere.

'Then of course that explains it,' she said after a moment. 'I'm sorry – I should have thought.'

'No reason why you should,' Fleur replied briskly. 'Owen, could you order some more coffee, please?'

Lynn let out her held breath. So Fleur hadn't changed her mind. She wondered yet again at what stage she'd feel the girls deserved to hear the truth.

It had been a hateful evening. Holly had known as soon as she entered the restaurant that she was overdressed. Then, as if that wasn't enough, she'd somehow found herself telling them about Beth, which put a dampener on everything. And just as things were getting back to normal, she'd made that comment about the girls that had had such an odd effect – though why their adoption should apparently be a taboo subject, she couldn't imagine.

Owen and Fleur had dropped them off at their hotel, and as the bedroom door closed behind them she said tightly, 'I'm sorry, Stephen. I ruined the evening.'

'Of course you didn't,' he said, pulling off his tie. 'You looked lovely.'

'I looked like the Christmas fairy,' she contradicted, 'and every time I opened my mouth I made a faux pas.' Her voice wavered. 'You must have been sorry you brought me.'

He turned to look at her, aware for the first time of how upset she was, and quickly took her in his arms. 'The bit about Beth was unfortunate, but no more than that,' he said. 'And as for the adoption, that was my fault. I was remembering in the shower that there'd been some problem about their having children, but I just dismissed it. I could have spared you that if I'd only thought it through.'

'But why should adoption be such a big deal?'

'God knows. Come to think of it, though, at Owen's stag do when there was all the usual ribbing about future sleepless nights and dirty nappies, he said, "You can laugh, but as it happens I can't wait to be a father!" It seems he did have to wait to be a biological one, but Lynn said Verity's inherited Fleur's artistic talents, so it sounds as though they got there in the end.'

'But it wasn't Owen who reacted.'

'Well, I suppose Fleur felt the same, though after twenty-five years and three lovely girls, you'd think she'd have got over it. And you were right – they don't look alike.'

He kissed her gently on the lips. 'But enough of all that. Hurry up and take that gorgeous dress off, Mrs Penrose, because I want to make love to you.'

My best friend died of breast cancer. Hours after the dinner party broke up Fleur lay rigid in bed staring up at the invisible ceiling, cold fear in her heart. On their return she'd surreptitiously felt for the lump, willing it to have gone, but it was still very much there.

Surely people didn't still die of breast cancer if it was caught soon enough? Not in this day and age? But catching it early meant seeing Dr Price next week and her heart quailed. Would he be able to tell her straight away that she'd nothing to worry about? Or would a biopsy be taken, and she'd have to wait unbearable days or even weeks for the result? And suppose it proved malignant? She shuddered.

Should she tell Owen and ask for his advice? But she knew unequivocally what his response would be. If only Sue hadn't had to leave early she could have confided in her, but despite her many friends in St Cat's there was no one with whom she felt able to discuss her worry. Oh, please God, let it have gone by the morning!

THREE

Rachel Firth lay back on her sun lounger and tried to summon the energy for a swim. Beside her, Jess's even breathing suggested that she was asleep and Rachel was loath to wake her, knowing she'd not been sleeping well since their arrival.

'Jet lag!' she'd said facetiously, when Rachel had commented on her restlessness.

'Between Bristol and Pisa?'

'Well, you know what I mean.'

Rachel didn't, and now admitted to herself that she was a little concerned. They'd been looking forward to this holiday for months, but ever since they'd met at the airport Jess had seemed subdued. There was clearly something on her mind, and Rachel had been hoping to hear what it was, that Jess would perhaps ask for her advice as she had in the past. They'd known each other since schooldays and had stayed in touch as their career paths diverged, managing despite commitments with various boyfriends to get together for a holiday each year.

Rachel glanced at her watch. Just time for a quick swim, after which they must decide whether to have lunch here by the pool or seek a brief respite from the heat in the hotel restaurant. One decision, however, she had already reached. If Jess hadn't told her what was bothering her before this evening, she would ask outright. Two heads were surely better than one.

She took off her watch, glanced at her still-sleeping friend, and, avoiding a group of wildly splashing children, slid into the pool.

It was seven o'clock and they were sitting on the hotel terrace with their *aperitivi*. Around them fellow guests, skin glowing after a day in the sun, laughed and chatted in a variety of languages. Several backs and shoulders were red rather than tanned, not boding well for a good night's sleep. Which reminded Rachel of her decision.

Twirling the swizzle stick in her glass, she began cautiously, 'You haven't said much about your new flatmate. What's she like?'

Jess shot her a quick glance. 'Maggie? She's OK, but if I'm honest we're not exactly on the same wavelength.'

'How so?'

'Well, for one thing people keep dropping in all the time and staying till well after eleven – often as many as five or six at a time. It's very disconcerting; I can never relax and just slob out because I never know when someone might turn up. Sometimes Maggie will just announce we're going out for a meal, then on to a club. Not my scene, but they won't hear of me not going.'

'A bit much, I'd have thought, but presumably Maggie doesn't mind?'

'Quite the reverse, but I'd welcome the chance to relax occasionally after a busy day. And, of course, they're her friends, not mine.' She paused. 'I say "friends", but actually they don't seem to have much in common.' She gave a short laugh, remembering. 'When I first moved in, one of them said, "Welcome to Maggie's Lonely Hearts Club!"'

'So who are these people? Haven't they got homes of their own?'

Jess shrugged. 'From what I gather most of them are either separated or divorced, so she's probably doing them a kindness. Individually I quite like them – or most of them – but I'd like them more if I didn't see them so often!'

'Why don't you have a word? Suggest you have a quiet evening now and again, with just the two of you?'

'I can't do that. After all, it's her flat and this routine was established before I arrived.'

'Then why not look for somewhere else, if it's getting you down?'

Jess sighed. 'I had been thinking of it,' she admitted, 'but now—' She broke off and bit her lip.

'Now what?'

Jess shook her head dismissively. 'It would be awkward, that's all.'

'Why would it?'

'It just would. Look, I'm beginning to get hungry; shall we go in?'

Rachel sat back and folded her arms. 'Not until you tell me what's wrong.'

Jess stared at her, but her eyes were the first to drop. 'I don't know what you mean.'

'Oh, come on, Jess! How long have we known each other? There's been something on your mind ever since we set off, and it's more than not getting on with your flatmate.'

Jess's fists clenched beneath the table. In this sun-soaked paradise the events of that day in Bristol seemed unreal, even ludicrous. 'It's nothing,' she said.

'Sorry, not good enough.'

'OK, I *was* worried about something, but as there's nothing I can do I'll just have to forget it.'

'Blood from a stone!' Rachel muttered. 'And what exactly will you have to forget?'

'You're not going to let this drop, are you?' Jess said after a minute.

'Got it in one.'

'OK, well, if you must know, I saw something I shouldn't have, but no one knows so I'm quite safe.'

'Safe?' repeated Rachel sharply. 'I think you'd better start at the beginning.'

Jess bit her lip. She'd almost confided in Patrick, but she realized now that had she told him he'd have tried to make her report it, which she dared not do. Yet she badly needed to tell someone, and who better than Rachel?

'It was last Friday,' she began slowly, 'just before I set off for home. That morning I'd put my case in the car to save going back to the flat, so after work I went straight to the basement car park. Then I remembered I'd left my paperback in my room, so as I was in good time I decided to go and collect it.'

'Yes?' prompted Rachel when she came to a halt.

Jess took a deep breath. 'I went up in the lift and . . . let myself in. And . . . oh, God!' Her hands flew to her face. 'If the door hadn't clicked shut behind me, I'd have run straight out again.'

Rachel, increasingly alarmed, waited.

'Someone was there,' Jess continued from behind her hands, 'lying on the floor.'

Rachel frowned. 'Your flatmate, you mean?'

Jess shook her head. 'A man. Someone I'd never seen before.'

Rachel was confused. 'You mean he was asleep?'

'No,' said Jess starkly, lowering her hands. 'He was dead.'

The sound of laughter around them cut off abruptly like the pressing of a mute button, locking them in their own frozen space. Rachel said shakily, 'God, Jessie, are you sure? Mightn't he just—?'

'His eyes were open,' Jess said, shivering in the heat, 'and there was a red stain down the front of his shirt.'

Rachel stared at her in horror. 'What did you do?' she whispered.

'Just stood there. I wanted to run but I . . . couldn't move. Then I heard someone outside and fled to my room, but I couldn't close the door because when I'm out it's always left open and if I had, whoever it was would have known I was there. I scrambled into the fitted wardrobe and slid it almost shut, and only just in time. The flat door opened and some people came in.'

'How many?'

'Two, I think. They were talking in low voices, but I couldn't make out any words.' Jess shuddered. 'I was expecting them to be as shocked as I was but they didn't seem to be. Then the noises started, thumps and grunts and a dragging sound and someone swore.'

She looked across at her friend, reliving the horror. 'God, Rachel, I was terrified, standing shivering in the half-dark with my clothes brushing against my face. It was illogical, but I was sure they knew I was there.'

Rachel leaned across the table and laid her hand over Jess's. 'But they didn't, did they?' she asked urgently.

Jess shook her head. 'Then I heard the door open and close, and after that there was silence. I waited several minutes before daring to come out.' She stared at Rachel, her eyes wide. 'And the incredible thing is that if I hadn't seen that man with my own eyes, I'd never have known he'd been there. There was absolutely no trace of him – nothing at all. It was . . . creepy.'

There was a short silence, then Rachel said, 'The odds are one of them must have been your flatmate.'

'I suppose so. Actually, I've just remembered – Maggie said she was taking the afternoon off. She'd have finished work at lunchtime.'

'Then it's even more likely. And looking at it logically,' Rachel added carefully, 'whoever removed him must have had a hand in killing him.'

Jess nodded and took a quick drink of her *aperitivo*.

Rachel thought for a minute. 'What did he look like, the dead man?'

Reluctantly Jess recalled her first horrified glimpse. 'Older than us; in his forties, I'd say. Brown hair, grey eyes. Tanned.'

'What was he wearing?'

'Jeans and a T-shirt.'

'And you're sure you'd never seen him before?'

'Absolutely certain.' She shivered. A slight breeze had got up, cool on their sun-warmed bodies, and Rachel pushed back her chair.

'Come on, let's go in for dinner. You need some hot food inside you, and after hearing all that, so do I.'

For the next fifteen minutes or so they were occupied in settling at their table and studying the menu, though neither felt much like eating. But as the waiter moved away with their order, Rachel said curiously, 'What did the police make of it?'

Jess was silent, looking down at her lap.

'Jess?' Rachel's voice sharpened. 'You did contact them?'

Jess met her eyes defiantly. 'To tell them what? That I saw someone I didn't know lying dead on the carpet, but some people – I don't know who – came and removed him? They'd think I was hallucinating. I've no proof any of it happened at all.'

'But Jess, you *have to* report it!' Rachel said urgently. 'Someone must be missing him, his wife or someone.'

'Then I'm sorry, but I'd be no help. And if the police *did* pursue it, whoever killed him would know it was me who'd contacted them.'

'I don't see why; someone else in the building might have noticed them arriving or leaving – or seen the dead man, for that matter. There must be security cameras. And if it *was* Maggie and her crew – and who else could it have been? – they'd think you were safely out of the way en route for Somerset.' She paused. 'After all that, did you collect the paperback?'

Jess gave a rueful smile. 'No. Though it was highly unlikely, I was afraid Maggie might have seen it on my table and noticed later that it was missing. As you know, I bought one at the airport, which I should have decided to do in the first place and saved myself this nightmare.'

Rachel sipped thoughtfully at her wine. 'Tell me about these friends of hers.'

Jess lifted her hands helplessly. 'Surely none of them—'

'Well, *someone* did! Look, start with the men – they're the most likely.'

Jess frowned, staring into her glass. 'If it *was* one of them, my money would be on Laurence.'

'Why?'

'For one thing he's the closest to Maggie – he quite often stays the night.'

'Doesn't make him a murderer!'

But Jess didn't smile in response. 'There's something about him that makes me uneasy. I wouldn't like to be alone in a room with him.'

'OK. Who else?'

'Well, there's Dominic. He's a bank manager, I think, and recently divorced. Maggie said he's on the rebound and he certainly drinks more than the others.'

'Anyone else?' Rachel prompted when she didn't go on.

'Connor. I know him a bit better than the others because we sometimes sit together.'

'Do you now? Might he be a successor to the amorous doctor?'

'Oh Rachel, for heaven's sake!' Jess protested laughingly.

Their antipasti arrived and claimed their attention for the next few minutes. Then Rachel said, 'What about the women?'

'Well, Maggie, of course. She runs a fairly prestigious garden design business-cum-garden centre. She's just won some prize or other; her photo was in the local paper and she was interviewed on TV.'

'Good for her. Who else?'

'Di and Sarah are the most regular. I don't know either of them well, but I like them both.'

'Are any of them couples, would you say, apart from Maggie and Laurence?'

Jess shrugged. 'Possibly Dominic and Di, but it's all pretty fluid.'

They lapsed into silence, both pursuing their own thoughts. At one point Rachel said, 'What do you think they did with the body?'

Jess didn't reply.

The meal continued with only sporadic conversation, Jess's admission having cast a pall over the holiday that neither seemed able to shake off. Their first and then second course plates were removed, and it was as they were having coffee that a heavily accented voice above them said, 'You two ladies look very serious, and that is not allowed!'

They looked up into the smiling faces of a couple of Swedish men they'd spoken to briefly by the pool.

'Too much sunshine making us dozy!' Rachel said.

'Not something we Swedes complain about!' laughed the one called Anders. 'We have to soak up all we can to make up for the long dark winters! We're about to take a stroll into town and visit a bar we discovered yesterday. If you're not too sleepy, would you care to join us?'

Miraculously the cloud hanging over the women lifted. 'We'd love to!' Jess said.

Lars and Anders proved interesting and attentive companions for the rest of the holiday. As a foursome they visited all the tourist attractions, including climbing the famous Leaning Tower for a tilted view of the city. Another highlight was a day trip to Florence to marvel at its many wonders. The constant activity, together with congenial company, had the welcome effect of banishing thoughts of Bristol to the back of Jess's mind. However, as the holiday neared its end, fear reasserted itself and she began to dread her return to the flat.

As they prepared for bed the final evening, she suddenly burst out, 'I wish I could go back to London with you!'

Rachel paused in the act of brushing her hair. 'Oh, hon, I know.'

'It would help if I knew whether or not he's been found. If he has, and has been identified and everything, someone might even have been arrested by now.'

'Well, that would be great, wouldn't it?'

'It would certainly absolve me of responsibility for not reporting it.'

Rachel turned to look at her. 'So you agree now that you should have done?'

'Oh Rach, I always knew that, but I was too frightened. If I'd had more time to think about it I probably would have, but I was on the point of driving home for Cassie's birthday and then coming away, and it all just . . . panicked me.'

'It still wouldn't be too late.'

Jess shook her head. 'But don't you see? If more facts suddenly came to light just after my return to Bristol, it would point the finger at me even more.'

'As I said before, not necessarily, but I understand your concern. Is there anyone you could confide in? I really don't know what advice to give you.'

Jess made a face. 'Anyone I tell would say the same as you – I must report it.'

And Rachel, knowing this to be true, could only nod in reply.

FOUR

Jess's holiday wasn't the only one that ended that weekend, and Jenny and Ron Barlow had a painful conversation on the long drive home.

'You have to remember, love,' he began, 'they're not kids any more. A day on the beach with people they hardly know—'

'*Hardly know?*' Jenny echoed, and Ron winced at the pain in her voice.

'Well, you could count on the fingers of one hand the number of times we've seen them since they moved down here. Added to which, we're earlier this year because of Cassie's birthday, which means the school term hasn't ended. That leaves only the weekends, which they obviously want to spend either studying for exams or with their friends, rather than traipsing down to see us – especially since they saw us at the party.'

'But we hardly spoke to them there!' Jenny wailed.

'And with Jess being in Italy,' Ron continued doggedly, 'it wouldn't have been the same. She was always the chatty one, wasn't she?'

'I feel I'm losing them all over again,' Jenny said, rummaging in her handbag for a tissue.

'Perhaps it would be as well to cool it for a bit – go somewhere else next summer, abroad, maybe.' He flicked her a sideways glance. 'We could even ask Gemma or Freddie if they'd like to join us.'

Jenny snorted. 'No guesses what their answer would be!'

'Oh, I don't know. They might appreciate that we're taking a break from the annual pilgrimage. In any case, Cassie could well be at university and off travelling during the long vacation. We're coming to the end of an era, love, and we have to face it.'

Jenny's control finally gave way. 'Why can't things stay as they are?' she sobbed.

To that, Ron accepted, there was no reply.

*   *   *

They parted in Bristol, Rachel making for her train to London and Jess for hers to St Catherine's, where she'd left her car.

'Let me know how you get on,' Rachel said, as they hugged goodbye. 'And as soon as you think it's safe, look for somewhere else to live.'

'Oh, I shall!' Jess replied fervently. 'I don't trust any of them at the moment.'

She was glad to be going home, albeit briefly, before returning to the flat. It would give her a chance to draw breath, and arriving late tomorrow would reduce time spent with Maggie and whoever else happened to be there. It would be a strain having to be constantly on her guard, ensuring that she behaved naturally and gave no grounds for suspicion that she might know more than was good for her.

Fleur was in the garden deadheading when the station taxi turned into the drive, and in the seconds before her mother saw her, Jess had a fleeting sense that she looked downcast. Then she smiled and came to greet her, and by the time Jess had paid the driver and retrieved her case she'd forgotten the impression.

'You're as brown as a walnut!' Fleur exclaimed. 'I hope you put on plenty of sunscreen!'

'Oh, Mum, really!'

'Ignore me! Did you have a wonderful time?'

'It was great, yes. Super hotel, super food, super weather, and a chance to catch up with Rachel.'

'Any dashing young men on hand?' Fleur enquired mischievously as they went into the house.

'A couple of Swedes, since you ask. Perfect holiday companions and no strings to complicate things. How's everything here? No alarums and excursions?'

Her mother's eyes flickered away, and again that spurt of unease. But she answered lightly, 'No, all well. Exams are finished, so the girls are just cruising along until the end of term. Incidentally, Gran's invited herself to lunch tomorrow. She wants to see you before you go back to Bristol, and says she didn't get a chance to speak to you at the party.'

Owen appeared from the direction of the kitchen. 'Ah,

the wanderer returns!' He gave her a quick hug and kissed
her cheek. 'We gather from your texts you had a good time.'

'I did, yes. I'll tell you all about it, but if you don't mind
I'll take my things up now and have a quick shower. We didn't
have time for one this morning and I'm all sticky after travelling. Can I dump everything in the washing machine, Mum?
No point taking them back to Bristol – they're hardly work
clothes.'

Music was coming from Cassie's room as Jess reached the
top of the stairs. She tapped on her door and put her head
round it. 'Hi!' she said.

Her sister looked up from her tablet. 'Oh, hi yourself! Have
a good time?'

'Great, thanks. I'm just going for a shower to get rid of
travel grime.'

Cassie nodded. 'OK. There's something I want to talk to
you about, but it'll keep.'

'Sounds pretty serious!'

'It'll keep,' Cassie repeated, and turned back to her tablet.

With a resigned shake of her head, Jess went for her shower.

Fleur had still done nothing about the lump in her breast, and
Jess's return from holiday brought home to her that it was
now two weeks since she'd discovered it. She was well aware
that had it been Owen or one of the girls she'd have insisted
they go to the doctor immediately, for reasons that applied
equally to her: if, as was most likely, it was nothing serious,
they could spare themselves needless worry by having the fact
confirmed; if, on the other hand, it *was*, the sooner it was
treated the better.

So why, when it came to herself, was she such a coward?
She had even kept putting off phoning Sue Davenport, her
long-term best friend and the only person with whom she felt
she could discuss her plight. Admittedly a phone conversation
was far from ideal for such a topic, but since Sue lived in
Oxford there was no other option. Fleur had, in fact, reached
this decision several times over the last two weeks, but each
time she was alone in the house and the ideal opportunity
offered, she'd thought up excuses to postpone it.

Enough! On Monday, when Jess was back in Bristol and Owen and the girls at school, she would pluck up her courage and make the call, and this time she would carry the decision through.

It had been a pleasantly relaxed evening. As promised, Jess regaled her family with an account of the holiday, including their day trip to the Ponte Vecchio and the Uffizi Gallery, and illustrated it with photos on her phone. Once the meal was over, Verity left them to join a group of friends at a local gig and the rest of them exchanged odd snippets of news and general chat until, after watching *News at Ten*, Jess excused herself and went upstairs. It had been an early start in Pisa, followed by a long day, and she was exhausted.

But once in bed she found it impossible to switch off all the fears and anxieties she'd kept at bay for the last two weeks but which now, with her imminent return to Bristol, threatened to swamp her.

After tossing and turning for half an hour, she decided to read for a while in the hope that it would make her sleepy. She plumped up the pillows behind her and prepared to immerse herself in her book, but she'd read only half a dozen pages when there was a tap on the door and Cassie, clad in pyjamas and dressing gown, came in bearing a tray with two mugs.

'I saw your light was still on,' she said, 'so I thought you might like some hot chocolate.'

'Thanks,' Jess said gratefully, laying down her book. 'I just couldn't get to sleep; overtired, I expect.'

'This should help, then.' Cassie handed her a mug and perched on the side of the bed with her own.

Jess sipped at it appreciatively. 'You wanted to talk about something?'

'Yes.' Cassie stared down at her drink for a moment. Then she looked up and said in a rush, 'Have you ever thought about trying to trace your birth mother?'

Jess stared at her. 'God, Cass, I wasn't expecting that!'

'Well, have you?'

'I can't say I have, no. Mum's the only mother I need.' She paused, surveying her sister's troubled face. 'Have you?'

Cassie sipped her drink. 'Not till very recently. It started with one of the girls at school. I hardly know her, so Lord knows how she found out I was adopted; I've never tried to hide it, but I haven't shouted it from the rooftops either. Anyway, a group of us were talking about my eighteenth and she suddenly said, "Now you'll be old enough to search for your birth mother!"'

Cassie looked up, meeting Jess's eyes. 'It was like she'd slapped my face. I suddenly felt like a . . . displaced person.'

'Oh, Cass!' Jess said softly.

'But it did start me thinking. And it struck me that when I have children of my own, I'll want them to know where they came from.'

'You have a point,' Jess conceded, 'but that won't be for a while, I trust!'

Cassie gave a half-smile. 'I'd probably have put it on hold, if something else hadn't come up.' She drew a deep breath. 'I popped in to see Gran the other day, to thank her properly for my birthday present.' She paused. 'You know when she moved out of here she left several boxes of stuff in the attic, because there's not much storage space at the bungalow?'

Jess nodded, wondering where this could possibly be leading.

'Well, she and Henry had been to the Vermeer exhibition and she wanted to re-read a book about him called *Girl with a Pearl Earring*. She searched everywhere but couldn't find it, and wondered if it was in one of the boxes she'd left here. So she . . . asked me to have a look for it.'

'And did you find it?' Jess prompted, when she didn't go on.

'Oh, I found it all right. And when I lifted it out of the box' – Cassie reached into her dressing gown pocket and removed a folded sheet of paper – 'this fell out. It must have been used as a bookmark.' She sat staring down at it.

'Well, are you going to tell me what it is?' Jess asked impatiently.

'Read it yourself!' Cassie thrust the paper into her hand. Unfolding it, Jess was surprised to see their mother's handwriting. Scrawled on one side of the page, it was a letter dated 12 October 2000 and read:

> *Dearest Ma, please don't be angry with us. I know you don't approve – you made that very plain! – but if it's on my behalf there's no need to worry. I really don't mind one way or the other as long as we have a healthy baby, and it means so much to Owen. Talk it over with Pops – I think he understands, but I need you to be happy too. I love you very much. Fleur.*

Jess looked up to find her sister watching her intently. 'What do you make of that?' she demanded, her voice trembling.

'I've no idea,' Jess said helplessly.

'From the date it has to be me they're talking about, but what doesn't Gran approve of, for pity's sake? They'd already adopted you – she should have been used to the idea.'

Jess shook her head. 'It doesn't make sense. You didn't mention this to either Gran or Mum?'

'Of course not. What do you take me for?'

'Well, you might at least have got an explanation.'

'Suppose Gran still doesn't "approve"? Does that mean she doesn't approve of *me* either?' Cassie's voice broke on an angry sob and Jess reached quickly for her hand.

'Oh, Cass, of course not! She loves you to bits, but you know what she's like. She gets these ideas in her head and hangs on to them like a terrier. I've seen Dad bite his lip more than once when she goes off on one of her rants.'

'Nevertheless,' said Cassie bleakly.

'So what are you going to do?' Jess enquired after a minute. 'Ask one of them – which would be the quickest way – or start to look for your birth mother?'

Cassie lifted her shoulders. 'I just wish Trudy had kept her big mouth shut and Gran hadn't asked me to find the book and things could have gone on as normal.'

'Turning back the clock,' Jess said reflectively. 'We all wish that from time to time.'

Cass looked up. 'Oh? What would you change?'

'I was speaking generally. I shouldn't worry about it; there's probably a simple explanation. Anyway, whatever it was is well in the past now, so it can't have been that important.' She finished the last of her chocolate. 'Thanks for this, Cass. Let's hope we can both sleep now.'

Cassie took the letter from her and slipped it back in her pocket. 'No harm in hoping,' she said.

Since its windows had been closed for two weeks, the Bromley house felt close and stuffy and Jenny had gone round opening them all – though, as Ron had pointed out, she was only letting in more heat. Due to a break for lunch and the slow holiday traffic it had taken them almost four hours to reach home, and the headache brought on by her earlier tears was still lingering, despite a couple of paracetamol. She felt tired, lethargic and miserable, and though she was supposed to be unpacking the cases that had been brought up earlier, she sank down on to the bed, her head in her hands. Thunderstorms were forecast and Ron was hurriedly cutting the grass before they arrived. She could hear the sound of the mower through the open window.

Was he right, she wondered, that their Somerset holidays had virtually come to an end, breaking any worthwhile connection with the Tempest family? She wasn't sure she could bear it, but what else could she do? She was well aware that Fleur resented the prolonged contact, spasmodic though it was, and was unlikely to offer any alternative.

A host of images of the Tempest children through the years flickered through her mind – Jess a freckled five-year-old, Cassie a toddler, hunting in the garden for Easter eggs. That must have been before Verity was born. Then, a few years later, trips to the cinema, strictly monitored by Fleur . . .

A rattle of rain against the window broke into her reverie, followed by a crash of thunder. Wearily she brushed a hand across her face and, hearing the back door open as Ron took shelter from the storm, she at last began to unpack their cases.

By the next morning the rain had reached Somerset and after a disturbed night Jess woke to its pattering against the window. Various other sounds filtered through from the house around her: Minty mewing near at hand and her mother calling him from downstairs; music drifting from both her sisters' rooms in discordant harmony; and, from nearby St Barnabas, bells summoning the faithful to prayer. Sounds which, in various permutations, she thought drowsily, had punctuated her life.

Gran would be at church and Jess pictured her sitting upright in what had always been the family pew. Though not approving of the modern services she bore them stoically enough when there was no alternative.

Jess smiled to herself. Dear Gran: she was a complex character, politically incorrect to the nth degree and frequently dismissing other people's opinions out of hand. As a child, Jess had been hurt by the undeniable favouritism shown towards Verity, whom, Jess suspected, Rose regarded as her only true grandchild, but she was also capable of unexpected acts of kindness and more than once had surprised her by understanding her teenage worries when her parents had failed to do so.

She slipped out of bed and padded to the window, staring down the length of the garden to the gate at the far end. It was a sorry sight in the relentless rain, the branches of trees and shrubs bowed down with the weight of it and a few bedraggled birds pecking at the lawn. Very different from the fairy-lit surroundings of two weeks ago.

Her thoughts turned to Cassie and last night's disclosure. What was the meaning of the mysterious letter tucked inside that book and then forgotten? Had Gran ever replied to it? *It means so much to Owen*, her mother had written. What did? And why the need for assurances that Fleur herself was happy? Did this mysterious something explain why Gran often seemed over-critical of her father? Though admittedly, while always scrupulously polite, he didn't let her wilder assertions go unchallenged, a fact she obviously resented. A state of armed neutrality! Jess thought.

Turning from the window, she went for a shower before replacing her washbag and night clothes in an overnight bag, the only luggage she'd be taking back to Bristol that evening, wishing as she did so that she had several more nights to spend in the safety of home.

*   *   *

Sandstone was, as Rose always maintained, a family house, solid, unpretentious and comfortable. Adhering to its traditions, Sunday lunch always consisted of a roast and was partaken of in the dining room at the rear of the house, its French windows giving on to the terrace and garden. Today, as the rain continued to fall, it had been necessary to switch on the lights.

Jess, remembering her earlier musings, surreptitiously regarded her grandmother across the table. Her high cheekbones and large heavy-lidded eyes showed traces of the beauty she must once have been. As always she was perfectly groomed, her silver hair – impossible to think of it as either white or grey – impeccably coiffed thanks to her weekly visit to the hairdresser.

'So how was the new vicar, Ma?' Fleur enquired, passing her the potatoes.

'Ghastly!' replied Rose unequivocally. 'Would you believe he began his sermon by asking everyone to call him Josh? *Josh!* How can one discuss theological matters with someone called Josh?'

'Joshua is a biblical name,' Owen pointed out, straight-faced.

'It was bad enough,' Rose continued, ignoring him, 'when people spoke of our previous incumbent as "Reverend" or "the Reverend Jones".' A retaliatory glance at Owen. 'Presumably, since grammar is no longer taught correctly, no one had told them the word "reverend" is an adjective, and that without the courtesy title they were baldly addressing him as the equivalent of "Handsome" or "Incompetent".'

'"The Handsome Jones!"' Verity said with a giggle. 'What should it be, Gran?'

'The Reverend *Mr* Jones, of course.'

There was a slight pause, then Fleur said a little desperately, 'This must be the first rain you've seen in a while, Jess.'

'Yes – good old England!'

Rose, having had her say, was willing to be diverted. 'I hope you have some photographs to show me, Jessica? Your grandfather and I honeymooned in Florence and it would be good to see whether much has changed.'

'I've loads, Gran, but they're on my phone. I'll show them to you on the TV after lunch.'

'That will be interesting, though I must say I prefer flicking through an album.' She turned to Verity. 'I believe your exams are over now, my dear? When will you have the results?'

Verity grimaced. 'Not till nearly the end of August. It's a total waste of time having to go to school for the rest of the term,' she added, with a glance at her father. 'It's not as though we're really doing anything.'

'A perennial argument,' he responded mildly.

Rose helped herself to gravy. 'Did I tell you Mrs Hill's grandson goes to the college? She was saying there's been a lot of concern about bullying this term. I'm surprised you allow it, Owen.'

He flushed and Jess noted the tightening of his jaw, though his voice remained steady. 'We hardly *allow* it, Rose; the school has a very strict anti-bullying policy and anyone caught flouting it is severely reprimanded.'

'Well, it doesn't seem to be working,' Rose said serenely. 'I hear several of the younger boys have gone home in tears. This beef is very good, darling,' she went on, in almost the same breath. 'Are you still going to Dewhurst's?'

It took Fleur a moment to switch her train of thought. 'Yes; they're marginally more expensive, but worth the extra, I think.'

Rose having apparently shot her barbs for the day, the rest of the meal passed peacefully, and as soon as it was over Owen excused himself and went to his study. How was it, he thought furiously, closing the door behind him with a sense of relief, that the damn woman always went for the jugular? It was as though she deliberately sought out his most vulnerable areas and dug her knife in. He was well aware of the outbreak of bullying in the latter half of term and had taken stringent measures to contain it, but it was proving hard to eliminate completely. If it continued next term, they might be forced to consider exclusion, a move they were loath to take.

He walked over to his desk and bent over it, hands flat on its surface. Rose was getting worse, he thought despairingly.

For Fleur's sake he'd always tried to contain his anger at her constant needling, but the limit of his tolerance was fast approaching.

Truth to tell, he'd been in two minds about applying for the St Catherine's job, precisely because of the proximity of his mother-in-law. But he'd been thinking of moving from the Bromley school for some time, and it was Fleur who'd seen the ad in the *Times Educational Supplement* and begged him to apply. And he was forced to admit that Rose had been more than generous in handing over her house to them at a ridiculously low price. Also, he reminded himself, there were times when she was charming and seemed almost fond of him, but they were few and far between and getting fewer.

He straightened, telling himself he couldn't allow one opinionated woman to mar his enjoyment in the job he loved with a passion. If all it took to keep the peace was for him to hold his tongue, so be it.

The flat was in darkness when, with some trepidation, Jess arrived just after nine o'clock that evening. A scrawled note was propped against a candlestick on the table, reading *Gone to the Peacock. Come and join us if you're not too late. M.*

She *was* too late, Jess thought thankfully, grateful to have some time alone in the flat as she forced herself to look down at the carpet where, unbelievably, a man's body had lain. What had happened to him? Where was he now? Above all, *who* was he? All questions to which she was unlikely ever to find the answers.

Breakfast at Sandstone. Although it was Monday the girls were still in bed, not having to be in school until later, and their parents were enjoying the unusual calm. Fleur was trying to calculate the best time to phone Sue, while Owen skimmed through the local paper.

'Good God!' he exclaimed suddenly, making Fleur jump. 'That body that was washed up a few miles down the coast – it seems the man didn't drown, he was murdered! And even more incredibly, I met him! There's an artist's impression here.'

'You *met* him?' Fleur repeated, laying down her cup. 'Where and when?'

'The day before Cassie's birthday. If you remember, I had to go to Bristol to collect her present, and arranged to meet Charles for lunch. He was late as usual and I was at the bar having a pint while I waited for him. This guy came and perched next to me and we started talking. Just general stuff really. He said it was his first visit to the UK and was asking about Bristol. Then Charles arrived and we went through to the restaurant, and that was the last I saw of him.'

He glanced back at the paper. 'The police are appealing for anyone with any information to get in touch, but I hardly think a couple of words over a pint would count for much.'

'It would prove he was in Bristol that day,' Fleur said.

'True. Well, I'll give it a thought.' He glanced at his watch. 'I must go. Have a good day, sweetheart.' And after a quick kiss he was gone. By the time the front door closed behind him, Fleur, intent on her worries, had forgotten all about her husband's encounter.

FIVE

As Patrick was leaving for work that morning, a brightly coloured postcard dropped through the letter box, and since he was running late he slipped it in his pocket and promptly forgot it until half an hour later as he was opening office mail. The picture on the front was, predictably, the Leaning Tower of Pisa.

Guess where I am! Jess had written.

> *Italy is glorious – I can highly recommend it! We visited Florence yesterday and it was breathtaking – too much really to take in on one visit. Good excuse to go back! Food, weather and hotel all great. As they say, Wish you were here! Love, Jess.*

It was dated a week ago; she was probably back by now, and the realization awoke his previous worries about their brief conversation on the stairs at Sandstone. He'd give her a call later and hope to get some more information out of her, but with luck whatever the crisis had been would now be resolved. With which comforting thought, Patrick returned to his correspondence.

To Jess's heartfelt relief, her encounter with Maggie that morning passed off smoothly. In fact, she was so exactly the same that Jess could almost have believed she'd dreamt the whole thing. But then, she told herself, she'd had two weeks to prepare.

'Thanks for the card,' Maggie said. 'We were all very envious!'

'I'm surprised it arrived before I did!' Jess replied.

'Only just; it came on Saturday. What time did you get back last night?'

'Around nine. Not late by your standards, I know, but I didn't feel up to changing and going out again. Did you have a good evening?'

'It was OK. Connor was disappointed you didn't show,' Maggie added slyly.

'I'm sure he got over it.'

She laughed. 'We're going to try that new Thai restaurant in Park Street this evening. It's had good reviews. Table booked for eight p.m. OK?'

'OK.' So this evening would be the test, Jess thought; meeting the group en bloc and trying to guess which of them might be a murderer. She felt slightly sick at the prospect.

During the coffee break at work, however, there was a further development. A copy of the local paper was lying on a table, and while awaiting her turn at the coffee machine Jess picked it up. She was idly flicking through it when a headline caught her eye and she came to an abrupt halt.

BODY ON BEACH FOUND TO BE MURDER VICTIM

Her heart suddenly pounding, her eyes raced down the rest of the column:

> *At a press conference last night police revealed that the man whose body recently washed up on Clevecombe beach had not, as assumed, drowned, but died from a knife wound to the chest. Torquay landlady Mrs Emma Noble, 65, recognized the deceased from an artist's impression and identified him as Bruce Marriott, an Australian who was staying at her B&B. He'd told her he'd be away for a couple of nights and had taken only his briefcase with him.*
>
> *Police are anxious to speak to anyone with information concerning Mr Marriott's movements since his arrival in this country and especially after 19th June, the date on which he left Torquay.*

Below the report was a sketch of a face strongly resembling the one that had haunted her for the last two weeks.

Jess's mouth was dry. Did Maggie know? If so, would it be noticeable when they met this evening? And why was a man recently arrived from Australia lying dead on their carpet?

'Jess?'

Her colleague's slightly raised voice penetrated her musings and she looked up.

'If you've finished with my paper, I'd like a shot at the crossword before getting back to work.'

Jess flushed. 'Sorry, Jan, I didn't realize it was yours.' She paused. 'What's all this about a body? It must have happened while I was away.'

'Oh yes; he was found on the beach at Clevecombe – fully dressed, which seemed odd, and he'd been in the water some time. Bit of a shock to hear he'd been murdered, though. No one's been reported missing so it was assumed he was a holiday-maker who could have come from anywhere in the country – or the world, for that matter. As, it seems, he had. At least thanks to his landlady he now has a name.'

'He'd no means of identification on him?'

Jan shook her head. 'But now they know who he was there's sure to be much wider coverage.'

Her prediction proved well founded, for as Jess hurried out of the office two hours later in search of lunch her mobile rang, identifying the caller as Rachel.

'Is this guy in the paper who I think it is?' she asked without preamble.

Jess moved off the busy pavement into a doorway. 'It must be, mustn't it?'

'I presume you've still not contacted the police?'

'Give me a chance!' Jess defended herself.

'Well, here's your opportunity. Now they're actually *asking* for information.'

'I'd still be chief suspect as whistle-blower.'

Rachel's sigh came down the line. She changed tack. 'How was Maggie when you saw her?'

'Exactly the same. No hint of any trouble. We're meeting some of the others this evening, and since I've no idea which, if any of them, was involved, I'll have to be wary of everyone. Frankly I'm terrified I'll give myself away.'

'Tell you what: how about phoning the police and just saying you saw this man going into the block of flats? That doesn't tie you down but it'd give them a lead. They'd interview everyone in the building but none of your lot would suspect you, specially since they thought you'd gone home before it happened. Admittedly it mightn't lead anywhere, but you'd have done your "civic duty".'

'It's an idea certainly, provided they'd guarantee not to release my name.'

'There you are, then,' Rachel said with satisfaction. 'I'll get off the line so you can call them now.' And without giving her a chance to comment further she rang off.

Jess stood for a moment longer in the doorway, her appetite gone. Despite her apprehension she'd felt guilty about not reporting her involvement, and as Rachel said this presented a safer way of complying. But she didn't want a lengthy phone call, being put on hold while she was passed from one extension to another and having to explain herself a dozen times. Better to go to the police station now and speak to someone in person.

In the event it was not all that straightforward. It transpired that the station was inundated with reported sightings and her request to speak to someone in charge met with short shrift.

'No one's available at the moment, madam, but if you could leave your contact number someone will get back to you.'

Jess shook her head. 'This is important information. I saw this man go into a building on Friday the twenty-first.'

The civilian behind the desk hesitated. 'If you could give us the address—'

'No!' Jess heard her voice rise in frustration and as she drew a breath to steady it a man emerged from an internal door, pausing as he caught sight of her. He glanced at them with raised eyebrows.

'A problem, Bill?'

The man shook his head. 'Just another alleged sighting, Sarge.'

Jess had had enough. 'There's no alleged about it!' she said heatedly. 'I saw him with my own eyes, but if no one believes me I'm obviously wasting my time.'

She turned to go but the detective put a hand on her arm. 'Just a minute, ma'am. I'm DS Rob Stuart and I'm working on the Marriott case. Am I right in assuming you have some information?'

Jess held his eye unflinchingly. 'Yes, I have.'

'Then if you'd like to come with me, I'd be grateful to hear what you have to say.'

With a look of triumph at the hapless clerk, Jess allowed herself to be led to a door across the foyer which her companion opened, ushering her into a small room containing little but a table and several chairs. While she seated herself he made a phone call and shortly afterwards a tap on the door heralded another officer, who identified himself as DC Masters and took his place next to the sergeant.

'Now,' Stuart began, 'perhaps we could start by taking your name and address?'

Jess hesitated. 'Do I have to give them? I'd be much more comfortable remaining anonymous.'

'I'm afraid it's necessary for our records, ma'am, but don't worry, your details won't be made public. So, you are Ms . . .?'

'Tempest,' she said reluctantly. 'Jessica Tempest.'

'And your address?'

Again, she paused. 'This is where it becomes difficult. He went into the building where I live, but I don't want to be known as the one who reported it.'

'Ah, I see your point, but as I explained we never reveal our sources.'

Perforce accepting his assurance, Jess gave them the address of the flats and the date on which she'd seen the man who'd been identified as Bruce Marriott, making a rough guess at the time he'd arrived at the building.

'What makes you so sure it was him?' the constable enquired.

She improvised. 'I was able to have a good look at him, because he was going in as I came out, and he held the door for me.'

'Did he say anything?'

Should she hint at an accent? But his landlady would know whether or not he had one, so better play safe. 'No, he just smiled,' she replied. 'Could you say a passer-by had seen him?'

DS Stuart smiled reassuringly. 'Still worried, Ms Tempest? Don't be. We always keep some things back and what you've told us, valuable though it might well be, is unlikely to be made public.'

'Thank you.' He was being so considerate that Jess briefly wished she'd given him the true facts, though as Rachel said she'd pointed the police in the right direction and the rest was up to them.

'So now will you read through your statement which DC Masters has taken down, and if everything is correct, please sign it.'

Jess had a moment of panic. Would she be committing a crime by confirming she'd met Marriott outside the building? Too late to think of that now, and at least she'd reported seeing him. Biting her lip and mentally crossing her fingers, she signed the statement.

Stuart pushed back his chair and came to his feet. 'Thank you. We're very grateful to you for coming forward; this could well be the lead we've been looking for.'

Out in the foyer he shook her hand, asked her to get in touch if she remembered anything else, and handed her his card so she could reach him directly.

As the heavy doors swung to behind her Jess felt a huge sense of relief. She'd done what was required of her – or almost – and a weight had been lifted. Whether logically or not, she felt a great deal safer – and she still had time to grab a sandwich before going back to the office.

An hour earlier, Patrick had set off for a meeting in Exeter, Jess's postcard in his pocket as a reminder to contact her.

His appointment wasn't until two thirty, and although he knew there was little chance of Natasha being free at such short notice, he'd allowed extra time on the off-chance they might manage lunch together. However a quick call had established that she was in France. Elusive as smoke! he thought frustratedly. No reason, though, why he shouldn't have a decent meal himself. Lately sandwiches at his desk had been the norm.

Having parked his car he started to walk towards the cathedral, glancing at displayed menus as he passed without finding anything that appealed. He'd decided to settle on the next restaurant he came to when he remembered his father mentioning a few weeks ago that he'd had a good meal at somewhere called L'Aperitif, and resolved to give it a try. It could go on expenses, too, he thought with satisfaction. A quick check on his mobile established it was only a couple of minutes' walk away and he quickened his steps, already anticipating an enjoyable lunch.

It was obvious as soon as he entered the restaurant that it was busy – a good sign, but he hoped service would be quick or he'd be pressed for time. Obeying the notice *Please wait to be seated*, he glanced idly round the room and his eyes skidded to a sudden halt. At a corner table his father was in earnest conversation with a woman, his hand resting lightly on hers. Patrick hesitated, wondering whether to beat a hasty retreat; but he'd been looking forward to this meal and didn't see why he should forfeit it.

Before he could change his mind he went over to their table, registering the shock on Justin's face as he caught sight of him.

'Patrick!' he exclaimed, his face reddening. 'What are you doing here?'

'I have a meeting with John Simpson at two thirty,' Patrick answered steadily, 'and decided to give your recommendation a try.' Now, as he turned to the woman awaiting an introduction, he realized he'd seen her before, though he couldn't remember where.

Justin moistened his lips. 'I believe you've met Mrs Grant? We did some probate work for her earlier this year.'

'Of course.' Patrick nodded at her. She too had flushed and was looking decidedly uncomfortable.

'Shall I bring another chair, sir?'

Patrick turned to the waiter who'd followed him across. 'No, that won't be necessary, thank you,' he said quickly. 'There are some notes I must look over while I have my meal.'

'Very well, sir. A table for one, then? I believe one's just become available, if you'd care to follow me?'

Patrick nodded to the couple motionless in front of him, turned on his heel and followed the waiter. My *God*! he was thinking; what have I stumbled on? Was it possible Dad and this Grant woman were having an *affair*? Did this account for his changing moods during the last month or two, his banishment from the marital bedroom?

His thoughts continued to collide as he studied the menu and placed an order. If there *was* some truth in all this, Mrs Grant was an unlikely mistress. Not only was she a fairly recent widow, but in Patrick's view she'd little to recommend her. Aged about fifty, she was pale and ordinary-looking – not a patch on Mum, he thought with fierce loyalty. What the *hell* was Dad thinking?

His steak arrived with exemplary swiftness, cooked exactly as requested, but he gave it little attention. From Mrs Grant his thoughts had turned to his father, regarding him in the totally unaccustomed light of a lover. The idea was ludicrous, yet on reflection he was a good-looking man, tall and straight, his horn-rimmed spectacles giving an air of dependability. Huh! Patrick thought viciously. Thank God he didn't have to go back to the office this afternoon. How Dad would react next time they did meet, he couldn't begin to imagine. Well, that was his problem. Patrick certainly wouldn't make the first move.

He'd deliberately seated himself with his back to the couple and when, twenty minutes later, he left the restaurant he didn't so much as glance in their direction. Whether or not the table was still occupied he neither knew nor cared.

The closer she came to meeting the others the more Jess's feeling of safety dissipated. Mouth dry, throat closed – suppose she was unable to eat? They'd wonder what was wrong with her. How many would be there this evening, she wondered fearfully, and, whether they were implicated or not, how many knew what had happened? Would she be the only one supposed to be in ignorance?

She had reached the restaurant and, drawing a deep breath, pushed her way inside, meeting a blast of ice-cold air conditioning. She saw them at once; Connor, who had been watching the door, stood up and waved to her and she threaded her way between the tables to join them.

'Welcome back!' he said, pulling out the chair next to him. 'Had a good time?'

'Very, thanks.' *Had the police been to the flat yet?*

'Great tan!' Sarah commented, glancing up from the menu. 'I'm counting the days till I go away.'

Maggie said, 'She brought me back some of the local dried pasta and a packet of seasoning – a mix of spices, including chilli flakes. Can't wait to try it!'

'Save it for when we're round for supper!' Laurence put in.

They all seemed so *normal*, Jess thought, as she tried each voice in turn against the whispers she'd heard from the wardrobe; but she'd been unable to tell even at the time whether they were male or female.

It was halfway through the main course that Di remarked casually, 'Did anyone see that thing in the paper today, about the body that was washed up?'

'What "thing", exactly?' asked Dominic.

'Well, apparently the guy was murdered!'

Sarah raised an eyebrow. 'How did they come up with that?'

'A knife wound. The police have only just released that fact.'

'Gruesome!' Sarah commented, and returned to her curry.

Jess kept her eyes firmly on her plate, terrified she might intercept an exchanged glance she wasn't meant to see. *Keep eating!* she instructed herself, though each mouthful was sticking in her throat.

'Probably a bar-room brawl,' Dominic suggested. 'Remember that case a few years ago? Two seamen got into a fight, one pulled a knife. It's surprising it doesn't happen more often, now knife crime's on the increase.'

Maggie hadn't made any comment, Jess noted. Nor had Laurence or Connor. Was that significant, or were they just not interested? But as she and Rachel had deduced, Maggie, as owner of the flat, must surely be involved. She repressed a shiver, thankfully conscious that the conversation had moved on.

'You OK, Jess?'

Connor's voice startled her back to the present. God, this was just what she hadn't wanted to happen! She gave him a bright smile.

'Fine, thanks.'

'You're making heavy weather of that curry!' His voice was teasing, but there was an underlying note of concern. *Please don't let it be Connor!*

'Hangover from the holiday!' she said. 'First day back at work, and all that. Sorry if I'm being a drag; I should probably have opted out and gone home to bed!'

'I'm glad you didn't,' he said quietly. 'But I'll run you back now, if you're wilting. My car's just down the road.'

'Thanks, but so is mine. I'm OK, really.'

Di leaned across the table. 'You said you'd been to the Uffizi, Jess. What was it like?'

And to Jess's infinite relief the conversation moved from the personal and remained innocuous till the end of the evening.

There was a full moon, and in the light seeping through the curtains shadows chased themselves across the bedroom ceiling. His right arm had gone to sleep, but Owen was loath to move it. It had taken Fleur a long time to drift off, tears drying on her cheeks, and he didn't want to risk waking her.

Why the *hell* hadn't she told him weeks ago? he thought helplessly, worry gnawing at him. A lump, for God's sake! She was a sensible woman; she knew the risks of delay. What would he do if he lost her? The thought flashed into his head before he could stop it and he clamped down on it before it took hold. Think of something else! he commanded himself.

But a lesser worry lay waiting to surface – the spate of bullying at school, young Jamie Coulson's tear-stained face, and his mother-in-law's acid voice: *I'm surprised you allow it, Owen.*

He gritted his teeth in the darkness. If that woman didn't ease up on her criticisms, so help him he'd throttle her! He imagined her surprise if he suddenly seized her round the throat, and a reluctant smile came to his face. A pretty pass when the only thing to calm him was imagining violence towards his mother-in-law! Yet, oddly, it had the desired effect and after a while he too sank into sleep.

SIX

'God, Patrick, are you sure?'

'Well, it's a bit of a no-brainer, isn't it, all things considered? Holding hands in an expensive restaurant, where you wouldn't expect to see anyone you knew?'

Amy said in a small voice, 'Do you think Mum knows?'

'She must have some idea, if she banished him to the guest room.'

'It's worse than we thought, then.'

'Yep.'

'Look, you're on hand; it's much easier for you to see them than for me to get time off.'

'We didn't get very far last time I went round.'

'But it's different now; Dad knows you know, or at least suspect. He'll probably try to find out how he stands.' She paused. 'Perhaps he was only trying to comfort her over the death of her husband.'

'One way of putting it.'

She sighed. 'No, you're right. Besides, if you handled probate earlier in the year, he'll have died some time ago. They've obviously kept in touch.'

Patrick glanced at his watch. 'Anyway, I just wanted to put you in the picture. I'll keep you posted, but I'll wait for Dad to make the first move. Must go, sis, duty calls.'

'Me too. Thanks for letting me know. I think.'

Patrick started his car. The other phone call he wanted to make was to Jess, but he wasn't sure of the best time to call her. Around lunchtime, perhaps. With his mind still full of family problems, he drove to work.

'There's more on that Australian guy,' Owen remarked at breakfast, laying down his newspaper. 'It seems he was a successful businessman until a few years ago, when there was some kind of scandal and his company slumped.'

'Not had much luck, has he?' Fleur commented. 'Did you tell the police you'd spoken to him?'

'Yes, but I gather they've been deluged with people phoning in. I doubt if they'll get back to me.' He folded his napkin. 'Must go, love. Let me know if you get an appointment.'

Ten minutes later Fleur was still at the kitchen table, the phone in her hand. There'd been a cancellation at the surgery and she'd been allocated an appointment with Dr Price later that day. So much for her hope of avoiding him! What would she know by supper time?

The answer, of course, was very little. Unless Dr Price was able to give her instant and categorical assurance that the lump was non-malignant – a most unlikely hypothesis – the most she could hope for was that she'd have the result of a biopsy within a few days. Somehow, she'd have to live through those days.

As promised she sent a quick text to Owen, then made a cup of coffee and carried it upstairs to her studio – a grandiose name for what was basically one of the attics. Nonetheless, a studio it had become – a pleasant, comfortable room with clear northern light, a large table at which she worked, a computer and bookshelves filled with books she'd illustrated. The deadline for the one she was working on was fast approaching and she needed to get back to it.

Resolutely pushing worries aside, she re-read the emailed text and began to make preliminary sketches.

Justin Linscott had seriously considered not going in to the office today. However, delay was unlikely to help matters and he was anxious that their work colleagues should be unaware of any atmosphere between himself and Patrick. Accordingly, after glancing briefly at his mail, he went down the corridor to his son's room, tapped on the door and went in, closing it behind him.

Patrick looked up from his computer and across the room the two men eyed each other in silence. Then, steeling himself, Justin said, 'She's a client, for God's sake!'

'Was,' Patrick corrected. 'Months ago.'

'I was in Exeter on business and we happened to bump into each other. What would be more natural than asking her to join me for lunch?'

Patrick leaned back in his chair, hands behind his head, his eyes never leaving his father's. 'Sorry, Dad, not good enough.'

Justin ran his hand through his hair, came further into the room and sat down, leaning forward with his hands between his knees. 'Look, I don't know what you think you stumbled on but we really were just having lunch.'

'Holding hands?'

To his annoyance Justin felt his face redden. 'We were *not* "holding hands", as you so quaintly put it. When you came over, I was patting her hand to reassure her on a point I'd just made.'

'Why are you sleeping in the guest room?' Patrick asked abruptly.

His father stared at him, thrown by the change of direction. 'None of your damn business!' he snapped.

'Just putting two and two together.'

Justin's temper started to rise and with an effort he held it down. 'All right, as you're determined to be intrusive, I *have* met Hilary Grant a couple of times over the last month or two. She's been having a bad time one way or another since her husband died and wanted my advice. And yes, since you've brought it up, your mother and I *have* been going through a difficult patch. It happens in the best of marriages and will blow over.'

'Not if you meet other women for lunch,' Patrick said. 'Did you tell her your wife doesn't understand you?'

Justin stood up angrily. 'There's no point in continuing this if you insist on being offensive. I've tried to explain the position and it's up to you whether or not you choose to believe it.'

And with that, he left the room. Patrick leaned forward slowly and put his head in his hands. He could have handled that better, as Amy was sure to tell him. So what, if anything, would happen now?

*   *   *

Jess stared down at the text she'd just received. *Meet me for lunch, 1 p.m. at Giraffe? (Maggie says that's your lunch hour!) Please come! Connor.*

Oh God, what should she do? She liked him, but was it wise to develop any kind of relationship until she knew whether or not he was involved in the murder? The obvious answer was very definitely no; the trouble was that she really wanted to.

She read the text again. Well, one lunch was innocuous enough, and she'd have the legitimate safeguard of a time limit. Also, it would be the first occasion they'd be together without the rest of the crowd, so a chance to get to know each other better. And if she didn't like what she learned, she needn't pursue it and there'd be no harm done.

OK, thanks, she typed rapidly, and sent it before she could change her mind.

Jess's mobile rang as she was leaving the office, identifying the caller as her cousin.

'Hi, Patrick; I'm just on my way to lunch.'

'Which I was hoping would be a good time for a chat.'

'Afraid not, actually; I'm meeting someone and running a bit late.'

'Anyone interesting?'

She smiled. 'That's what I aim to find out!'

'Ah! Well, far be it from me to stand in the way of young love!'

'It's hardly that!' she protested, hurrying along the pavement. 'Can I call you back this evening? Sixish?'

'OK, do that. And make sure he gives you a good lunch!'

She was still smiling as she turned into Cabot Circus and made her way up to the café. Connor stood to greet her as she went in. 'Thanks for coming,' he said.

He held her chair while she seated herself. 'Let's order straight away,' he suggested, passing her the menu. 'Then we can settle down to talk without interruption.'

Everyone seemed to want to talk to her, Jess thought. After a brief discussion they made their choices – Pulled BBQ Beef for Connor, Katsu Chicken for Jess – and, as the waiter moved

away, they sat back and smiled at each other tentatively. There
was a momentary pause.

'Long time no see!' she said facetiously, to break it.

'Actually, it's because of last night that I contacted you.
Despite your assurances, you didn't seem yourself and I
wondered if I could help in any way?'

'I told you, it was post-holiday fatigue.'

'And nothing more?'

'Nothing more,' she said firmly.

'Well, that's good.' He paused and gave a little laugh. 'You
know, it must be at least six weeks since we first met, and it's
just struck me that all I know about you is your name!'

She smiled. 'What do you want to know?'

'Well, certainly more than that! Your likes and dislikes,
where you work, your taste in music. How about your family,
for starters. Any brothers or sisters?'

'Two younger sisters, both still at school.'

'Are you close?'

She shrugged. 'Fairly close to the elder, but the younger
one's a nightmare!'

'And your parents?'

'My mother illustrates children's books, my father's a deputy
headmaster.'

'Wow! Impressive! What school?'

'St Catherine's College.'

'And I suppose you went there yourself?'

'No, by the time we moved down here I was at university,
but my grandparents lived in St Cat's – my grandmother still
does – so I've always known it. Now it's your turn! What
family do you have?'

'Parents, one in insurance, one in IT, and an older married
brother.'

'And where do they live?'

He laughed wryly. 'Oh, we're all Bristolians, born and bred.
None of us have strayed far, except for uni.'

Jess tried to sound casual. 'So you've known Maggie and
the others for some time?'

'No, actually, only Dom.' He paused. 'A long-term relationship had just ended and he took me along with him one night

to cheer me up. To be honest I needed a bit of persuading, but he insisted it was open house and I'd be welcome, and that was how it started.' He smiled a little. 'Though to be honest, I've only started going regularly since you arrived!'

'As it happens,' Jess said quickly, 'a break-up was one of my reasons for coming to Bristol.'

'There you go! I knew we had something in common!'

'So you knew the person who was sharing with Maggie before me?'

'Not really; I met her a couple of times, but she was leaving to get married so she spent most evenings with her fiancé.'

Their food arrived, causing a natural break in the conversation. The waiter poured sparkling water into their glasses, hoped they'd enjoy their meal, and moved away. Snippets of conversation from the neighbouring tables reached them, and as they unfolded their napkins Jess admitted to herself that her initial liking of Connor had strengthened. Also, since he was relatively new to the group, she persuaded herself he was unlikely to have been one of those who'd sanitized the crime scene.

His voice broke into her thoughts. 'A penny for them!'

She flushed, shaking her head. 'Not worth it!' she said.

He took the hint and there were no more personal questions, both of them accepting that enough information had been exchanged for the moment. At the end of the meal they left together.

'Can we do this again?' Connor enquired as they emerged from the Circus and prepared to go their separate ways.

'I'd like to,' Jess acknowledged. 'And thank you for my lunch.'

'You're more than welcome. See you this evening, perhaps?'

'I don't think so; Maggie's staying on at the centre for a late delivery.'

'Tomorrow, then?'

'Probably,' she said.

'Before too long, anyway. Bye, Jess.'

'Goodbye, and thanks again.'

As she walked back to the office, Jess replayed their conversations in her head, analysing her overall reaction. Favourable, she decided, but she'd no intention of becoming too close to Connor till she knew a lot more about what had happened in the flat the afternoon she left for St Cat's.

The first person Fleur saw as she reached the surgery was Dr Roger Price, Jess's erstwhile boyfriend. Instinctively she hesitated, but it was too late to withdraw; he'd seen her, and after a corresponding flash of embarrassment, was coming towards her with a smile.

'Fleur!' he said, holding out his hand. 'Good to see you.'

'You too, Roger. How are you?'

'Busy as always. What's the news of Jess? Has she settled in Bristol OK?'

'I think so. She and Rachel are just back from a holiday in Italy.'

'The obligatory girls' jolly!' he commented. 'I remember it well! Nothing was allowed to interfere with that!'

Fleur smiled distractedly. 'I'd better report to Reception,' she murmured.

'Yes, of course.' He hesitated and she realized he was refraining from asking how she was. The mere fact that she was here meant something was amiss and even the most conventional query might breach medical ethics. She was his father's patient, not his.

'Good to see you,' he said again, and she nodded, moving towards the desk to register her arrival.

It was sheer bliss to have the flat to herself that evening. Jess kicked off her shoes, poured herself a G&T and settled on the sofa. After a day in a busy office she craved some quiet time to herself, which, as she'd complained to Rachel, Maggie's social arrangements usually denied her. But her peace was soon interrupted by the ringing of her mobile and, glancing impatiently at the ID, she remembered her promise to phone Patrick.

'How was lunch?' he asked in greeting.

'Very good, thanks.'

'Where did he take you?'

'Giraffe, in Cabot Circus. I'd recommend it.'

'Right. I'll look in next time I'm up. Are you going to tell me the name of the latest Lothario?'

'He's not that, I told you, but if you must know, his name's Connor Ross.'

'Connor Ross?' Patrick repeated, his voice rising. 'Honestly? You had lunch with Connor Ross?'

Jess sat up straighter. 'You know him?'

'Not well, but we were at school together and I see him at reunions. The last I heard he was on the point of becoming engaged.'

'It fell through,' Jess said. 'I'd forgotten you lived in Bristol then.'

'So how did you meet?'

'He's a friend of my flatmate's.' She paused. 'Did you like him?'

Patrick gave a short laugh. 'Jess, I hardly knew him. He's a couple of years older and at that age it makes a huge difference; we didn't come into contact, though he was quite a hero of mine – very good at sport and in all the school teams.' He paused. 'More importantly, do *you* like him?'

'I think so.'

'Poor chap! Treats you to lunch, and that's the best you can come up with!'

'I'm just being cautious, after Roger.'

'Point taken. Now, enough about Connor Ross. What the hell were you on about at Cassie's party? I don't mind telling you, you gave me a few sleepless nights worrying about it.'

'I'm sorry,' Jess said contritely. 'I shouldn't have said anything.'

'But you *did*, so you at least owe me an explanation.'

It was as well that she'd talked it over with Rachel, Jess reflected thankfully, since as Patrick knew Connor, albeit slightly, there was no chance now of confiding in him.

'Really,' she said, almost truthfully, 'it's all been . . . settled now.'

'But you said someone had *died*, for God's sake!'

'Patrick, honestly, it's nothing for you to worry about. I was probably a bit tipsy.'

There was a brief silence. Then he said resignedly, 'I'd forgotten how stubborn you can be!'

Jess breathed a sigh of relief. 'Tell me about your love life,' she invited. 'Is the gorgeous Tasha still on the scene?'

'As much as she's ever been.'

'Still being elusive?'

'I haven't a hope in hell, Jess. I've always known that.'

'Faint heart never won fair lady!'

'There's such a thing as being realistic.'

'Then why not make a clean break?'

'For the simple reason that I can't let her go. Pathetic, isn't it?'

'So you'll just go on feeling sorry for yourself? Come on, Patrick! You've more backbone than that.'

'Very clever!' he said heavily. 'I phone you to ask for an explanation and you turn the tables on me!'

'It's for your own good.'

'Which doesn't make it any easier to hear.'

'I love you really!'

'Glad someone does!' He paused. 'Sorry, scrub that. Things are somewhat fraught on the home front, so I'm a bit thin-skinned at the moment.'

'Oh? What's happened?'

'I had a run-in with the old man so I'm in the doghouse. It'll blow over, don't worry.' His voice changed. 'Talk of the devil! Tasha's calling on my landline.'

'Right!' Jess said. 'Here's your chance to sweep her off her feet!' And heard his low laugh as he rang off.

'Look, love,' Ron Barlow said desperately, 'it's her *birthday*! She'd love to see you.'

'That would be a first!' Gemma retorted, hating the bitterness in her voice. She heard him sigh. Poor Dad, it wasn't his fault; he seemed to spend his life trying to smooth things over.

Across the room she caught Brad's eye and he raised a reproving eyebrow, which she ignored.

Ron tried again. 'It would only be for lunch. You could make some excuse and leave straight after, but a family lunch on her birthday—'

'Is Freddie going?' she interrupted.

'Yes. Come on, Gem, make it a full house!'

Hearing the pleading in her father's voice, Gemma felt the prick of unwelcome tears. It always seemed to end like this.

'Gemma?'

'I'll think about it,' she said sullenly, knowing the battle was lost.

'Thanks, love.' Ron knew it too. 'That'll be just great.'

She cut the connection and stood for a moment, still holding the phone, before turning to Brad, who was lounging on the sofa. 'Why do I always give in? Why?' she demanded angrily. Then she drew a deep breath. 'All right, I know you think I'm a cow but you don't know the half of it!'

'Then tell me.'

She shook her head dismissively but he held out an arm and, still seething, she went and sat down next to him, feeling that arm come round her.

'How come I've never met your parents?' he asked idly. 'We've been together for a while now.'

'I prefer to keep my life in compartments,' she replied, making herself speak lightly. 'Work, relationships, family. It's less complicated that way.'

'And never the trey shall meet?'

'Exactly.'

'And if, heaven forfend, you should decide to get married, what then?'

'I'll cross that bridge when I come to it. Now, pour me a drink and I'll make a start on supper.'

Patrick's satisfyingly long phone call with Natasha was drawing to a close. He'd managed to persuade her to spend the weekend with him, a major coup, and was already planning where to take her when she said suddenly, 'Oh, I forgot to tell you – the strangest thing! You know that man who was washed up near you a week or two ago? He's been identified as Bruce Marriott from Oz, and guess what? I met him once, at a function in Sydney!'

'God, how creepy! The police are saying he was murdered. What was he like?'

'Quite a big cheese but seemed pleasant enough. We only talked for a few minutes, but after I'd left Oz an aunt told me he'd been involved in some sort of scandal, though I don't remember the details.'

'Even creepier! Do you think the police here know?'

'Bound to; they'll be digging around over there, I have no doubt, but I guess they'll play it close to their chest. Probably nothing to do with his murder anyway. So: Friday evening; OK if I drive up around seven?'

'Perfect. See you then.'

It had been easy enough to end the conversation with Brad, less easy to shut off the tumult of emotions that followed any contact with her family. Lying next to him later that night, weary of fighting her memories, Gemma let them come.

It hadn't always been like this. With an ache of the heart she remembered bedtime stories, goodnight kisses, running to her mother with grazed knees for them to be kissed better, aware – though she'd never thought to question it – of being loved. Then, when she was eight or nine, Jenny had become pregnant and, though initially surprised that such things happened at her mother's age, Gemma had been quite excited. It would be good to have a little brother or sister; Freddie, three years her senior, was always off with his friends, who didn't appreciate her tagging along. She could help Mummy bathe the new baby, wheel it out in its pram.

But the baby was stillborn, and everything changed. For a long time – weeks, it seemed – her mother had spent her days crying, and she and Freddie were forbidden ever to mention it; incredibly, they still didn't know if it had been a boy or girl. As a result a barrier had grown up and the sense of separation grew until it struck Gemma that her mother must have loved the dead baby more than herself. That idea took root, strengthened and festered. It was only now, lying sleepless in the dark, that she realized her own withdrawal had been a defence mechanism, protection against being hurt.

Eventually, of course, Jenny had made an effort to resume her role as mother but it was too late, and when Gemma had continued to rebuff her advances, she'd turned instead to the

Tempest family, and their young children seemed to take the place of herself and Freddie in her affections.

Gemma turned restlessly on to her side, pulling the pillow under her chin as the memories continued to plague her. For years, though, she'd been unaware of the extent of her mother's interest in the Tempests; in the early days she'd been at school all day, and on leaving she'd moved into a flat with a girlfriend. It came as a shock when, after the family moved to Somerset, her parents forsook their annual European holiday, always a highlight of their year, for a fortnight near Weston-super-Mare.

'I can't believe it!' she'd fumed to Freddie. 'It's not as though they were particularly friendly with Owen and Fleur! To the best of my knowledge they've never even been to our house, nor the parents to theirs. It's those bloody girls that are the draw! *Why*, in heaven's name? Aren't we enough for them?'

Her brother had shrugged. 'No skin off our noses, is it? It's not as though they try to drag us down there with them. Be thankful for that!'

But Gemma would privately have preferred it if they had. They'd been down again last month, she remembered, with the usual rush of emotion she unwillingly recognized as jealousy. And therein lay the trouble: at some level she still loved her mother, and knew to her shame that that was why she lashed out.

In an attempt to escape the admission, she again turned over, pulling the duvet with her, and Brad grumbled in his sleep. 'Sorry!' she whispered.

Sorry. Sorry for so many things. For the lost little brother or sister, for not trying to understand her mother's loss, for being spoilt and jealous and causing her father such pain, for so many things in her life. And as the slow, hot tears soaked into her pillow, they brought enough relief for her to be able to slide into sleep.

SEVEN

Sydney, Australia. New Year's Eve 2012

The scene in front of her was breathtaking, as ships of all sizes decorated with rope lights sailed across the water in the fantastic Harbour of Light Parade.

Mel, leaning on the rail, marvelled at her luck in being afforded such a vantage point; this balcony, with its grandstand view over the bridge, the harbour and the opera house, belonged to Dave Brooks, a work colleague of Jack's, who'd invited a group of friends to a New Year party, thereby saving them the hassle of fighting for space among the heaving crowds down on the waterfront. Which confirmed her belief that friends certainly had their uses.

Her own feelings, as at every New Year, were ambivalent: slight apprehension about stepping into the unknown – and possibly over a precipice – while at the same time welcoming the challenges it offered of new beginnings, a fresh start. And this particular New Year was certainly the time to take stock of her life, and what she'd achieved since arriving in Oz five years ago.

Admittedly she couldn't complain; since coming over as temporary maternity cover in a well-known hotel, she'd been systematically promoted until she'd attained a position of authority as Head of Housekeeping, with commensurate rises in salary. Lately, however, what had originally been cause for self-congratulation had begun to feel stale, and she was beginning to think it was time to move on. A fresh start was indeed what she needed – a point reinforced by Jack's proprietary arm round her shoulders. She gave a little shrug to dislodge it.

'Time to charge your glasses!' Dave called from inside. 'The midnight hour approacheth!'

Mel and Jack, along with others on the balcony, returned

to the room to take a brimming flute from the table. But as she bent to claim hers another hand, large and tanned, reached for the same glass and she automatically drew back, as did the man beside her.

'Sorry!' they said together, and laughed.

'Please!' He indicated that she should take it and she turned to thank him, meeting smiling grey eyes in a lean, tanned face. He held her glance for a shade longer than required before taking a couple of glasses himself. A current of excitement ran through her; a man with decided potential – just what she needed!

'Who was that?' she asked Jack casually. 'Another of your work colleagues?'

He glanced after the man, who, with his companion, had joined a group across the room. 'No, never met him. Probably one of Dave's tycoon mates.'

The countdown started and they all crowded back on the balcony as midnight struck. A great roar rose from the revellers round the harbour and the world-famous fireworks began, painting the sky in a stunning sequence of gold and blue and red and silver. Everyone was hugging and kissing and Dave edged his way between them, topping up their glasses as general chaos reigned.

It was some time later, when they'd all returned inside, that she felt a tap on her shoulder and a voice said, 'After trying to steal your drink, the least I can do is wish you a Happy New Year!'

He bent his head, but what began as a conventional New Year kiss suddenly deepened, taking them both by surprise, and it was with a palpable effort that they drew apart.

'Wow!' he said softly. 'And I don't even know your name!'

'Mel,' she supplied, heart hammering.

'Hi Mel! I'm Bruce.'

And as though in confirmation, a woman's voice called, 'Bruce! Hurry up with those canapés!'

For a second longer their gaze held, then he called back, 'Coming!'

Jack reappeared at her side, bearing a selection of the savouries now being laid out.

'OK?' he asked, glancing at her flushed face.

'Fine, why?'

'You look a bit . . . bemused!'

She forced a smile. 'It's all this champagne! Let's go back on the balcony, I need some fresh air.'

God! she thought incoherently; she'd been looking for a change, one that would, she hoped, advance her career, but physical attraction was an unexpected bonus and one she intended to make full use of.

It was three weeks before she saw him again. In that time, having adroitly learned his surname – Marriott – she'd looked him up online and discovered he'd established an interior decorating company three years ago, that he was born in 1978 and had married Sonia Mary Jessop in June 2009. There were two children of the marriage. Pity; that could be an obstacle.

She'd still not decided on the best means of approach when, as she was hurrying along Pitt Street one Saturday, a voice behind her said, 'Well, hello again! I thought it was you!'

She knew it! she thought, with a surge of triumph. Fate was on her side! She turned slowly to meet the grey eyes, the lopsided smile that had never been far from her thoughts.

'Hello,' she said.

He hesitated. 'You do remember me? Bruce? We met at New Year.'

'I remember,' she said.

'So: has 2013 started well for you?'

She shrugged. 'Room for improvement.'

'Oh? Might a coffee ease things along?'

Finally she returned his smile. 'It just might,' she said.

Ten minutes later they were seated at an outdoor table under a striped umbrella, cups of coffee in front of them.

'So,' he began, 'you're Mel. And that's absolutely all I know! Since you've got a British accent, I presume you weren't born here. Am I right?'

'Quite right. I've been here five years.'

'And what brought you in the first instance – holiday? Part of a world tour?'

She took a sip of coffee. 'It's a long story; a school friend of mine had come over two years earlier to work as a chef at the Beaufort Hotel. She'd been trying to persuade me to join her; then, just as things at home were beginning to go pear-shaped, she phoned to say a job was coming up for maternity cover in their restaurant. I had a degree in hotel management, so I applied for the job, did an online interview and was lucky enough to get it.'

He reached for a biscuit. 'What happened when the cover period ended?'

'Since my work permit was still good, I simply switched to housekeeping, where there was a vacancy.'

He raised an eyebrow. 'You make people's beds?'

'I did for a while, but now I'm head of department, which is much more interesting.'

'How so?'

'Well, for a start I order supplies, supervise the staff, schedule their rotas, liaise with the general manager, oversee budgets and maintenance reports – you name it!'

'Wow, multi-tasking on a large scale! We could do with someone like you in our business!' Bingo! Though her heart leapt she kept her face neutral as he added, 'Presumably you enjoy it?'

'I do, yes, but I've been there a while now and feel in need of a change. I'm tired of shift work, for one thing – it plays havoc with my social life!' She looked at him with a hint of challenge. 'But how about you? What's your line of work?' As if she didn't know!

'Oh, I started an interior decorating business a few years ago and I'm glad to say it's flourishing. In fact, we're in the process of widening our range, branching out a bit.' He paused. 'You said you came out because things had gone pear-shaped?' He made a dismissive gesture with one hand. 'Sorry, just being nosy.'

'It's fine. My parents had died within a year of each other' – she registered his exclamation of concern – 'and I'd no other family. They were in their late forties when I was born and had given up all hope of a family.' She smiled wryly. 'At the school gates, the other kids thought they were my grandparents!

Anyway, they'd left me a fair bit of money and there didn't seem any immediate chance of promotion at the hotel where I was working. So when Barb called about the job here, I decided to stretch my wings. And here I still am,' she ended.

'You're not thinking of going back to the UK?'

She lifted her shoulders with a little laugh. 'I'm not actually thinking of anything!'

'What about your friend? The one who persuaded you to come here?'

Mel grimaced. 'She got married last year and went to live in Perth.' She glanced at her watch. 'I must get back; my shift starts in twenty minutes.'

He said quickly, 'Perhaps we could finish this conversation later?'

She stood up and retrieved her bag from beside her chair. 'We've come full circle, haven't we? It *is* finished.'

'By no means! At least,' he amended, 'I hope not! Could we fix another meeting? If you could give me your number . . .?'

She smiled. 'Thanks for the coffee,' she said, and walked quickly away.

He'd contact her, she was sure of it; he knew where she worked. She'd wasted enough time with Jack and he was holding her back now. Bruce Marriott, on the other hand, had a thriving business, was wealthy, influential – and undeniably attractive. And he was interested, the more so since she'd not seemed eager to meet again. This could be just the break she needed. In the meantime, she had things to do.

As always, Jack was lounging in front of the television when she reached home just before midnight. He raised a lazy hand in greeting, his eyes still on the screen, and suddenly everything coalesced in her head – her general dissatisfaction, accentuated by a difficult conversation that evening with the general manager, Jack's placid assumption that they were together indefinitely and, above all, Bruce Marriott. Her future, she felt sure, lay with him, and it was time to clear the decks.

She walked over to the television and switched it off.

'Hey!' Jack looked up indignantly. 'I was watching that!'

'I've been thinking,' she said crisply. 'It's time for you to go home.'

'What?' He looked at her in bewilderment. 'I *am* home!'

'To your own flat. Not immediately, obviously. I'll give you a week to turf out your pals who're slumming it there.'

He struggled to his feet, unable to take in what she was saying. 'Mel, what is this? We were fine this morning!'

'No, Jack, we weren't fine. We haven't been fine for some time.'

'But – hell, we can talk it over, can't we? No cause for an ultimatum like this!'

'I've tried to discuss it, you know I have, but you always brush it aside and now the time for discussion is past.'

She walked towards the bedroom. 'I'll get the spare duvet and you can sleep on the sofa,' she said.

'The sofa?' he repeated incredulously. 'God, Mel! What brought this on?'

'I'm making a new start,' she said over her shoulder, 'and I'm afraid you don't feature in it.'

EIGHT

The result of Fleur's visit to the surgery was much as she'd expected: a biopsy had been taken and she would be informed of the result in a few days. Somehow she must try to put it out of her mind till then, and hours alone in the studio with too much time to think was the last thing she needed.

A little retail therapy should help, she decided, brightening. There were several things she needed, so she'd drive to Taunton and if possible meet her sister-in-law for lunch. They'd not had a chance to speak at Cassie's party.

'Hi Kathryn, it's Fleur!' she said quickly when her call was answered. 'I'm coming into Taunton on a shopping trip and wondered if you're free for lunch?'

'Hello, Fleur.' Kathryn sounded a little guarded. 'Yes, I think I could make it; I have an appointment this morning but it should be finished by twelve. What kind of food do you like – French, Italian, Chinese, Indian?'

'Goodness!' Fleur laughed. 'Just somewhere relatively central where we can have a reasonable meal and a good chat. You choose.'

'Then I'd suggest Mangetout; it's in the shopping centre, so easy to find. Would twelve thirty suit you?'

'Perfect. See you there!'

Kathryn was frowning as she put her phone down. Why on earth had she said she'd an appointment? It had been a purely instinctive reaction, leaving open the option of excusing herself later by claiming the meeting had overrun. An *excuse*? To avoid meeting *Fleur*?

She gave an exclamation of annoyance. She was becoming paranoid, suspecting Justin might have primed Fleur to find out how much she knew. Which, of course, was ridiculous, first because Justin and his sister had never been close, and second because, knowing he was in the wrong, he was very unlikely to broadcast the fact.

And the frustrating truth was that in fact she knew very little. Her suspicions had first been aroused by an increasing number of evenings 'working late', followed by the surely incriminating cliché of a lipstick-stained handkerchief in the laundry. When challenged with it, he first insisted it must be hers, and when told she never wore that colour, completely lost his temper and refused to discuss it further. Over-reaction, she'd surmised, and there the matter had rested.

Which led her to wonder what the children had deduced; there'd been pointed questions about Justin's move to the guest room and Amy had telephoned with unusual regularity since her return to college.

Kathryn straightened her shoulders. She positively refused to be regarded as a victim. If her husband was foolish enough at his age to run round after other women, she would continue to behave with dignity until he came to his senses, when she'd decide what course to take. In the meantime she would certainly *not* be confiding in Fleur over a bowl of bouillabaisse, and if by any chance he was hoping otherwise, he'd be disappointed.

Fleur was about to leave the house when Rose phoned, and she cursed under her breath. This was not the time for one of her mother's leisurely, long-drawn-out telephone conversations.

'This isn't really a good time, Ma. Would it be all right if I call you back later?'

'And where are you off to in such a hurry on a Wednesday morning?'

'Taunton, actually, to do some shopping. I'm meeting Kathryn for lunch.'

'Ah!'

'And what does that mean?' Fleur enquired, in spite of herself.

'I meant to ask if you noticed any signs of strain between her and Justin at the party.'

'No, I can't say I did, but I was too busy to notice anything much. Why, did you?'

'Yes indeed; treating each other with kid gloves while Amy watched them anxiously, poor child.'

'Oh Ma, I'm sure you imagined it! But if you're hinting that you'd like me to sound her out, I'm afraid the answer's no. I refuse to spy on my lunch companion.'

'As you wish. Still, this wasn't the reason for my call: I met Miss Culpepper from the Rosemount at the shops, and she mentioned seeing you at the surgery yesterday.'

Fleur closed her eyes and counted to ten.

'Fleur?'

She crossed her fingers. 'I was collecting a repeat prescription for Verity's eczema. Sorry I didn't tell you I was going!'

'There's no need to take that tone with me, Fleur. Naturally I was concerned.'

'Sorry. It's just that your bush telegraph can be a bit wearing. It's like living in a goldfish bowl.'

'Aren't you mixing your metaphors, dear?'

'Probably,' Fleur said heavily. 'Look, I really must go, but there's nothing to worry about.' Please God.

'Very well; we'll speak later.' And Rose ended the call.

Taunton looked positively festive in the summer sunshine. It was the height of the tourist season, the streets were crowded and parking was at a premium. It took Fleur over ten minutes to find a space, by which time she was beginning to regret her decision. She hoped her efficient sister-in-law would have booked the lunch table.

Though she'd never admit it, she'd always been slightly in awe of Kathryn, and in fact when Justin first brought her home, both she and their parents had been taken by surprise. Previously his girlfriends had been of a type – blonde and scatter-brained. Kathryn was neither. For a start, she had a first-class degree in classics and was research assistant to an eminent professor at Exeter University. Tall, pale and reserved, her dark hair framed her face in a smooth pageboy and her voice was low, her smile grave. They hadn't quite known what to make of her, but Justin was obviously besotted and they married six months later.

And, Fleur reflected as she put her money in the machine, all these years later she didn't know her any better.

The tourists had naturally invaded the shops as well as the streets, resulting in thronged aisles and queues at the tills. Fleur became increasingly flustered, unable to find anything she was looking for. The sandals she wanted were not available in her size, the dress she'd seen advertised was sold out and her favourite shade of lipstick had been discontinued. She was therefore in a thoroughly irritable frame of mind when she went in search of Mangetout.

Kathryn was, of course, there before her, cool and composed in lime-green linen. She raised a hand as Fleur hesitated in the doorway, and greeted her with a smile.

'Successful shop?'

'Far from it,' Fleur answered ruefully, seating herself. 'The entire sum of my purchases this morning is a copy of next week's *Radio Times*, which I could have bought in St Cat's!'

'Oh dear, so a wasted journey? Let's hope a good lunch helps to redeem it.' She passed the menu to Fleur, who studied it.

'Any recommendations?' she asked. 'I couldn't face anything hot.'

'I've chosen tomato salad to start with, which is just tomatoes sprinkled with basil in a delicious dressing.'

'Sounds good.'

'Followed, I think, by pork terrine and a green salad.'

'Perfect!' Fleur laid down the menu and nodded as Kathryn raised the carafe of iced water.

'I guessed that with the drive home ahead of you, you wouldn't want anything stronger.'

And Fleur, who might have bent the rules to include a glass of white wine, nodded reluctant agreement.

'We did so enjoy Cassie's party,' Kathryn said after a minute. 'She looked lovely, and so happy.'

'We were lucky with the weather. There was that storm a couple of days later, if you remember.'

'The English summer!' Kathryn commented, and they both smiled. They sounded, Fleur thought, like two strangers making polite conversation. She wondered fancifully how her sister-in-law would react were she to say boldly, *Is everything all right between you and Justin?* Instead she commented, 'It was good to have all the family there. We don't often manage that these days, do we?'

The waitress appeared .They gave their order and continued their inconsequential chat, Kathryn quizzing Fleur on the book she was illustrating, Fleur enquiring about Kathryn's job. For several years now she'd been a freelance researcher, which had resulted in some fascinating work.

'I could be immersed in Ancient Rome for months at a time, then have to switch to the life cycle of some obscure insect!'

'Does it involve travelling?' Fleur enquired. 'Or are most things available online these days?'

'I do have to travel sometimes, usually to specialist libraries, but not often abroad, more's the pity.'

'But you've had some exotic holidays, haven't you – Africa, Vietnam, Japan? Actually, we've decided to spread our wings ourselves this year. As soon as school breaks up we're heading off— Oh, God!' She broke off as an unwelcome possibility occurred to her and in the brief silence the waitress reappeared with their tomato salads.

Kathryn looked at her curiously. 'What is it?'

Fleur shook her head. 'Nothing.' Mechanically she picked up her knife and fork, but made no attempt to start eating.

'Fleur?'

She drew a deep breath. If that lump proved malignant they'd have to cancel the holiday of a lifetime that they'd spent the last few months planning. Her eyes filled with sudden tears and she blinked them rapidly away.

Kathryn leaned forward, laying her hand over Fleur's. 'What's the matter? Don't you feel well?'

'Sorry. I'm OK, really.'

Kathryn was not convinced. 'For God's sake, Fleur, you're worrying me! Tell me what's wrong!'

Fleur looked up at her concerned face. 'I've got a lump in my breast,' she said.

Kathryn sat back. 'Oh, no!'

Fleur swallowed. 'I've been to the doctor and we're awaiting the result of the biopsy. I'm so sorry, Kathryn; I didn't mean to bring this up. It was just that I suddenly realized if things don't go well we might have to cancel the holiday.'

'Let's not cross that bridge,' Kathryn said briskly. 'As I'm sure you know, a large percentage of lumps turn out to be benign. You've done the right thing going to the doctor, so for now try to put it out of your mind.'

Fleur smiled shakily. 'That's why I came shopping! Owen's the only one who knows, so please don't say anything to Justin.'

'I wouldn't dream of it. Now, eat your tomatoes and we'll talk about something else. Will Cassie be going to university in September?'

Slowly Fleur began to eat. 'If she gets the grades, yes,' she answered after a minute. 'She wants to continue with modern languages, though I don't know what she'll do with them. I suspect Owen would like her to go into teaching, but I doubt if she has the patience.'

Kathryn smiled. 'And I imagine teachers need plenty of that!'

'What about Amy? What will she do after college?'

'At the moment she's keeping an open mind. She's doing well, though: one of her paintings was on the front of the brochure for the last exhibition.'

'That's excellent! Well done!'

'You've an art degree yourself, haven't you?'

Fleur nodded.

'She's always admired you, you know. Perhaps she'll go into book illustration herself.'

'I'd be glad to talk to her, answer any questions she might have.'

'That's good of you, thanks. I'll tell her.'

Their next course was served and for the rest of the meal safe topics of conversation were maintained. As they were finishing their coffee, Kathryn said, 'What are you going to do now? Attack the shops again and hope for better luck?'

Fleur shook her head. 'It's obviously not my day. I'll just head home. I've enjoyed lunch, though, and it's been good to catch up.'

'Yes, we should do it again.' Kathryn hesitated. 'And you'll let me know how things go?'

'Of course.'

They parted outside the café and Fleur returned to her car. Although her shopping trip was a failure, it had been good to see Kathryn and she felt marginally better. Now, she thought resignedly as she drove out of the car park, she must face her mother's telephone inquisition.

'Hi there, handsome!'

Patrick smiled and settled himself back on his sofa. 'Hi to you too.'

'Change of plan about the weekend.'

His heart dropped. 'You're not going to cancel?'

'Not cancel, just amend.'

'Go on.'

'It turns out I'm stuck here in Gloucester for the next few days, added to which the new Ayckbourn play, which I've been wanting to see, is on at the Bristol Old Vic. I've called in a few favours and managed to get us a couple of tickets for Saturday, so how about I break my journey there, you come up to join me on Friday evening and I book us into a hotel for a couple of nights?'

'That sounds great, Tasha!'

'And if you come up by train, I can drop you off at Taunton on my way back to Exeter.'

'Even better!'

'Fine. Meet me in the bar at the Bristol Harbour about seven, then. Must go – see you!' And she ended the call.

It was a warm evening and despite the open windows the flat felt stuffy with the day's stored heat. Supper was imminent and, although Jess would have preferred a salad, Laurence had prepared mountains of spaghetti bolognese. Sarah was complaining about her office's air conditioning when she was interrupted by the arrival of Di and Dominic.

'Odd thing,' Dom remarked, setting down a pack of beer cans. 'A guy in the lift was saying the police have been round, knocking on doors. Did they come here?'

Jess's heart set up a rapid thumping that must surely be audible, and she kept her eyes firmly on her glass as Connor poured her some wine.

Maggie emerged from the kitchen with a handful of cutlery. 'Yes, I was going to tell you. They were asking about that man in the papers; someone had reported seeing him enter this building.'

Sarah frowned. 'This Aussie guy they pulled out of the sea? Why the hell would he come here?'

'He probably didn't,' Connor replied comfortably. 'They get hundreds of sightings in these cases. Next thing we'll hear he was seen in Timbuktu.'

'All the same,' Di said nervously, 'it's a bit close to home, isn't it? Especially with him being murdered, I mean!' She shuddered.

'*When* was he supposed to have come here?' Connor asked.

Maggie shrugged. 'Didn't ask.'

'Well, I suppose they have to follow up all leads.'

There was a moment's uneasy silence. Then Laurence called from the kitchen. 'OK, grub's up! Come and get it!' And as everyone got to their feet the subject, to Jess's intense relief, was dropped.

'I really don't think we should, Justin. Not now your son's seen us.'

Justin sighed irritably. 'For God's sake, Hilary! He's not going to say anything!'

It was certainly to be hoped not, she thought fervently. Justin had told her from the outset that he was putting his professional life on the line in conducting their affair, a fact that had startled her, stressing as it did its importance to him.

'Even so, I've been feeling guilty ever since. I'd been fooling myself that we weren't hurting anyone, but—'

'Well, we're certainly not hurting Patrick. He disapproves all right, but we're hardly breaking his heart. And I want to see you, Hills. Very much.'

She closed her eyes as a wave of weakness engulfed her. This voracious need, unsuspected until three months ago, had taken her totally by surprise when Justin Linscott had come into her life.

'Hills?'

A spurt of anger came to her rescue. It was he, after all,

who had instigated this, even if she'd proved a willing partner, and he was also the one who was married. 'Don't *you* feel guilty?' she cried.

There was a pause. Then he said, 'Marginally, I suppose. But quite honestly, I doubt if Kathryn would mind very much.'

'That's scarcely the point.'

'Let's leave ethics out of this, shall we, and start again. May I come round this evening?'

Tears of helplessness filled her eyes. 'I suppose so,' she said.

She put down the phone and stared through the window, her thoughts in turmoil. If she could have foreseen all this when engulfed with grief over Howard's death, it would have seemed not only ludicrous but totally impossible. It was only marginally less so now.

So how in God's name had it happened? Time to be honest with herself. She felt for the chair behind her and lowered herself slowly, thinking back to their first contact with the firm of Seymour and Linscott. It would have been twelve years ago, when they moved down south and were buying the house in Taunton, and Howard switched from their Lincoln solicitors for the sake of convenience.

The next time she could recall using their services again involved house purchase; Clive, having excelled at his A-levels, had been offered a scholarship at an American university, and without him and all his accoutrements the Taunton house was suddenly too big. So they moved again, to a cottage in Honiton. Yet on neither occasion had she had any personal contact with the firm.

But then, two years ago, Howard's health began to deteriorate and life became a constant round of hospital appointments and visits to consultants, ending, after twelve anxious and painful months, in his death. The next few months were a blur of misery. Clive had flown home on compassionate leave, and he accompanied her to the firm's offices to instruct them to apply for probate. That was the first time she'd met Justin, and she remembered being grateful for the calm and sympathetic manner in which he had dealt with them.

It was a month or two later, some time after Clive had

returned to his job in the States, that she received an email from Seymour and Linscott wondering whether she might be considering updating her will, something that hadn't occurred to her. Should this be the case, they wrote, they'd be happy to talk her through the questionnaire which they'd 'taken the liberty' of attaching.

Taking out a copy of her original will, she'd immediately seen this needed to be done; she and Howard had left their estates to each other and appointed their then local bank in Lincoln to act as executor.

She had contacted the firm, which resulted in her going to their office and again meeting Justin, who had guided her through the procedure with tact and compassion. She appointed Clive and the firm as executors and, thinking back now, remembered vaguely noticing that Justin was a good-looking man, tall and broad, with greying hair and brown eyes behind horn-rimmed spectacles. But he was very definitely 'Mr Linscott' and it had never occurred to her that he could be anything else.

Until that afternoon in Exeter when she had stumbled on an uneven paving stone, twisting her ankle in the process. She would have fallen had not a strong arm reached out to support her, and turning, wincing with pain, she had seen who her rescuer was.

But, she acknowledged to herself, there was an underlying reason why she'd been such an easy conquest. She had loved Howard deeply and they'd had an undeniably happy marriage, but the physical side had never been satisfactory for her, though she hoped he hadn't noticed. She'd certainly never known that wild passionate desire she'd read about, and often wondered what all the fuss was about. Until that first physical contact with Justin, when her body, previously dormant, responded with an urgency that left her breathless and at the same time painfully guilty that she'd not experienced it with her husband.

It was perhaps as well that at that point in her musing the phone interrupted her, and she hurried to answer it with a feeling of relief.

*   *   *

As Jess was preparing her breakfast the following morning she heard Maggie's mobile ring and smiled to herself. Maggie wouldn't be best pleased; she was going in later today as she had to call on some suppliers, and was bound to resent an interruption to her lie-in. A few minutes later she joined Jess in her dressing gown.

'Bloody nuisance!' she grumbled. 'Laurence had managed to get a couple of tickets for the new play at the Old Vic on Saturday. Now he's called to say his mother's had a fall and he'll have to go up there at the weekend.'

'That's bad luck,' Jess sympathized, buttering her toast. 'Is she badly hurt?'

'What? Oh, I don't think so. He didn't sound too worried, but his sister's been looking after her and expects him to do his share at weekends.'

'Fair enough, I suppose.'

Maggie poured herself some coffee and sat down opposite her. 'He's going to give me the tickets this evening,' she said. Then she looked up, meeting Jess's eyes. 'I suppose you wouldn't like to come, would you?'

Jess stared at her. 'Me?'

'Obviously I wouldn't expect you to pay, but it's not much fun going to the theatre by yourself and the play's had good reviews. I was looking forward to it.'

'Well, I— That's very kind of you.'

Maggie shrugged. 'It's to my advantage as much as yours. If you're not doing anything on Saturday?'

'No, no plans.' Jess had been half-considering going home for the weekend; she was concerned about Cassie's search for her birth mother and hoping to persuade her to abandon it, at least temporarily. It seemed a stressful and complicated procedure and, she felt, could safely be shelved for a year or two. But she'd not made any arrangements and there was always next weekend. Besides, it was some time since she'd been to the theatre.

'OK, that's fixed.' Maggie stood up. 'Right, I'll take my coffee back to bed. I needn't get up for another hour.'

'Thanks!' Jess called after her, and she raised a hand in acknowledgment as she disappeared down the passage.

NINE

The phone rang on Friday morning as Fleur was halfway upstairs with a pile of clean laundry, and she swore under her breath. Quickening her steps, she dumped it on the bed and reached for the upstairs extension.

'Hello?'

'Mrs Tempest? This is Dr Price.'

Her knees abruptly gave way and she sank on to the bed, toppling over the pile of clothes. 'Good morning, Doctor.'

'I'm pleased to tell you the result of the biopsy is that the lump is benign. No follow-up needed, but do get in touch if you've any further problems.'

'Thank you,' Fleur managed and, as the call ended, burst into tears.

Jess also received a phone call that morning, from Connor, inviting her to dinner the following evening.

'Oh, Connor, I'm sorry! I'm going to the theatre with Maggie. Laurence has to go and see his mother so she had a spare ticket.'

'Ah well, win some, lose some. What are you seeing?'

'The new Ayckbourn. It's had very good reviews.'

'Well, enjoy it. Next week, perhaps?'

'I'd like to. Are you coming round this evening?'

'No, a guy at work has got engaged so we're going out to celebrate.'

'Thanks for the invitation, anyway.'

'You're welcome,' he said.

Patrick arrived at the hotel before Tasha and was shown to the room she had booked for them. One reason for his prompt arrival was that he'd left the office early in order to avoid seeing his father, who sometimes looked into his room before leaving for home. Not, admittedly, that he had done so this week. Patrick had still not decided what his attitude should be when they did meet again.

He opened his overnight bag and took out his toilet things, arranging them on one side of the shelf in the en suite. It occurred to him that he'd have time for a quick shower before Tasha joined him, and he had started to take off his shirt when his phone sounded. The ID showed his sister's name and he stifled a sigh.

'Hi, Amy.'

'Hi there. Just wanted to let you know I'll be home for the weekend – in fact, I'm on the way now – hands-free, before you ask! I've been worrying about Dad ever since you called, and I think we just have to talk to him.'

'One small problem: I'm in Bristol for the weekend.'

'Oh, sugar! Why?'

'Tasha and I are going to the theatre tomorrow and decided to make a weekend of it.'

'I wish you'd let me know!'

'Why on earth should I? It never occurred to me you'd take it into your head to go home!'

'Well, we have to do *something*, don't we? We can't let them drift into a divorce without lifting a finger!'

'I doubt whether anything we say would make a difference.'

'So you're just going to sit on your bloody backside and let it happen?' She sounded suddenly close to tears and he felt a pang of guilt.

'Look, Ames, I'm really sorry. If I'd been home of course I'd have helped out, but as it is—'

'"But as it is,"' she mimicked savagely, 'I'm on my own! Fine!'

'Let me know how you get on.'

She rang off without replying, and Patrick was spared any further feeling of guilt by Tasha's arrival.

That first evening was a perfect beginning to the weekend. They enjoyed an excellent meal that stretched over a couple of hours, followed it with a brandy in the bar and retired to bed to make slow and passionate love. It has to be said that parental worries didn't trouble Patrick again for the rest of the weekend.

*   *   *

It was just before eleven when the coach arrived at St Catherine's and Rose had to admit she was tired. It had been a long but most enjoyable day visiting the Eden Project, and she'd done more walking than she had in a long time. There'd been so much to see and her head was spinning from all the facts she'd learned.

The coach drew to a halt just off the main square in a street known for its profusion of bars and cafés. A group of young people were reeling about on the pavement, laughing and shouting, some of the boys waving bottles, and her lips tightened. In a doorway a couple was entwined, the boy's hands moving systematically over his partner's body.

She'd been about to make a comment to Henry, who was extracting his brochure from the pocket in front of them, when the headlights of a passing car lit up the couple just as the girl turned her head, and Rose saw with a shock of disbelief that it was Verity.

She must have gasped, because Henry turned towards her enquiringly, but she shook her head and, stumbling to her feet, followed the other passengers down the steps. The coach screened her from the opposite side of the road and she waited impatiently for Henry to join her, still shaken. Obviously she must take some action, but that was for the next day; in the meantime she'd no intention of letting Verity catch sight of her, nor of telling Henry what she had seen.

Joining her, he tucked her arm through his and they followed a stream of fellow passengers to the multi-storey where they'd left his car.

After a leisurely start the next morning Patrick and Tasha set out to explore Bristol. Although he'd lived in the city until his late teens, Patrick had paid little attention to its historical context, a subject which fascinated Tasha, and he was now keen to fill in some gaps.

They began with a tour of the SS *Great Britain*, designed by the great Isambard Kingdom Brunel, once the longest passenger ship in the world and now a museum permanently moored in the harbour. Then, still in a nautical mood, they took a tour of the harbour on a packet boat before finishing their waterside visit with a drink and tapas on the quayside.

Finally, to end their sightseeing, they visited the M Shed history museum which told the story of Bristol from prehistoric times. Then, satiated with facts and figures, they returned to the hotel to relax before their early pre-theatre dinner.

Ron Barlow was laying the table and wishing, to his mortification, that the birthday lunch was over, the kids had gone home and he and Jenny were able to relax for the evening. Though she claimed to be looking forward to it, he knew she was on edge – as always prior to a visit from Gemma.

Ron sighed, straightening the table settings. He loved his daughter – of course he did – but there were times when he could happily shake her. If only he could find the root of her problem with her mother, which he was totally at a loss to understand. *Why* had she changed from a happy, loving little girl to, first, a stroppy teenager – which hadn't worried him unduly, because weren't they all? – to a prickly and at times downright hostile adult? And only towards Jenny, which was the most puzzling aspect.

A wave of protective anger swept over him; it wasn't right that Jenny should be under this strain each time she saw her daughter – walking on eggshells, having to think before she spoke – least of all on her birthday. He sent up a silent prayer that this time would be different, that Gemma would bring a suitable gift and not just a bunch of garage-forecourt flowers, and that she'd refrain from making any cutting comments. Or, Lord help him, he just might – as Freddie would say – really lose his cool.

He surveyed the table, made a minor adjustment and went to get changed.

'Sorry about this, hon,' Freddie Barlow said. 'Partners not included in the invitation.'

'From what I've heard of your family get-togethers,' Lucy rejoined, 'I'm probably well out of it!'

'Too right; wish I was!'

'Seriously, though, it can't be that bad, surely?'

'I suppose not.' He shrugged into his blazer. 'It's just that Gem always sets the cat among the pigeons.'

'What cat and what pigeons?'

He shrugged. 'The Mummy-doesn't-love-me-any-more kind.'

Lucy raised an eyebrow. 'How old is she?'

'Oh, this goes way back, but God knows what brought it on. We get on fine when we're away from home – not that we see that much of each other – but she's a totally different character when Mum's around.'

'Just your mother?'

He nodded, picking up his car keys. 'Poor old Dad tries to keep the peace, with varying degrees of success.' He bent and kissed the top of her head. 'See you later. Be good!' And he swung out of the flat.

The conversation was still in his mind during the brief drive to his parents' home. She was an odd girl, his sister, he reflected, aware that she was highly thought of at the advertising firm where she worked and by her wide circle of friends. The guy she was shacked up with had seemed OK too, on the few occasions Freddie had met him. But put her in the same room as Mum and sparks began to fly. Personally he thought she should see a counsellor and had said as much to his father, but Dad shied away from it. Well, all he could hope was that she'd keep the lid on it today, for Mum's birthday.

He glanced at the small package on the seat beside him and smiled to himself. It was a Royal Doulton spaniel that bore an uncanny resemblance to a dog they'd once owned, and he knew Mum would go into raptures over it. As she would over Gemma's offering, whatever it was. God, he hoped she'd remember to bring something!

His parents' house was in a leafy avenue in Shortlands and Freddie felt a tug of nostalgia as he turned into the drive, recalling cycling through these gates on his return from school. There was no sign of Gemma's Golf.

Bracing himself, he picked up his offering and got out of the car.

*   *   *

It was another twenty minutes before Gemma arrived, by which time everyone had begun to wonder privately if she was coming.

The sound of her car turning into the drive ended the speculation, replacing it with renewed tension. Then the front door opened, they heard her call, 'Greetings, family!' and she appeared in the sitting room doorway, her chestnut hair caught up in a ponytail and a slightly challenging smile on her face. To her father and brother's relief, she was holding a gift-wrapped parcel.

Jenny went quickly to greet her and Gemma submitted to her kiss before handing over the package. 'Happy birthday, Mum!' she said.

The gift proved to be a toiletry set of soap, shower gel and talc. 'Oh, how lovely, darling!' Jenny enthused. 'Now I can really pamper myself! Thank you so much!'

'And now,' Ron said, handing round flutes of champagne, 'it's time for a toast! To Jenny/Mum!' He raised his own glass and launched into a somewhat shaky rendition of 'Happy Birthday', joined, after a moment's embarrassed hesitation, by his son and daughter.

Jenny laughed and flushed. 'Thank you. Now, lunch won't be for another half hour so let's go and sit in the garden. It's a shame to be indoors on a day like this!'

They dutifully filed through the patio doors and seated themselves on chairs grouped round the old wrought-iron table with a hole in the middle for an umbrella long since rotted and disposed of. This too stirred Freddie's memories, of tea in the garden – and breakfast, during summers that were warm enough – or of relaxing after long bike rides with boys from school, cans of Coke in their hands.

And now, he thought with an inward smile, it was champagne he was drinking. *Sic transit* something or other. He glanced at his sister and followed her gaze down the length of the garden to where the old apple tree still dropped its windfalls, the tree she'd tried to climb after him only to fall and break her wrist. Were hers happy memories? he wondered.

As though she'd registered his glance, she switched abruptly back to the present, took a sip of her drink, and said with studied casualness, 'We've not seen you since your pilgrimage. How did it go? Were the Tempest girls as beautiful, gifted and charming as ever?'

It hadn't taken her long, Freddie thought bitterly during the brief silence. Then Jenny gave an uncertain laugh and Ron said steadily, 'I don't know about that, but everyone seemed on good form.'

Freddie forced himself to say, 'It was Cassie's eighteenth, wasn't it?'

'That's right. Rather more formal than usual – godparents and so forth, so Tony and Lynn were there, which was nice for us.'

Jenny stood up suddenly. 'If you'll excuse me, I'll go and put the potatoes on.' And she disappeared through the patio doors.

Freddie turned accusingly to his sister, noting the secret smile on her lips, but before he could upbraid her Ron continued quickly, 'It was quite a posh affair, buffet meal and best bib and tucker. Frankly it was quite a relief to escape to our familiar bolthole in Weston and just relax.'

'Did you see those people who are usually there at the same time?' Freddie asked.

'Sadly not. We were earlier this year, because of Cassie's birthday.' He went on to tell them of several outings they'd enjoyed during their holiday, and of the storm that had struck days after the party. 'It was spectacular, standing at the window and watching it roll in across the sea while the thunder crashed overhead. I'd visions of rain for the rest of the week, but fortunately the sun was back the next day.'

Jenny appeared at the window to call them in to lunch, and as they made their way to the dining room Freddie hoped that now Gem had shot her bolt they could all relax. And for a while it seemed that might be the case; her barb having had limited effect, she remained largely silent throughout the meal, speaking only when specifically addressed, while the rest of them kept up a somewhat artificial-sounding conversation.

Jenny had served a side of salmon with béarnaise sauce, new potatoes and a salad.

'It's delicious, Mum,' Freddie said appreciatively, 'but you shouldn't have had to do all this work on your birthday!'

'That's what I told her,' Ron responded. 'I wanted to take her out for a special meal, but she insisted she'd rather have lunch at home with the family.'

Dessert was a strawberry pavlova, which Freddie remembered had been a favourite of Gemma's when they were growing up, but it seemed wiser not to mention it.

'That's a pretty bracelet, Mum,' he said instead, as she handed him his plate.

She smiled, glancing down at it. 'Yes, isn't it? My birthday present from Dad.'

Gemma spoke for the first time in a while. 'What did Freddie give you?' she asked, spooning up a mouthful of pavlova.

'A dear little china spaniel,' Jenny replied. 'He looks just like Spike!'

'And the Tempests?'

Her mother looked bewildered. 'The Tempests don't give me presents, darling.'

Gemma raised an eyebrow. 'That's a bit off, considering all you do for them.'

Ron tensed, but before he could speak Jenny said hesitantly, 'I'm not sure what you mean, dear. I don't do anything—'

'Oh, Mother, don't give me that! For a start, how about abandoning your foreign holidays? You used to look forward to them all year till the Tempests left Bromley, when you promptly switched to a B&B in Somerset!'

'Gemma, that's enough!' Ron said, but now there was no way of stopping her as years of hurt and imagined slights ignited.

'And don't try to pretend you go to see Owen and Fleur,' she stormed, her spoon clattering back on to her plate, 'because you were never specially friendly with them! It's those blasted girls, who obviously mean more to you than Freddie and I do! So tell me, what's so special about them that you can hardly bear to have them out of sight?'

Jenny's eyes brimmed with tears. 'Gemma, that's not fair! You *know* I love you both! It's—'

Gemma shook her head vehemently. 'That's just what we

don't know, so why don't you tell us? *Why* is it necessary to see the Tempests on every conceivable occasion?'

Suddenly Jenny flung her napkin on the table, taking them all by surprise. 'Because Cassie's my daughter!' she cried. Then, registering the shock on the faces around her, her trembling hands went to her mouth. She held their gaze for a moment longer before pushing back her chair and running from the room.

Ron rose slowly to his feet and Freddie tensed. He had never seen his father so angry.

'I think you'd better leave,' he said, his voice shaking from his effort to control himself.

Gemma was staring at him, her face suddenly white. 'Dad . . .' she began hesitantly.

'I said leave! Now! I'm going to your mother, and I want you gone by the time I come down.' His eyes, two brown stones in his white face, moved to Freddie and his tone softened. 'You too, son. The party's over. We'll speak later.'

And he too left the room. They heard his footsteps going slowly up the stairs.

'Now you really have done it!' Freddie said heavily.

'But what did she mean, Freddie?' Gemma whispered, her lips trembling.

'God knows.' He was equally shaken by his mother's words. 'You'd better go,' he added. 'I'll clear the table, and be right behind you.'

She said falteringly, 'I didn't mean—'

'Of course you did!' he contradicted harshly. 'You always "mean".'

She gave a little half-sob, stumbled to her feet and ran out of the room. A minute later the front door opened and closed, and he was alone with the abandoned birthday table, lovingly set with the 'best' china which had been used for special occasions all his life. The pavlova had subsided into a crumpled heap, and remnants of it smeared all four plates.

Cassie's my daughter! What the *hell*?

Then his eyes widened. Could Cassie have been the 'dead' baby, all those years ago?

* * *

Jenny was sitting at her dressing table, tears streaming down her face. Ron put a hand on her shoulder and she met his concerned eyes in the mirror.

'What have I done?' she whispered.

'"Cat" and "bag" come to mind,' he said.

'If only we could have told them at the time, but Fleur was so insistent! They must be feeling so *hurt*!' She swivelled to look up into his face. 'What happened after I'd left the room?'

'I told them to leave.'

'Oh, Ron!'

'My one thought was to get to you as quickly as possible.'

She reached up to lay her hand over his on her shoulder. 'But how must they be feeling?'

He gave a deep sigh. 'Admittedly I didn't handle it well, but I was so furious with Gemma I could barely speak. This time she really went too far.'

'She still didn't deserve my outburst. That wasn't how she should have learned the truth.'

Downstairs they heard the front door open and close a second time. 'They've gone,' Ron said heavily. 'Come down again and I'll pour us both a drink.'

She shook her head. 'We must think of the best way to explain.'

'We can do that with a glass in our hands. I reckon we're both in need of it.'

She patted his hand and turned back to the mirror. 'You go on down,' she said. 'I'll join you in a while, but I need a little time to myself.' A smile touched her lips briefly and was gone. 'You could stack the dishwasher!' she said.

He frowned. 'Are you sure?'

'Really. I'm all right. A cup of tea, perhaps, in half an hour or so?'

'If that's what you want.'

And as she nodded confirmation, he reluctantly left her and returned downstairs.

How could she have been so brutal? she wondered achingly. Yes, Gemma had withdrawn from her, repulsed all her attempts at affection, but perhaps with reason. It had taken her too long, eighteen years ago, to accept her enforced separation from the baby she had carried, and that interval had done untold damage to her relationship with her other daughter.

Jenny sighed, her thoughts going back. Incredible to think that if she hadn't bumped into Lynn Dawson in Bromley High Street that day and they'd gone for a coffee together, her life would have been quite different. And it must surely have been fate that two young mothers and their babies came to sit at the next table, and because she was feeling a bit down, ridiculous tears had come into her eyes. Which of course Lynn had noticed.

'Feeling broody?' she'd enquired with a smile.

'All the time,' Jenny replied, 'but finances don't allow.'

'Then be thankful for the two you have,' Lynn said quietly. Lynn, who had no children at all. But she dismissed Jenny's embarrassed apologies with a shake of her head. 'It's all right, I accepted my lot a long time ago, but it's still raw for you, isn't it?'

Jenny nodded. 'It's all I ever wanted – to be married with a large family. I never wanted a career – I wasn't clever or academic.' She gave a half-laugh. 'In fact, my colleagues at the office called me Scatty Jenny, maintaining I didn't have a thought in my head other than make-up and the latest pop group. And they were right.

'Then I met Ron and we married and I couldn't wait to get pregnant. I just loved those months! It's such a happy time, full of anticipation. Everyone smiles at you and offers you their seat and there's this incredible knowledge of a new life growing inside you, the first fluttering movements, then the overwhelming joy when the baby's born. Looking back, it was the happiest time of my life. And when Freddie was a toddler, Gemma came along and again I was in my element. But when she was two and I was about to ask Ron if we could try for another, his business lost a valuable contract and it became clear we couldn't afford a third child. I cried myself to sleep for weeks.'

So the years had passed, but the sense of loss persisted, intensifying when Gemma joined Freddie at school, and though

Ron's business had to a large extent recovered, its future remained uncertain and she'd never felt able to raise the subject.

She'd glanced at Lynn with a half-laugh. 'By this stage I'd almost settle for a time-share baby – have all the joy of the pregnancy and its sense of achievement, then hand the baby over so that it didn't incur any expenses!'

Lynn had looked at her thoughtfully. 'You mean that?'

She was slightly taken aback. 'It was a joke, but actually I think I do.'

Lynn topped up both their cups. 'I have some friends who've had all sorts of difficulties starting a family,' she said slowly. 'Several courses of IVF and so on, which sadly only resulted in a couple of miscarriages. Eventually they adopted a little girl, and they'd dearly love another baby. But Jessica's now eighteen months and the process of adoption is getting longer and longer. It could be years before they can give her a little brother or sister.'

Jenny waited, unsure where this was heading. There was a lengthening silence, filled with coos and gurgles from the next table. Then Lynn looked up and said abruptly, 'Have you heard of surrogacy?'

And that was how it had started. She'd rushed home, full of excitement, to discuss the possibility with Ron, who'd taken a great deal of convincing. Lynn then spoke to the couple involved, and eventually, with Lynn and Tony as facilitators, they all met for what proved to be an awkward and embarrassing discussion.

She and Ron learned that the attempts at IVF had failed due to Fleur's eggs being few in number and of poor quality, so it was suggested that Jenny's should be fertilized with Owen's sperm. And it was at this stage that Fleur, who'd so far remained silent, interrupted. 'I thought a donor was used,' she'd said, her voice rising.

The others looked at her in surprise.

'Well, yes, darling,' Owen said after a pause. 'And that would be me!'

She'd looked wildly from one of them to the other. 'But shouldn't he be anonymous? Isn't that how it works?'

'Actually, no,' Tony said uncomfortably. 'I thought it as

well to check; one of the couple must be the child's biological parent.'

Fleur's eyes filled with tears. 'Then I'd rather wait for adoption!' she said.

Owen leaned forward, taking hold of both her hands. 'But don't you see, darling, this would be the best of all worlds! It will be our own biological baby, without laying you open to the danger and heartbreak of more miscarriages.'

His biological baby, Jenny remembered thinking. Fleur had risen to her feet. 'I want to go home!' she said.

Owen took her arm, giving them an apologetic smile. 'We'll be in touch,' he promised. She'd later learned it had been only after storms of tears and much pleading on his part that Fleur had finally agreed, with the proviso that no hint of surrogacy should ever be revealed and that the baby should be regarded as adopted.

What was it she'd said to Lynn that morning nineteen years ago, about going through all the joy of the pregnancy and then being able to hand the baby over? How little she'd known! For though she told herself repeatedly that the child she was carrying was not hers, her body refused to believe it and all her latent maternal instincts rose to the surface, only to be remorselessly crushed. She would never forget her first sight of Cassie's tiny face, her baby-blue eyes staring trustfully up at her, and the bitterness of knowing she'd have to betray her.

With a sigh, she pulled open the dressing table drawer and began to blot out the trace of tears. Looking back, she accepted that she'd not even tried to come to terms with her position. On the contrary, while not actually stalking Fleur, she'd constantly engineered 'accidental' meetings as she wheeled Cassie out in her pram, as well as frequently calling at the house with little gifts for the baby. All in all, it was no wonder that Fleur had always been coolly distant with her, while Jenny had indignantly felt she should be grateful. Would she ever have gone into this, she wondered, had she known the heartache that lay ahead?

She gave her pale face a last, assessing look, and went downstairs to join her husband.

TEN

Earlier that day, Rose had phoned her daughter, and Fleur knew from the tone of her mother's voice that something had displeased her. After a couple of general enquiries, Rose moved on to the purpose of her call.

'I'm wondering, Fleur, if you have any idea where Verity was last night?'

'Verity?' Fleur, who'd swiftly run through a number of possible causes for complaint, had not remotely considered her youngest daughter.

Rose was waiting for a reply.

'I believe she was going to the cinema with some friends,' she said after a minute.

'You believe?'

Fleur's patience snapped. 'Please don't play cat and mouse, Ma. What are you trying to tell me?'

'That at about eleven o'clock last night she was canoodling in a shop doorway with a boy with wandering hands.'

Fleur held back what would have been an unsuitable retort. 'Were they . . . alone?'

'If you mean was anyone else about, there was a group of young hooligans shouting and waving bottles and reeling about on the pavement. Would these have been her friends?'

Fleur bit her lip. 'I shall of course have a word with her.'

'I think it needs more than a word, Fleur. I'm only thankful that it was I, rather than any of my friends, who saw her.'

'Tell me, Ma, which concerns you more: Verity's welfare or what other people might think?'

There was a tight silence. Then Rose said, 'There's obviously no point in continuing this conversation.' And she rang off.

Oh, damn, damn, damn! This she could have done without. On the principle of getting it over as soon as possible, Fleur ran upstairs to her daughter's room, from which loud pop music was issuing. After a brief knock she opened the door, to see Verity lying back on her bed, her face screened by a magazine.

Locating the source of the music, Fleur went in and turned it off. Verity sat up with an exclamation of annoyance.

'I was listening to that!' she complained.

'And now you can listen to me,' Fleur said crisply. 'Where were you last night?'

An apprehensive flicker crossed her daughter's face, but she answered sullenly, 'I told you. A group of us went to the cinema.'

'And afterwards?'

The girl's eyes fell. 'We came home.'

'Not immediately, I think.'

Deciding attack was the best form of defence, Verity demanded heatedly, 'Do I have to account for every minute now?'

'Please answer my question, Verity.'

'Well, if you must know, some of us went to the all-night café in Belvedere Street. OK?'

Tired of fencing with her, Fleur said succinctly, 'Your grandmother saw you being fondled by some boy in a doorway.'

Verity's face flamed. 'The interfering old bat!' she exclaimed.

'*Verity!*'

'Was she on that coach of oldies that pulled in? I bet she couldn't wait to tell you!'

'Who was he?' Fleur demanded, holding on to her temper.

'Who?' Verity held her gaze for a moment, then her eyes dropped. 'Matt,' she muttered, barely audibly.

At least it was someone Fleur had met. 'Was Lizzie with you?'

'Not at that particular moment, obviously.'

'Don't be impudent, Verity. Do you realize how embarrassing it was for me to have to hear about this from Granny?'

Verity shrugged, her eyes on the bed. 'We were only kissing,' she muttered.

'He was apparently very free with his hands.'

'We weren't doing any harm. Granny should mind her own business for once!'

'That's enough. I'd been prepared to let it go this time, but since you persist in being rude, you're grounded for a week.'

She turned to go as Verity cried out, 'Mum! You can't do that! It's Simon's party tonight!'

'Then you'll miss it,' Fleur replied.

'OK, I'm sorry!'

'Too late.'

'Mum!'

Fleur closed the door on the howl of protest and returned downstairs.

Freddie was opening the door of his flat when Gemma phoned.

'Did you see them after I left?' she demanded without preamble.

Freddie sighed, pushing the door closed behind him. 'No; as I told you, I cleared the table and left just minutes after you.'

Across the room, Lucy frowned enquiringly and he lifted his shoulders in response.

'But what did she *mean*?' Gemma continued, her voice rising. 'What *could* she have meant, for God's sake? Did she have an *affair* with Owen Tempest?'

Freddie dropped his car keys on the table and sank down on the sofa. 'God knows,' he answered flatly. 'I've been going over it in my head on the way home. It just doesn't . . . compute.'

'And where does Dad fit into all this? Is he Cassie's father? If so, what the hell has she to do with the Tempests? And if not, how much did he know at the time? And Fleur, for that matter? Did she go along with Cassie's adoption not knowing she was actually Mum's?'

Freddie closed his eyes and leaned his head back against the sofa. 'Again, your guess is as good as mine.'

'I think we should go straight back and demand an explanation. They owe us one!'

'Calm down, Gem. As things stand they'd just throw us out again.'

'Throw *me* out, you mean.' She paused. 'But I was right, wasn't I? She does prefer that family to us, and now we know why.'

*　　*　　*

Owen had been in school for a senior staff meeting so it was late afternoon before Fleur was able to tell him about Verity.

'She's not come out of her room since,' she ended. 'No doubt venting her spleen on her mobile!'

'On the whole I'm inclined to agree with her,' Owen commented. 'Surely kissing in doorways is par for the course in your teens?'

Fleur flushed angrily. 'You don't think I was right in grounding her?'

'I think it was a bit harsh.'

'She compounded it by being very rude about Ma,' she defended herself.

He grinned. 'Well, your dear mamma does like to put her oar in, doesn't she?'

Fleur would have retorted but they were interrupted by the ringing of the house phone and he lifted it. 'Owen Tempest,' he said.

'Owen.' The voice was hesitant. 'It's Ron. Ron Barlow.'

He raised an eyebrow at Fleur and switched the phone to speaker. 'Hello, Ron. What can I do for you?'

'Well, this is a little awkward.'

'Yes?'

'We . . . we had a family lunch today, for Jenny's birthday.' Oh God, Owen thought, were they supposed to have sent a card? 'And . . . I'm afraid things got rather heated.'

'Yes?' he prompted again.

'Things were . . . said.'

Owen frowned, meeting Fleur's suddenly worried eyes. 'What things, exactly?'

'I'm afraid it came out that Jen is Cassie's mother,' Ron said in a rush.

'*Surrogate* mother.'

'Yes.'

There was a silence. Fleur felt for the chair behind her and slowly lowered herself on to it.

'I'm really sorry, Owen. We both are. We know Fleur didn't want it made public. We just . . . thought you should know.'

'Thank you for telling me.'

'Yes. Well, if there's anything we can do?'

'No, thank you.' *You've already done enough*, Owen added silently.

'Goodbye, then.'

'Goodbye, Ron.' He made himself add, 'Thanks again for telling us.'

'Yes,' Ron said miserably, and rang off.

Slowly Owen replaced the phone and met his wife's wide eyes. 'So what happens now?' he asked.

Maggie had suggested that they have a pre-show supper at the theatre, to save the hassle of cooking at home. It was clear a lot of people had the same idea, and Jess was glad they had a table booked.

'It's very good of you to invite me this evening,' she said, when they'd selected their dishes. 'Especially when there are other people you could have asked!'

Maggie smiled. 'Not all of them are theatre-goers, and I thought it might appeal to you.'

'Oh, it does! How did you all meet? I've never liked to ask!'

'Ah, a long story! I'd been living abroad, and when I first came back to the UK I felt a bit lost so I decided the best way to meet someone was to share a flat. Which is how I met Jill, your predecessor, though from the company angle she wasn't a good choice; she was already engaged and out nearly every evening.

'I'd taken a temporary job in an office while I decided what to do with myself, and not wanting to go home to an empty flat, I formed the bad habit of stopping for a drink at a hotel bar. I'd worked in a hotel and felt at home there, with people about me. That's how I met Di. She was also lonely, having just divorced. She said the daytime was OK when she was at work, but she hated being alone in the evenings. So I suggested she come to supper. That was the start of it.'

The waitress arrived to take their order, and as she moved away Jess asked, 'And she knew the others?'

'Only Dominic – he worked in the same bank. He'd also divorced recently and in her opinion was drinking too much. She asked if she could bring him along one evening. It was he who coined the phrase "Maggie's Lonely Hearts Club". I suppose it has a ring of truth.'

And, Jess knew, Dominic in turn introduced Connor.

Maggie took a sip of wine. 'Actually, it was through Di I got the garden centre. It belonged to a friend of hers who was retiring, and as soon as I heard about it I realized it would suit me perfectly – something quite different, a fresh start. I'd worked in interior design and enjoyed the creative aspect; this was my chance to put it to good use. Even better, I didn't need any formal qualifications, though I took an evening course at the Royal Horticultural Society so I'd at least know what I was talking about! And once I was more sure of myself, I started the design side of it.'

'And made a great success of it!' Jess commented. 'What about Sarah and Laurence?'

'I can't remember now who first brought Sarah.'

'And Laurence?' Jess persisted.

'No, he didn't come recommended!'

Jess wasn't surprised, but could hardly press the point. Instead she said, 'And you don't mind them dropping in all the time?'

Maggie laughed. 'Is our pace of life too fast for you? Sorry about that, but instead of one or other of them phoning to ask if they could come round, it seemed easier to make it open house. As you know, they always turn up with some contribution. When it's not convenient I send a group email. Admittedly it gets a bit hectic at times but I've become addicted to it. And at least it keeps them off the streets!'

Their meal arrived, and as they settled down to it, Jess reflected that this was the longest conversation she'd ever had with Maggie, and felt she knew her a little better.

Patrick saw Jess the minute they entered the foyer and, to Tasha's surprise, went straight over to tap her on the shoulder.

'Greetings, cuz!' he said.

Jess spun round. 'Patrick! What are you doing here?'

'The same as you, I imagine.' He turned to Tasha, who'd joined them. 'Tash, this is my cousin, Jess. Jess, meet Natasha.'

Jess smiled at her. 'I've heard a lot about you!' she said.

'This is Maggie, my flatmate,' she added, turning to her companion. 'Cousin Patrick, Mags, as you'll have gathered – and Natasha.'

Patrick bought them drinks and they moved to the side of the room. 'Have you come up just for the play?' Jess asked Patrick.

'We'd arranged to meet anyway but Tasha's been in Gloucestershire most of the week. She'd been hoping to see the play so she decided to stop off on the way home. I came up to join her and we're making a weekend of it.' He smiled ruefully. 'We've spent the day exploring Bristol, and I'm shattered!'

Tasha, who'd been glancing at Maggie from time to time, suddenly said, 'I keep thinking I know you! Have we met before?'

Maggie looked surprised. 'Not that I'm aware of.'

'Sorry; you must remind me of someone, but I'm not sure who!'

'You probably saw her on TV,' Jess put in. 'She was interviewed after winning a gardening prize.'

'Oh, well done you! What was it for?'

'Designing a small garden,' Maggie replied. 'I combine bespoke design with running the centre, so I thought it worth having a go. Good for publicity, if nothing else – and it's certainly paying off! I've been invited to be a guest on *Gardeners' Question Time*, and there's even talk of a guest appearance on TV's *Garden Rescue*.'

They murmured their congratulations, then Tasha turned to Jess. 'And to change the subject, I've been wanting to ask where you got that fantastic tan?'

'She's just back from a holiday in Italy,' Patrick said.

They talked for a few minutes about various holidays abroad until the bell sounded for the start of the performance, when they split up to go their separate ways.

'Talk about all your successes made me feel guilty,' Jess admitted, as she and Maggie took their seats. 'I've never been to your garden centre – I don't even know where it is!'

'Well, since you haven't a garden I don't suppose it's of much interest,' Maggie replied. 'Don't worry, my business life is quite separate from my private one. Laurence is the only one who's been there.'

And, conscience assuaged, Jess settled back as the lights dimmed and prepared to enjoy the play.

Owen had fallen asleep long since but Fleur's mind was in turmoil and she was unable to settle. Eventually, afraid of waking him with her restlessness, she slid out of bed, shrugged into a dressing gown and slippers and crept downstairs in the dark, holding on to the banisters for safety. In the hall a measure of light seeped through the fanlight over the front door, illuminating her way to the kitchen.

As she entered the room something soft brushed against her and she gave a low cry before realizing that of course it was Minty, surprised at the unexpected invasion of his domain. She pushed the door shut and switched on the light as he weaved himself ecstatically round her legs, nearly tripping her and purring loudly.

'Hush, Minty – basket!' she ordered automatically as she filled the kettle, knowing full well he'd take no notice until she tipped some biscuits into his bowl. Who was it who'd said dogs had masters and cats had staff?

Having poured herself a mug of tea and administered the required biscuits, Fleur seated herself at the table. The room looked alien at this time of night, as though resentful of her intrusion. A hub of family life during daylight hours, it was eerily quiet, only the ticking of the clock and an occasional hum from the fridge breaking the silence, with unrelieved blackness beyond the windows. But this apartness was what she needed while she forced herself to recall painful memories. What crisis, she wondered, could have forced Jenny to break the promise Fleur had wrung out of her nineteen long years ago?

The trouble had always been that those involved had expected her to be grateful, while all she was conscious of was a deep and burning resentment. Why, when for years she had longed – ached – to have Owen's baby, had this woman whom they barely knew been able to give him one? Jealousy also played its part, tormenting her with an imagined deep and lasting bond between her husband and Jenny, Cassie's natural parents, while she, Fleur, had had no part to play.

She'd hidden these feelings during the pregnancy, counting the months till the time they could wave Jenny goodbye and pretend that none of it had happened, that the baby, like its elder sister, had simply been adopted. But as time for the birth drew closer, resentment turned to fear as it became clear Jenny was growing deeply attached to the child she was carrying. They'd been warned from the start that a surrogate mother could legally change her mind and keep the child, and for terrifying weeks they'd not even known if she'd go through with the arrangement.

Nor did the nightmare end when Cassie was born. The law required the baby to be handed over almost at once, but Fleur hadn't realized that Jenny and her husband Ron would be considered the legal parents until such time as they 'fully and freely' gave their consent for the Parental Order that would transfer legal parenthood. Even more worrying was the fact that the surrogate mother could not by law give her valid consent until the child was six weeks old.

During those interminable weeks Jenny had haunted their house, coming round at odd times of the day and begging to be allowed to see the baby, or waiting just round the corner for Fleur to emerge with the pram. And Fleur, terrified of antagonizing her, had had to concede. She knew, from Ron's telephone calls, that Jenny was suffering severe post-natal depression similar to that after a stillbirth, and she forced herself to be patient.

To add to the strain, the granting of the Parental Order was repeatedly postponed because Jenny, constantly in floods of tears, refused to sign it, pleading for 'just a little longer', until finally Owen, increasingly concerned for Fleur, asked Ron to put his foot down and the precious Order was at last completed.

Even then, when Fleur had thought her ordeal over, Jenny continued to stalk her at every opportunity and her patience wore thin, giving way to the deep dislike of her supposed benefactor that still existed today. Under sufferance and in line with Owen's quiet but firm directive she had through the years invited Jenny to Cassie's birthday parties and allowed the child to go, with Jess, to the Barlow home 'for tea', and to visit the pantomime or circus with their family.

Unbidden, a long-buried memory surfaced, of three-year-old Cassie, seated at this very table, spooning cereal into her mouth and asking casually, 'Did me and Jess have the same mummy and daddy?'

Like her sister, she'd been told at an early age that she was adopted.

Fleur had answered sharply, 'Of course you have – *we're* your mummy and daddy!'

Cassie shook her head, 'No, I meant *before!*'

There'd been a tense silence, then Owen had answered quietly, 'No, darling, you didn't, but Mummy's right: you both have us now.'

Which, thank God, had seemed to satisfy her, and – though they'd not known at the time – what seemed a miracle had already occurred and Fleur was finally, unbelievably pregnant with her own naturally conceived child.

Even some twelve years later, Fleur knew that part of her joy at moving to St Catherine's had been because it offered an escape from her incubus. Now, in the shadowed kitchen, she gave a brief, bitter laugh, startling Minty from his nap; for the Barlows had immediately changed their long-time holiday arrangements in order to maintain the contact.

And now that her reminiscences had come full circle, the new and present crisis that had caused her sleeplessness reared its head again: the Barlow offspring now knew the reason behind their parents' link with the Tempests. What would they make of it – and, more worryingly, would they attempt to contact Cassie?

It seemed the time she'd fervently hoped would never come had, after all, arrived. She would have to reveal the truth to her daughter – and therefore also to Jess and Verity. The thought filled her not only with dread but with fear. Would family life ever be the same again?

ELEVEN

Sydney, Australia. March 2016

Well, she'd done it! She'd actually done it, and he had no idea!

Mel sat back in her seat, mentally ticking off the tasks she'd completed: tenancy of her flat ended and her belongings in the trunk in the hold of the plane; bank account closed, social media account deleted, new mobile, personal documents destroyed. Nothing left to give him the means to find her. And in a little under twenty-four hours she'd be back in the UK. A fresh start on the other side of the world! Her only regret was not being able to hold a leaving party for her friends; once settled, she'd send a joint email.

She glanced out of the window at the final preparations for flight, her thoughts drifting back over the eight years she'd spent in Australia – the Beaufort Hotel with Barb, the beach parties and barbecues, the various men she'd hooked up with – Steve, Harry, Jack. And Bruce.

Bruce. She'd never considered herself in love with him. Even in the early days it was his drive, his single-mindedness and business acumen that attracted her – and, of course, their insatiable appetite for each other. That was a bonus, but it wasn't love.

How had it all gone wrong? Well, if she wanted to trace back the sequence of events there was no better time to do it – long hours ahead of her, with no interruptions.

The loudspeaker issued instructions for take-off and safety procedure was being demonstrated in the aisle but she tuned them out, settling down to an in-depth analysis of the last three years.

*   *   *

It had been ten days after their coffee together that Suki tapped on her door, put her head round it and informed her that one of the guests wished to see her in room 303.

Damn! she'd thought, looking up from the schedules she was revising. What was the complaint this time? Reluctantly abandoning her lists, she went up to the third floor and tapped on the door. And Bruce Marriott opened it.

Taken entirely by surprise, she simply looked at him. After a moment his lips twitched and he stood to one side. 'Please come in,' he said.

Still unnerved by his unexpected appearance, she moved past him into the room and he closed the door behind her, indicating one of the easy chairs. In silence she seated herself and he perched on the edge of the bed.

'Sorry!' he said. 'That wasn't fair of me. But I need to see you and I didn't think you'd come if I'd suggested meeting somewhere.'

'So you decided to ambush me?' she accused, finding her voice at last.

'In a word, yes, since it's important. I have a proposition to put to you.'

Her eyes must have widened, because he laughed. 'No, not that! Seriously, I was most impressed by your obvious ambition and the breadth of your current responsibilities, which, I must confess, I went to some length to check.'

He held up a hand at her instinctive movement of protest. 'I'm not known for being impulsive – quite the reverse – but I also pride myself on knowing a good thing when I see one.' That quirky smile again. 'You said you were looking for a change, so I decided to go out on a limb and called a board meeting. And after some pretty heated discussion, it was agreed that subject to a successful interview, we'd like to offer you a position.'

He named a figure considerably higher than her present salary and went on to explain where he felt she'd be of most value to his company. 'We could call it a trial period if you prefer,' he ended, 'but it would be a job description tailored specifically to your skills and would give you a more or less free hand to exercise your initiative. We're about to widen our range, as I think I mentioned. We could make that your project and seriously consider any ideas you come up with. Obviously this is a very informal approach but if you'd agree to consider it, we would—'

'Yes!' she said.

He stared at her. 'I'm sorry?'

'Yes!' she repeated. 'If I'm formally offered the job, I'll take it.'

For a second longer he gazed at her, then his face broke into the smile that had first attracted her. 'Well!' he said. 'That was easier than I expected!'

'It sounds like just the challenge I'm looking for. Of course, I'd have to work out my notice, but I can't see—'

He interrupted her in his turn. 'That's fantastic, Mel! Look, it might be only four o'clock but I think this calls for a toast. After all, we met over a glass of champagne; it's only right it should seal our agreement!'

'There's still the interview to go through,' she reminded him, but he waved a dismissive hand, went to the minibar and took out a bottle and flutes.

'Are you really staying here?' she asked, watching him.

'Just for tonight. It had to be bona fide.'

He poured the drinks, expertly guiding the foaming liquid into the glasses, and handed her one. And as their fingers touched electricity sparked between them. This, she thought, raising her glass in response to his, could work to her advantage in more ways than one.

The next month or so passed quickly. Having succeeded in impressing the board of Marriott Interiors, Mel duly handed in her notice and began conducting interviews with applicants hoping to be her successor.

When her plans became known, however, several of her friends were dubious.

'Bruce Marriott has a name for being ruthless,' more than one person warned her. 'Don't be fooled by all that surface charm!'

'He's a businessman. I'd expect nothing less,' she retorted. 'Come to that, I'm pretty ruthless myself!'

'You're sure you know what you're doing?' they persisted.
'Never been more sure,' she replied.

And she was. Knowing the hotel was due for its three-yearly refurbishment, she had immediately approached the management and suggested they ask Marriott's for a quote. She'd seen enough, during her tour of the premises following her interview, to have a good idea of the quality and spread of what was on offer, and to be impressed by it. Her head was crowded with ideas for widening its appeal and she was impatient to discuss them with Bruce.

However, she had neither seen nor heard from him since her formal acceptance of the position, and when she phoned to speak to him his secretary informed her he was unavailable. It was a rude reminder that large though this new job might loom in her life, to him she was simply a prospective new employee with potential, who had yet to prove her worth. That, she swore to herself, would change.

And once she started working there, it did. Slowly and discreetly she set herself up to be indispensable; if she suspected an employee of shirking or being offhand with clients, she subtly made it known, sometimes resulting in dismissal. Consequently she was unpopular with junior members of the firm, but the more senior increasingly asked her opinion on a variety of matters. The acceptance of their quote by the Beaufort Hotel was another significant feather in her cap.

One of the initiatives she put forward soon after her arrival was to make better use of the ground floor store rooms and offices. At the moment samples of wallpaper and soft furnishings were displayed, artistically enough, in rolls and panels in the main showroom, but she made the point that they'd be shown to better effect if incorporated into actual room settings. The underused offices could be turned into replica bedrooms, sitting and dining rooms, presenting materials to much greater advantage, and the displays could be regularly updated.

And this would be still further enhanced, she suggested, if part of the planned expansion encompassed liaising with local furniture makers, china manufacturers and carpet warehouses to offer a complete package – tables laid with attractive modern china and cutlery, beds made up with luxurious covers, all available via Marriott Interiors.

After a considerable amount of prevarication, in-depth discussions, financial haggling and the emphatic proviso that any arrangement with Marriott's should not be exclusive, the respective businesses agreed to collaborate on a trial basis, and work began on the structural alterations and redecorations required.

During this time she'd seen little of Bruce. Occasionally they had passed in a corridor and nodded to each other, or he'd come into the office to confirm some point. He was unfailingly pleasant but very much the boss and she bided her time, suspecting he was waiting till he'd proved to the board that his investment in her had been validated.

She must have passed the test, because as she was about to leave the office one evening she received a text.

Since we've reached the end of the trial period which, incidentally, you passed with flying colours, I think a little celebration is in order. Dinner tomorrow at the Random Club, eight thirty?

Mel allowed herself a small, satisfied smile before texting back. *Thank you. See you there.*

That was when it really began. Over the meal in the candle-lit dining room the sexual tension that had existed between them since New Year and been ruthlessly suppressed intensified to such a degree that Mel wondered if they'd make it to the end of the meal. Conversation became sporadic and finally, abandoning their half-drunk cups of coffee, he got to his feet, muttering, 'Let's get out of here!'

She didn't own a car and had arrived by taxi but Bruce's BMW was in the club car park.

'You'll have to direct me,' he said as he started the engine. After negotiating busy streets for some minutes they drew up in front of her block of flats. Pre-empting any invitation, he took her arm as they hurried into the building and up in the lift, waiting with mounting impatience as she searched in her bag for her key. She had barely closed the door behind them when he spun her round and began to kiss her, continuing to do so as they made their way to the bedroom, leaving a trail of clothes behind them.

For a while nothing changed outwardly at the office. She continued to liaise with the firms involved in the new venture, suggesting fabrics and fittings with which to furnish the proposed new rooms, and Bruce maintained his normal routine. But most evenings he called at her flat on the way home.

Gradually they began to work together more openly, going in tandem to view equipment, meeting clients and discussing their requirements, where, he acknowledged, her suggestions and advice were much appreciated.

Then the time came when Bruce was invited to a dinner for leading businessmen, and asked Mel to accompany him.

'My wife's tied up with the kids and not really interested in business,' he told everyone, though Mel thought privately she'd have been interested in the dinner, had she been asked.

After that occasion they were regarded, in the business world at least, as a couple, and invitations sent to the firm began to be addressed to Mr Bruce Marriott and Ms Melanie Hunter. Increasingly she also accompanied him on social occasions both public and private – to the races, to the opera and theatre. By this time the replica rooms had been launched, and their impact was greater than anyone had foreseen. Marriott Interiors' reputation, not to mention profits, continued to rise.

But those months had not been without controversy. The first occasion was soon after they'd come together, when Mel had invited Bruce to dinner at her flat. In those early days she was still anxious to seal their relationship, and had made every effort to impress him, poring for days over recipes and for hours over preparing and cooking the meal. She'd even, though she ridiculed herself, indulged in a new dress for the occasion.

And he never came.

For a while she'd convinced herself he'd been delayed – though he could surely have phoned? – but her impatience and anxiety escalated as the hands of the clock crept round.

Pride prevented her from contacting him, so at ten o'clock the congealed food was tipped into the waste bin, a significant amount of the opened bottle of wine consumed, and she retired to bed angry, baffled and worried. Was this a deliberate snub, or had he genuinely forgotten? One reason was hardly preferable to the other. Had she congratulated herself too soon over her influence on him?

In the office the next day no mention was made of the missed date. Hurt and angry, she avoided Bruce where possible and sent her apologies for a scheduled meeting of senior management. She left the office slightly early to avoid seeing him, wondering if their brief collaboration was over.

But he arrived at the flat as usual. 'What the hell was that all about?' he demanded, the moment she opened the door.

'What, exactly?'

'You know damn well what. All but cutting me all day, then not attending the meeting.'

'I might ask the same of you,' she said coldly.

He frowned. 'Meaning?'

'You were expected here for dinner last night.'

His face cleared. 'Oh, is that what it was all about? Well, I'm sorry. It slipped my mind.'

Her voice was dangerously calm. 'Am I to take that as an apology?'

He made a dismissive gesture. 'Take it how you like. You of all people know I've a lot on my mind at the moment.'

'You arrogant bastard!' she said slowly.

His eyes widened, then flashed as his face reddened. 'Perhaps you should remember who you're talking to!'

'Believe me, I'm only too aware! I went to a lot of trouble, not to mention expense, over that meal, and the least you could do is show some sign of remorse! Or is common courtesy too much to expect?'

'You little—'

For a moment she actually thought he was going to hit her and took a quick step back. Instead he seized hold of her and started to kiss her ferociously while she fought to free herself until desire overcame her resistance.

That, though their affair continued unabated, was the

forerunner of many such outbursts. Once, when Bruce was out of the office, Mel's agreement to a course of action was sought and given, which resulted in fireworks on his return. 'Who the hell do you think you are, usurping my authority?' And so on. And as with all their disagreements, it ended in sex taking the form of a punishment. She had to accept that two strong personalities were bound to clash, and the continual seesaw of the relationship gave it added spice.

Sometimes, in the relaxed aftermath that followed love-making, they indulged in pillow talk, he with less caution than was perhaps warranted, and Mel tucked away various snippets that might, in less companionable times, come in useful.

And how that had paid off! she thought now, accepting a tray of food from the flight attendant. When the morning papers were delivered tomorrow, one such snippet would make the front pages. Then, perhaps, he'd regret how he'd treated her.

Starting on her meal, she resumed her reflections. One thing she hadn't anticipated, she admitted now, was that although not in love with him, she was far from immune from sexual jealousy, and as time wore on found herself, to her chagrin, increasingly on edge if any woman appeared to be paying him attention, or – worse – he seemed interested, even fleetingly, in someone else. His wife of course didn't count; their paths crossed only infrequently and Mel seldom thought of her.

Then came the day that, though neither of them realized it, heralded the end of their relationship. They were on their way back to the office after visiting a client, and she'd paused to glance in a jeweller's window.

'Isn't your birthday coming up?' Bruce enquired. 'Now's your chance to choose your present!'

She turned to him in surprise. 'You're serious?'

'Of course. It will save me having to rack my brains!'

She turned back to the window and almost at once pointed to a slim gold bracelet studded with turquoise. 'That would be absolutely perfect!' she said.

'Expensive tastes!' he commented, but waved away her embarrassed suggestion of an alternative.

'Just teasing!' he assured her, and they went on their way.

Shortly after that, though, his visits to the flat became noticeably fewer, and it grew harder to conceal her suspicions. And this time, as she discovered, they were well grounded. They came to a head when someone in the office asked how she'd enjoyed a play at the local theatre, and on hearing that she'd not yet seen it, the girl had flushed and stammered, 'Oh, I thought – someone saw Bruce there, and I just—' She'd floundered into silence and fled.

Instinctively Mel knew who he'd been with – a tall, leggy blonde by the name of Madeleine Connaught who, in Mel's view, had been flirting with him for some time. Confirmation wasn't long in coming.

A few days later while shopping in a department store she caught sight of Madeleine reaching up to take a lizard-skin handbag off a shelf, and to her numb disbelief registered the bracelet on her wrist. For a moment she felt physically sick, a toxic mix of anger, jealousy and betrayal. She turned and stumbled out into the fresh air.

That was when her decision was formed. She had to accept that her days of intimacy with Bruce were limited, and there was no way she was going to wait for him to end it. The humiliation after all they'd achieved together would have been insupportable, so there was no alternative. She must leave Sydney, and therefore Australia, before that could happen. Time, yet again, for a fresh start.

So she'd begun to plan, and when her birthday was marked simply with a large and exotic bouquet of flowers it was proof she'd made the right decision, though she'd greeted them with a show of delight. Her arrangements for leaving completed, she plotted that last act of revenge.

Mel pushed her tray away from her and looked out of the window at the grey clouds below them. Having brought herself up to date, it was time to think of the future. She'd decided from the beginning that she wouldn't return to London; rather than the desired fresh start, that would have been revisiting the past. Somewhere the other side of the country, then, and, after eight years in Australia, she wanted to be near the coast.

She'd checked various locations online, and eventually settled on Bristol as suiting her needs perfectly.

A decision still to be made was what field she'd work in, but it would be neither hotels nor interior design. Whatever she chose, though, she was determined to make a success of it, which meant possible publicity, and she couldn't risk any Australian tourists hearing of the latest achievements of Mel Hunter. So she'd need a new name, and the only stipulation, bearing in mind her luggage and various other engraved items, was that she keep the same initials.

Returning her tray to the steward, she settled back in her seat and began to think of one.

TWELVE

The day after his return from Bristol, Patrick's family conscience resurfaced and that evening he phoned his sister.

'How did it go?' he asked.

Her sigh came down the phone. 'A wasted journey, really. I mean, it was good to see them but it didn't resolve anything. I'd been determined to broach the subject somehow, but without you there to back me up I chickened out.'

'Sorry, Ames. It was bad timing, that's all.'

'I meant to ask – have you seen Dad in the office since?'

'Only the day after, when he came to my room and tried to bluff it out. Since then we've been keeping out of each other's way.'

'Well, how about having a go yourself next weekend? I can't get off again so soon, but you could tackle them, couldn't you? Invite yourself to supper or something, or Dad might be out again "playing golf".'

He caught the quote marks. 'You don't think he was?'

'Your guess is as good as mine.'

'I doubt I'd have any more luck. They'd probably just clam up, which would make for a thoroughly uncomfortable evening.'

'At least have a go, and let me know how you get on.'

He sighed. 'OK, will do.'

A week had now come and gone and Fleur had still not broken the news to her daughters. It had been the last week of term, Owen had had little time for family discussions and Cassie and Verity, excited at the prospect of the coming holiday, would in any case have been hard to tie down. Anyway, Jess was coming home this weekend, which would be the ideal opportunity. She and Owen had decided the wisest course was to tell all three girls together, so Cassie would have the support of her sisters. It had just remained to agree on the best time. Owen suggested after dinner on Saturday.

'But that's too late in the day!' Fleur objected. 'I don't want her to go to bed while it's all new and upsetting – she'd never sleep! She must have time to digest it before bedtime.'

'After lunch, then. It can all be thrashed out and questions asked during the afternoon, and by bedtime with luck the impact might have lessened.'

'I'm dreading it,' Fleur admitted.

'Well, it's not as though it makes any real difference. Our one mistake was in not telling them sooner, which gives it added impact.'

'*My* mistake, you mean.'

He shrugged. 'It was bound to come out sooner or later. I'm amazed it's taken this long.'

'I'd hoped that with our moving here, it never would,' she said.

As she drove home, Jess reflected on what had happened in the two weeks since she was last there. She'd learned the identity of the man she'd found in the flat, reported seeing him to the police, and come to know both Maggie and Connor a little better. She'd also met the glamorous Natasha, and could appreciate her cousin's obsession with her. And Patrick himself had, to her relief, stopped quizzing her about her incautious comments on the stairs.

It had been a strain, though, having to be constantly on her guard, not knowing for sure which of the group was a murderer. Maggie had presumably had at least a hand in it, but the curious thing she kept coming back to was what possible motive there could be to kill a man recently arrived from the Antipodes. And what was he doing in the flat anyway? A burglary gone wrong was surely too simplistic a solution?

Still, it was time to put those worries out of her mind and concentrate on the one that had brought her home: Cassie's intention to find her birth mother. These searches, she knew, could go on for a lifetime and cause much heartache, whether they were finally successful or not. She silently cursed the girl at school who'd first put the idea in Cassie's head. But then, she remembered, there was that strange letter from their mother discovered in the loft. What that had all been about Jess couldn't imagine.

She was approaching St Catherine's and felt herself relax as the familiar landmarks came into view. In ten minutes more she'd be home.

In Verity's bedroom she and Lizzie were sitting on beanbags, sharing a packet of crisps.

'Come on then,' Verity said, 'what did you want to tell me?'

Lizzie tensed. 'It doesn't matter,' she said.

Verity sighed theatrically. 'Then why phone needing to see me urgently?'

Lizzie shook her head.

Verity screwed up the empty crisp packet and aimed it at the waste basket, missing it by several inches. 'I stayed in specially because you were coming,' she complained. 'Penny's redecorated her bedroom and wanted to show it to me.' She made to get up. 'If there's nothing important, we can go round now.'

'No!' Lizzie laid a hand on her arm, then said in a rush, 'My period's late!'

Verity froze in mid-air before sinking slowly back on to the beanbag. 'God, Lizzie!' Then, 'Are you sure?'

She nodded. 'You know how regular I am, always spot on the day – you tease me about it. But it's five days late!'

Verity was silent for a moment. Then she said cautiously, 'Is there any reason you can think of?'

Lizzie started to cry.

Verity stared at her. All at once this was deadly serious. She said simply, 'Who?'

Lizzie sniffed and reached for a tissue. 'Paul,' she said.

'You mean you've been—?'

'No!' She shook her head violently. 'It was only once, and – oh God, Vee, I didn't even want to!'

Verity's thoughts spun. This was something well beyond her remit; she tried to remember agony aunts' advice they'd giggled over on social media. She took a breath and asked, 'What happened?'

Lizzie blew her nose and went on more calmly, 'It was at the school disco last week. You know how hot it was. Several of us went outside and me and Paul wandered down to the tennis courts. I knew he'd been drinking – all the boys had; they'd smuggled in cans of beer and hidden them in the grounds.' She paused, remembering. 'We'd gone out for a snog so I was expecting him to kiss me, but that night it was different, more – intense somehow, right from the start, and I tried to push him away.'

She looked earnestly at her friend. 'Vee, you know I like him, and we've been together now for several months. But I wasn't ready for this.'

'Did you tell him?'

'Yes, but he wouldn't listen. I broke away and started to run back towards the building but he caught me and then he – he pulled me down on to the grass.'

She started crying again and Verity passed her the box of tissues. 'I was screaming at him to stop, but although I could see several couples in the distance they didn't take any notice – probably thought we were just larking about. And then he – he did it. And it *hurt*, Vee! That's something they don't tell you! I was crying and struggling but he held me down. Then, when he'd finished, he'd the nerve to tell me to shut up! "What do you think we came out here for?" he said, and I said, "Not that!" and he just laughed.'

'And you've been upset about this ever since? Why didn't you tell me, Liz?'

'I was ashamed,' she answered in a low voice.

There was a long silence, then Verity asked, 'Have you taken a pregnancy test?'

Lizzie shook her head.

'Why not, if you're so worried?'

She shrugged. 'Afraid of what it might say.'

'We'll have to tell Dad,' Verity said after a minute.

'What?' Lizzie's head spun round. 'No! I told you in confidence! I don't want *anyone* to know, least of all your dad! And if it's OK after all, no one need *ever* know!'

'Lizzie, it happened on school premises, Paul is a student, and whether you're pregnant or not, it was *rape*!'

Lizzie stared at her. 'But – it was Paul!' she said.

'It doesn't matter who it was. You said no and he didn't stop.'

'But I can't get him into trouble! What would the gang think?'

'He's probably been bragging to them about it.'

Lizzie's hand went to her mouth. 'Oh *God*! I hadn't thought of that! How can I face them?'

'Have you seen him since?'

'Once, at Simon's party, but there were a lot of people and I was able to keep out of his way.'

Simon's party, which Verity had missed through being grounded, though the ban had been lifted the next day. It occurred to her that this was precisely what Gran had been worried about, after seeing her with Matt.

She brushed the thought aside. 'Look, you must tell your parents, at least. They'll know what to do.'

Lizzie looked at her wildly. 'They'll kill me!'

'If the worst happens, they'll have to know anyway. And he shouldn't get away with it – it's not right! Promise me you'll tell them. Otherwise I really will tell Dad.'

The tears began again. 'I've been *praying* every day that it would start!' she sobbed.

'Can you think of any other reason it might be late? Have you had a cold, or an upset tummy or anything?'

Lizzie shook her head, blew her nose and straightened. 'Look, let's give it a week – that's another two days. If it hasn't come by then I'll take a pregnancy test, and if – well, you know – I'll tell Mum. OK?'

'You ought to tell her anyway.'

'Two more days, Vee. And in the meantime don't you dare say anything!'

Verity nodded. 'OK.'

By mutual consent they got to their feet and as Verity moved to open the door, Lizzie gave her a quick hug. 'Thanks,' she said simply. 'There was no one else I could tell.'

During the evening meal Jess regaled the family with an account of the play she'd seen the previous week. 'If you get the chance, you should go,' she ended. 'Oh, and we ran into Patrick and his girlfriend in the foyer.'

'Is she as gorgeous as he makes out?' Cassie enquired.

'I'd say so. Exotic rather than beautiful – tall, with masses of red-gold hair. And she's very nice too.'

'Is it serious, do you think?' Fleur asked.

'On his part, but he reckons he's not in with a chance.'

'He'd be a very good catch for somebody,' Fleur commented.

'Really, Mum!' Jess protested. 'You sound like a Jane Austen novel! But tell me about this holiday you've organized. It's not long now, is it?'

'Only another week!' Owen replied. 'Just what we need after the hectic term we've had!'

'So where do you fly to?'

'Direct to Miami, then on to Lima.'

'Mum told me your Peru itinerary, which sounds incredible. Then it's – where?'

'Bolivia, Brazil and Argentina.'

'Wow! And I only got as far as Pisa!'

'What's more, you missed our one bit of excitement while you were away,' Fleur commented. 'A body was washed up just along the coast, and it turns out the man had been murdered!'

Jess froze. 'Murdered?' she echoed faintly.

'Yes; at first it was thought he'd drowned, but they found a knife wound in his chest.' She turned to her husband. 'There's more about him in today's paper, did you see?'

'Not today, but there's been quite a bit lately, with business contacts he met in London coming forward.'

'Well, the latest is he had some bad press a few years ago and there was a fair bit of animosity towards him. The police in Sydney are checking to see if anyone still bears a grudge, though of course he was killed here.' She glanced at Jess. 'We're interested, because incredibly enough Dad met him in Bristol!'

Jess felt a cold wave wash over her. She swallowed twice before she managed to say, 'You *met* him, Dad? How? When?'

'Well, "met" is a bit of an overstatement. He sat next to me at the bar while I was waiting for Charles Latimer.'

'But *when*?'

'The day before Cassie's party – I'd gone up to collect her present, and was meeting him for lunch.'

'Did you tell the police?' Jess asked out of a dry mouth.

'Yes, but it wasn't much help; apparently they've had hundreds of sightings.'

Jess's hands were clenched in her lap. Should she tell them? But how could she possibly, with all the family here ready to condemn her for not coming forward? Had it been only herself and Dad, she'd certainly have confessed her own 'meeting' with Bruce Marriott, and it would have been a great load off her mind. With luck she might get another chance later, but the coincidence that both she and her father had a personal connection to the murdered man was not one she wanted to dwell on.

In the meantime, she'd Cassie to worry about. Tomorrow, she promised herself, she'd quiz her about her birth mother search.

That evening, Natasha phoned Patrick from Paris.

'Thought I'd give you a call,' she said. 'I was just thinking of this time last week.'

'Me too. It was great, wasn't it?'

'What are you up to this weekend?'

He made a face, though she couldn't see it. 'Duty visit to the parents.'

She laughed. 'Enjoy!'

They chatted for a few more minutes, then, just as they were ending the call, she said suddenly, 'Oh, by the way; I've remembered where I saw that friend of your cousin's. You know I said she looked familiar? Well, it came back to me where I'd seen her. It was several years ago, in Sydney, of all places!'

'Good heavens! I'm surprised you recognized her after so long. She didn't seem particularly memorable to me.'

'Her hair colour was different, but I'm good with faces – part of my job. The point is, though, it was at some business dinner, and you'll never guess who she was with!'

'Then you'd better tell me.'

'None other than Bruce Marriott – your Body on the Beach!'

Patrick drew in his breath. 'Honestly? Surely you must be mistaking her for someone else?'

'No, it was definitely her. And I think she recognized me too, though she disguised it pretty cleverly.'

'Well, you'd be much harder to forget! Seriously, though, I don't remember any mention of her in the paper – coming forward to identify him or anything. Surely she would have done?'

'Can't help you there.' Tasha yawned. 'Well, we're an hour ahead of you here and I'm more than ready for bed. Night, lover!' and she rang off.

Patrick was frowning as he clicked off his phone.

Verity was just drifting into sleep when the phone on her bedside table vibrated and she fumbled to locate it.

'*Who* is it? What did you say?'

'It's *me*, Vee, and I said it's come! Panic over!'

'Lizzie?' Verity was still befuddled with sleep.

'*Yes*! Oh – were you asleep? Sorry, I didn't realize the time, but I've only just found out and I had to tell someone! *I'm not pregnant!* God, the *relief*!'

'That's great, Liz!'

'So no one needs to know anything about it!' Lizzie said firmly, and Verity was too tired to argue the point.

The next day promised to be a hot one, and at breakfast Jess suggested to Cassie that they go down to the beach together.

'I haven't swum in the sea since Italy!' she said.

'Prepare for a difference in temperature!' Owen cautioned.

'Even so, it's just the day for a dip. You game, Cass?'

'Yes, I'll come,' Cassie said. 'Not promising I'll actually go in, though. I'll test the water first!'

'Well, I want you all back for lunch,' Fleur said. 'I'm making one of my special salads.'

It was a ten-minute walk to the beach and they set off an hour later, beach bags in hand, swimsuits under their dresses and suntan lotion applied. It was already hot and the sky cloudless. If only her own life was! Jess thought.

The beach was already busy, with families staking their claims with chairs, umbrellas and rugs, but the sisters made for one of their favourite sites in the dunes, sheltered from the breeze and out of sight of those on the flat sand below. Jess spread out their rug and Cassie dropped down on to it.

'This is the life!' she exclaimed. 'School over, no more work till September, and an exciting holiday to look forward to!'

'I envy you South America,' Jess commented, pulling off her dress and joining her on the rug. 'It's on my bucket list! Will you be back before your A-level results?'

Cassie pulled a face. 'Why did you have to mention that? No, they come out our last week.' She grinned. 'If I don't get the grades, I'll run away and join the gauchos!'

'You'll get them,' Jess said complacently, lying back with her eyes closed. Cassie was hoping to study psychology at Liverpool.

They were silent for several minutes, feeling the July sun soak into their bodies. Then Jess said, 'Did you get any further with your birth mother search?'

'Oh, I've pretty well given up on it for now,' Cassie replied lazily.

Jess kept the relief out of her voice. 'Oh? Why's that?'

'Well, I made a few enquiries and nothing came up on the most likely adoption sites, added to which it was all more time-consuming than I'd realized.'

Jess remained silent. She'd forgotten how her sister could be wildly enthusiastic about a project, only to abandon it at the first hurdle.

'Do you ever think about yours?' Cassie asked after a minute.

'No,' Jess replied truthfully.

'When I was little, I used to imagine she was some sort of foreign princess locked up in a tower to stop her looking for me. Or the opposite, a beautiful serving maid in a rich household, and they took her baby because the son and heir was the father and they wanted to hush it up.'

'You should be doing creative writing rather than psychology!'

Cassie laughed. 'I can dream, can't I? Perhaps it's better

not to know, so I can go on dreaming, though I'm past the princess and serving girl scenario.'

'That's a relief, anyway!'

Cassie sat up suddenly. 'Well, you're the one who wanted a swim! Race you to the water!' And she set off, squealing as the hot sand burned her feet. In close pursuit, Jess was thankful that at least she had one thing less to worry about.

Patrick had become increasingly concerned after learning of Jess's flatmate's association with the dead man. If Tasha was right – and she'd seemed pretty certain – surely Maggie or whatever her name was would have come forward? Of course, he reminded himself, she might well have done so; people who'd contacted the police hadn't been named in the press. But surely she'd at least have told her friends that she knew him, in which case Jess would have heard? And if she hadn't told them, why not?

He was making far too much of this, he chided himself, but he knew he'd have no peace of mind till he'd spoken to Jess, and this new worry reminded him that he'd never got to the bottom of her unsettling comments at Cassie's party. All in all, he felt in need of a serious conversation with his cousin, and if he hadn't been committed to seeing his parents, he'd have driven straight up to Bristol to see her. Tomorrow would have to do, but he'd call now to make sure she could see him.

As it happened, she wasn't in Bristol anyway, and when he called had just returned from a morning on the beach. Patrick hesitated; true, it would be much easier for him to drive to St Cat's, but he didn't want to have that conversation at Sandstone, when any of the family could interrupt them at any time and where he could hardly ask to speak to her privately.

'What time are you going back tomorrow?'

'I'll be leaving here about six. Why?'

'There's something important I need to discuss with you.'

'You're not going to drag up that conversation on the stairs again, are you?' It was the very last thing she wanted to discuss.

'There's something you need to know,' he said, avoiding a downright lie. 'What are you doing Monday evening?'

'Meeting Connor for a drink.'

'What time?'

'Seven o'clock at the Wild Cat.'

'Could you meet me there beforehand, at six thirty? We could have our discussion, and when he arrives say we just bumped into each other. It would be good to see Connor again. Then I'll make myself scarce, I promise.'

'It all sounds very cloak and dagger!' Jess said cautiously. 'But OK, if it's that important I'll meet you first.' He heard a call in the distance. 'Have to go now – lunch is ready. See you Monday.' And she ended the call.

Not ideal, Patrick reflected. He'd have to leave the office early and dash up to Bristol for a half hour meeting before driving all the way back. But in the circumstances he felt he'd no choice.

Lunch, as always, was eaten at the kitchen table. Today the back door was open to the garden and Minty lay stretched on the mat, his fur glistening in the sunshine. Fleur, who prided herself on her salads, had produced one that incorporated spinach, artichoke hearts, avocados, black olives and toasted pine nuts, with flakes of salmon mixed in and a garlicky dressing to pour over it. The family did it full justice.

Verity finished her glass of Coke and pushed her chair back. 'Thanks for lunch, Mum. Can I go now? Penny's redecorated her room and wants me to see it.'

'Wait a minute, dear,' Owen said quickly. 'Mummy and I have something we'd like to discuss with you all.'

The three girls stared at him, each reacting in her own way to the seriousness of his voice.

'You're not getting divorced, are you?' Cassie asked, with a nervous half-laugh.

'No, nothing like that; and I want you all to remember that what we say now doesn't alter the family in any way at all.'

'Now you're really worrying us!' Jess protested. 'Whatever it is, please tell us!'

Fleur hadn't spoken, and now sat looking down at her hands folded in her lap.

'We've always told you,' Owen continued, after a quick

glance at her, 'that Jess and Cassie were adopted. Well, that isn't strictly true.'

Under the table, Cassie reached for Jess's hand and held it tightly as they both recalled their conversation on the beach that morning.

'For reasons we don't really understand, Mummy and I weren't able to have our own baby for a long time.' He smiled at Verity, who stared speechlessly back at him. 'So after a while we applied to adopt a baby – Jess – and she made all the difference to our lives. So, when she was about two, we decided we'd like a brother or sister for her. But at that time there were fewer children for adoption and more people wanting to adopt and we realized we'd have to wait years for our turn.'

He came to a halt. Jess and Cassie exchanged puzzled glances. He looked from one of them to the other, then asked abruptly, 'Have you heard of surrogacy?'

'No!' Cassie and Verity said in unison.

'I think so,' said Jess.

'In a nutshell, it's when a woman offers to have another woman's baby for her.' He went on to explain the procedure in general terms, ending lamely, 'So that's what we decided to do.'

There was a silence, then Cassie said uncertainly, 'And someone had me?'

Owen nodded, then glanced at Fleur again. She hadn't moved.

'But so what?' Jess broke in. 'Someone had me too! How is it any different?'

Owen cleared his throat. 'This is the technical bit, but the bottom line is that in surrogacy one of the intended parents has to be related to the baby.'

The three girls looked at him blankly.

'Which means that either the intended mother's egg is fertilized and inserted in the surrogate's womb, or the intended father's sperm is used. And for various reasons in Cassie's case it was my sperm.'

There was a moment's silence, then Cassie said on a high note, 'You mean you're my *real* dad?'

Fleur made an instinctive movement but still didn't look up.

'We're both your real parents, Cassie,' Owen said quickly, 'but I'm your biological father, yes.'

There was a silence, broken only by rapid breathing as unimaginable facts were slowly assimilated. There was one glaringly obvious question, and after a glance at Cassie's face, it was Jess who asked it.

'Then who's her mother?'

And at last Fleur looked up, her eyes going challengingly round the table. 'Jenny Barlow!' she said.

There was a gasp from all three girls.

'Auntie Jen is my *mother*?' Cassie asked incredulously. Her lips began to tremble, and Jess thought achingly of the foreign princess and the servant girl. 'But I don't even *like* her very much!' she said.

Verity said, 'Is that why she was always hanging around when we lived in Bromley? And why they come down here every year?'

It was Owen who answered. 'Darlings, what she did was a very brave and generous thing. She gave us Cassie and we can never thank her enough for that. The tragedy was that when the time came to hand her over to us, it nearly broke her heart.'

Tears had come into Cassie's eyes and were beginning to run down her cheeks. 'I'd rather have been adopted, like Jess!' she said.

Jess looked from her sister's devastated face to her father's and demanded accusingly, 'Why didn't you tell us years ago, and why are you telling us now?'

'Because,' Fleur replied, 'I was jealous of her having Daddy's baby when I couldn't, and I didn't want anyone to know. In fact, I made everyone promise never to say. Also,' she added in a quieter voice, 'I thought if Cassie found out, she might love her more than me.'

'Oh, Mum!' Cassie reached across the table and took her hand.

'So why are you telling us now?' Jess persisted.

'Because at a family lunch at the Barlows' last weekend there was a row and the truth came out. And we thought that as Freddie and Gemma know, it was only fair that you should.'

'And they might tell us,' Jess said shrewdly, and saw her mother wince.

'But as I said at the beginning,' Owen reiterated, 'it makes no difference whatever to who we all are. We're exactly the same people as we were at breakfast.'

Out in the hall the landline phone started to ring and Fleur, who'd had more than enough of the conversation, hurried to answer it. She was gone for several minutes, and when she reappeared she stood in the doorway, white-faced, leaning against the frame.

'That was Lynn,' she said, her voice shaking. 'She was phoning to tell us that yesterday Jenny fell under a bus in Bromley High Street. She's seriously ill in hospital and not expected to live.'

THIRTEEN

Cassie burst into tears.

Owen pushed back his chair, went to Fleur and took her arm. 'Come and sit down, darling,' he said, leading her back to the table.

She said shakily, 'I was so horrid to her!'

'What exactly did Lynn say?'

Tears welled in Fleur's eyes. 'Ron told her Jenny'd been upset ever since the row last weekend. And – oh God, this is the worst part! – witnesses said she seemed to step deliberately in front of the bus!' She took out a tissue and wiped her eyes. 'She was walking along the pavement, then suddenly just veered into the road.'

'I didn't mean that I didn't like her!' Cassie sobbed.

Verity said, 'This is turning into the most horrible day! I'm going round to Penny's. See you later.' And she left the room.

Fleur looked helplessly at her husband. 'What do you think we should do?'

'There's not a great deal we *can* do, except keep them all in our thoughts.'

'Lynn said she'd ring as soon as there's any news. We could send flowers?'

'Better wait a while and see how things go.'

Jess moved uncomfortably. 'Is it all right if Cassie and I go upstairs?' she asked.

Fleur stretched a hand towards Cassie and let it drop again. 'Of course, darlings,' she answered distractedly, and the two of them thankfully escaped.

She turned back to Owen. 'Ron met Freddie and Gemma during the week,' she told him, 'in an attempt to smooth things over. Lynn got the impression it didn't go too well.'

Upstairs, they sat side by side on Cassie's bed, Jess's arm round her sister who continued to cry quietly. 'At least you know your birth mother loved you,' she said. 'She still does. She only gave you away because it had been arranged beforehand, and she hated doing it. Whereas mine simply didn't want me.'

'You don't *know* that. She mightn't have had any choice either.'

'Perhaps.' Jess didn't sound convinced.

Cassie blew her nose. 'I wonder if I'd ever have found her, if I'd continued my search.'

'Probably not, since it wouldn't have gone through an adoption agency.' She stood up. 'Come on, we can't sit here moping. There's nothing we can do, so let's go out for a walk.'

And Cassie, with a final sniff, acquiesced.

Justin hadn't been pleased to hear his son was coming to dinner. He resented being put on the defensive and was unsure exactly what Patrick would come up with. Worst case scenario was that he'd mention the Exeter lunch twelve days ago. He'd been cursing himself ever since for arranging it; it had been a totally unnecessary risk and God knew where the repercussions might end.

The possible consequences had forced him to re-examine his feelings for Kathryn, and though he accepted that he didn't want to lose her, nor, selfishly, did he wish to give up the illicit excitement Hilary provided. He flattered himself that he'd awakened her with his lovemaking, and her passionate response had been unexpected and profoundly gratifying. After nearly thirty years of marriage, it was addictively thrilling to sample the allure of forbidden fruit. It wasn't love, he wasn't naive enough to believe that, but the attraction was still as undeniably potent as at the beginning of their three-month relationship. Even thinking of her now aroused him.

And it wouldn't have happened, he defended himself, if things had been better between himself and Kathryn. It was a long time since they'd made love like that. Could it, he suddenly wondered, be his fault? Had he allowed intimacy to become routine rather than passionate? But Kathryn was always so poised, so cool and in control of herself that perhaps subconsciously he'd held back. Now, he reminded himself, he might never have the chance to make love to her again.

* * *

'I don't know what we've done to earn this sudden display of
filial duty – first Amy, now you,' Kathryn remarked as they
sat over pre-dinner drinks.

Patrick, on edge from the moment he'd arrived and aware
he mightn't get such an opening again, took the plunge. 'It's
because we're worried about you,' he said, and from the corner
of his eye saw his father stiffen.

'Because Dad's moved to the guest room? We discussed
this before; I can't think why you're making such a big deal
of it. The bed in there is firmer than ours and more comfortable for his back. We've both been sleeping better.'

True or not, this was a new explanation. 'You just don't
seem – relaxed together, that's all,' he ploughed on. 'And—'

Justin said quickly, 'You'll discover for yourself, my boy,
that marriage isn't always plain sailing. Life goes more
smoothly at some times than at others, and being human we
react accordingly. But in case you're wondering, we're not
about to throw in the towel. Or at least, I'm not!' He forced
a laugh.

If he was waiting for Kathryn to agree with him, he was
disappointed. She merely said, 'Obviously we're delighted to
see you both, but we're not in need of marriage guidance,
thank you, particularly from our children who have no experience of it. Now, if we can consider the subject closed, I'll
serve dinner.'

It was not a comfortable evening. The subject might have
been closed, but the strained atmosphere continued, principally
because, though he strove to hide it, Justin remained on tenter-
hooks. Patrick wished uselessly that he'd had a more in-depth
conversation with Amy, so they could have established a clearer
course of action. As it was, he was tempted to drop his bombshell simply to force their hands. It was a relief to all of them
when it was time for him to go home.

Justin walked down the path with him. 'Thanks,' he said
gruffly.

'For what?'

'You know damn well for what.'

Patrick turned from opening the car door. 'Are you serious
about this woman, Dad?'

'No, of course not,' Justin blustered.

'Have you stopped seeing her?'

'Well, I . . .'

Patrick made a disgusted sound and turned away. Justin put a quick hand on his arm.

'Can't we be adult about it? These things happen, Patrick. You must know they do.'

'Not with my parents. I don't want Mum hurt.'

'Nor do I, for God's sake.'

'Then it's in your court. For the moment.'

And with the implied threat hanging in the air between them, Patrick got into the car and drove off, leaving his father staring after him.

Before putting her light out, Jess crept downstairs with the intention of retrieving the daily paper. Subsequent traumatic disclosures hadn't quite obliterated the comments her mother had made, both about there being further news of Bruce Marriott and about Dad actually meeting him.

But she was out of luck. The papers had been tidied away, and short of rummaging in the recycling bin she had no way of satisfying her curiosity. Disappointed, she went back to bed.

Gemma, white-faced and dry-eyed, sat holding her mother's hand. There had been no flicker of movement in the twenty minutes they'd sat with her. All was quiet except for the bleeping of machines, the odd murmur from another bed and the constant movement of the nurses as they adjusted tubes and checked monitors.

She looked across the still form at her father, who'd aged visibly in the last few hours. 'She'd want Cassie to be here,' she said.

Ron's heart lurched with love and pity for her. 'Sweetie, she's no idea who's here and who isn't,' he said gently.

'But I owe her that, Dad. All this is my fault.'

He sighed. Gemma had been claiming responsibility for her mother's accident for the last twenty-four hours and nothing he could say would dissuade her.

'We can't expect the girl to come hotfoot from Somerset,

when she might not even know the connection. I told you how Fleur—'

'It's time Fleur grew up and accepted her share of the responsibility!' Gemma snapped.

Ron could only agree. 'Lynn said she was going to tell them, but I don't know if she has.' He glanced at his watch. 'It's Freddie's turn now. I'll go and change places with him.'

Gemma released her mother's hand and stood up. 'No, you should stay, Dad. I'll go.' She bent forward and kissed her mother's forehead just below the swathe of bandages. Then, with a wan smile at her father, she went in search of her brother.

Jess hadn't slept well. The shocks that had been coming thick and fast ever since she arrived home – Dad's meeting with Bruce Marriott, Cassie's unexpected parentage and finally Jenny Barlow's accident – had reverberated in her head all night, and by six o'clock she'd had enough tossing and turning.

She swung out of bed, showered, dressed and went downstairs, leaving a scribbled note on the kitchen table. Minty approached her hopefully but she shook her head. 'It's not time for breakfast,' she told him, and quietly let herself out of the back door.

As on the afternoon she'd discovered the body, she made for the beach. The tide was coming in and there was a stiff breeze. In the distance a couple were throwing a stick for a dog but otherwise she seemed to have it to herself. She lifted her head, breathing in the salty air. God, how she loved this place! Perhaps she should never have exchanged it for Bristol: look at what that move had brought her! Should she have stilled her doubts about Roger, whom she'd loved – if not quite enough – since she was seventeen, and accepted his proposal?

He'd been her first serious boyfriend. They'd met when she was staying with her grandparents during the summer prior to university, when he was in his last year at medical school. They'd phoned and corresponded throughout her time at uni and he'd driven over several times to see her. And, of course, they'd both been ecstatic when the family moved to St Cat's.

Perhaps, Jess reflected sadly, the phrase 'absence makes the heart grow fonder' implied that presence might make it less so. Having graduated, she'd lived at home while she applied for jobs, but with Roger constantly available and wanting to see her every evening, she'd started to feel suffocated. Then to her delight she was offered a post as PR assistant at a prestigious public relations agency in Bristol, and her parents suggested that since it was so close she could save money by continuing to live at home and commuting daily.

But as her feelings towards Roger continued to wane, his grew stronger. She tried several times to suggest they slow things down, making increasingly frequent excuses not to see him, but when he consistently refused to comply she decided the only course open to her was to move to Bristol. Whereupon, greatly to her distress, he had asked her to marry him.

Suddenly, as though she had conjured him up, she saw him striding across the sand towards her, his Irish setter Fergus at his heels.

'Jess!' he called. 'I thought it was you! You're an early riser!'

She slowed to a halt as he approached. 'Hello, Roger. Hi, Fergus!' She bent to pat the dog, who was leaping up at her in delighted recognition.

'I didn't know you were home,' he said.

She looked up at him, his face flushed from his exercise, dark hair blowing in the wind. She'd forgotten how good looking he was. 'Just for the weekend,' she said.

'Then I'm very glad I caught you. I saw your mother at the surgery the other day. Did she tell you?'

'No?' Jess felt a tweak of alarm. What was her mother doing at the surgery?

But Roger, doctor that he was, ignored the implied question. As she started to walk again, he fell into step beside her, while Fergus raced ahead, flagged tail wagging.

'So how's Bristol?' he asked.

'Fine.'

He shot her a sideways glance. 'Damned with faint praise!'

'No, really! It's a very interesting place, with lots to do.'

'And the job? Still enjoying it?'

'I love it, yes; it's so varied and we have some really well known clients, which is great.'

'And socially – you've made friends?'

'Yes, quite a few.' Though she barely considered them friends, apart from Connor and perhaps Maggie.

'I've missed you,' he said quietly.

She didn't reply, and he gave a half-laugh. 'It's all right, I'm not going to go all maudlin on you. It's just that we were part of each other's lives for so long.'

'First love!' she said, trying to lighten his mood.

'They say you never forget it.'

'I won't.'

'Bless you for that.'

'What about you, anyway?' she went on quickly. 'Still playing tennis every weekend?'

He smiled. 'Yes, still the same old routine. When I'm not on call, that is. The crowd would love to see you; any chance of you dropping in at the club for half an hour?'

She shook her head. 'Not this time, I'm afraid. I'm going back this evening, and it's been a difficult weekend for the family. I want to be with them as much as possible.'

'Oh?' His face sobered. 'Nothing serious, I hope?'

'Serious enough, but not life-threatening, or you'd have heard! But they'll be waking up now; it's time I was getting back.'

'I'll walk up with you.'

They parted at the gate to Sandstone. 'Take care, Jess,' Roger said.

'You too. It was lovely to see you.' She reached up to plant a quick kiss on his cheek. 'Bye, Roger.'

And she turned and hurried up the path.

After the traumas of the previous day, Sunday passed quietly. There was no further call from Lynn, so presumably no change in Jenny's condition. Cassie remained subdued. Jess recalled ruefully that her main reason for coming home had been to see if there was any news on her birth mother. Well, she'd had that all right; they all had. In spades. It was a salutary lesson in not trying to trace her own origins. Who knew what murky secrets could be unearthed?

All in all, she wasn't sorry to be setting off back to Bristol, even though the atmosphere there was fraught with uncertainty. Still, she was meeting Connor tomorrow. And Patrick! she remembered suddenly. Subsequent events had put him entirely out of her mind. What could it be that he so urgently wanted to discuss with her?

The next evening was warm and sultry. It had been a rush to get back from work, have a quick shower and dash out again in time to meet Patrick at six thirty. She was glad to see that drinks were being served in the garden behind the pub, and seated herself at a vacant table. Her watch showed exactly six thirty, and as she looked up again, she saw the tall form of her cousin in the doorway, scanning the garden. She raised a hand and he came out, bending to kiss her cheek.

'Thanks for coming early, Jess,' he said. 'Now, what can I get you to drink?'

'Something long and cold, please. Don't mind what!'

He nodded and went back into the pub, returning minutes later with two brimming glasses of spritzer.

'So,' she invited, 'what's all this about?'

Patrick took a long draught of his drink. 'I needed that, after negotiating the rush hour traffic!' He put his glass down and looked across at her. 'This might seem an odd question, but what do you know about Maggie?'

Jess stared at him. Whatever she'd been expecting, it was not that. 'Maggie?' she repeated, and when he nodded, went on, 'Well, not much. Why?'

'Did you know, for instance, that she used to live in Australia?'

'Australia?' She must stop repeating what he said, but warning bells had started ringing before she fully understood why. 'Are you sure?'

'Pretty sure. At least, Tasha is. Remember at the theatre, she said she thought she recognized her? Well, later she remembered seeing her at a do in Sydney. And furthermore, she was with none other than Bruce Marriott!'

When she continued to stare at him speechlessly, he added, 'He was the man who was washed up on the beach.'

'I know who he was,' Jess said, just above a whisper.

'What is it, Jess?' Patrick asked sharply. 'Are you OK?
You've gone very pale.'

She'd no option now, and she desperately needed to share
her secret. 'He was in our flat,' she said expressionlessly.

'What?' Patrick frowned. 'Who was?'

Jess moistened her lips. 'Bruce Marriott. He was dead!'

Patrick leaned back in his chair, staring at her. 'What the
hell are you talking about?'

'I saw him,' she went on. 'The afternoon of Cassie's party.
That's why I tried to ask what I should do.'

Involving someone dying, she'd said. Why the *hell* hadn't
he followed it up?

'Let's get this straight,' Patrick said slowly. 'You saw Bruce
Marriott, dead, in your *flat*?'

She nodded.

He drew a deep breath. 'Suppose you take me through this
from the beginning.'

So she went through the sequence of that afternoon's events
– returning to the flat to retrieve her paperback, the body on
the floor, hiding when some people came in and removed it.

She came to a halt and there was a brief silence. Then
Patrick said, 'And what did the police say?'

She shook her head wordlessly.

He looked at her in disbelief. 'You're not telling me you
didn't report this?'

'Don't shout at me, Patrick,' she said, close to tears. 'I was
in shock. All I could think was that I had to get home for the
party. Then the next day Rachel and I flew to Italy. It was all
. . . complicated.'

'*Complicated?*'

Now he was doing the repeating, she thought dully.

'But I don't understand. Why didn't you at least tell your
father, if not me?'

She shook her head again. 'I should have done, of course
I should, but I was frightened. Whoever moved him had
presumably killed him. I didn't know who'd come in, I couldn't
distinguish their voices, but it had to be someone I knew. And
if I'd gone straight to the police, they'd have known it must
be me who'd reported it. Anyway, how would it have helped?

It's not as though I knew who he was then, and there was nothing whatever to back up my story, no trace of anyone ever having been there.'

'So you're telling me you *never* reported it?'

'I did when I got back from holiday,' she said defensively. 'By then he'd been found and a drawing of him was in the paper. I didn't say what had happened, but I told them I'd seen him going into the block of flats. That was at least pointing them in the right direction.'

She looked at him hopefully.

'God, Jess!' Patrick said helplessly. He had another drink. 'To go back to my original question, what do you know about Maggie?'

'Well, she did say she'd lived abroad, though not where, and I didn't think to ask. She worked in hotels at one time and she's also done interior designing. And of course she now has a garden centre and recently won a prize. That's all, really.'

He thought for a moment. 'You said there were two people; come to think of it, there must have been, to have moved the body of a full-grown man. Has she a boyfriend?'

'She's closer to Laurence than anyone else.'

'Laurence who?'

'I think his surname is Pope.'

'Know anything about him?'

She shook her head. He didn't come recommended, Maggie had said. She leaned across the table and put a hand on his arm. 'Patrick, I'm trusting you not to repeat any of this to anyone.'

'Jess, love, I have to! You could be in considerable danger, and—'

'Not as much as if you do! Look, I'm safe enough; no one suspects I know anything. They think I'd already left for my holiday, and I was away for the next two weeks. I promise that if anything changes in any way I'll go straight to the police.'

'But don't you see, it's different now! We know there was a connection between Maggie and the victim. The police would certainly be interested in that!'

'Again, we can't prove it.'

'But they probably could!'

'Promise me, Patrick!'

'My God!' said a voice above them. 'Patrick Linscott!'

Patrick pushed back his chair and stood up, holding out his hand. 'Connor! Good to see you again!'

'What are you doing here?'

Patrick glanced down at Jess. Fortunately her colour was starting to come back. 'We just ran into each other. Jess and I are cousins – not sure if you knew?' Connor shook his head. 'I've been in Bristol for the day, stopped for a low-alcohol drink on the way home and found her sitting here.'

'Cousins? Well, it's a small world, all right! What are you doing with yourself these days?'

Their words washed over her, comfortingly harmless. Apart from her father, they were the two men in the world she most trusted. She wished she'd had time to ask Patrick if she should take Connor into her confidence. Part of her longed to; he could surely have nothing to do with what happened. On the other hand, he'd only lecture her like Patrick and Rachel, and from the safety angle it was wise to limit the number of people who knew.

Patrick was saying, 'Well, I won't intrude on your date any further! Enjoy your evening, both of you!'

He stooped to kiss her. 'I'll be in touch,' he said and, with a pat on Connor's back, he left them.

Connor said, 'Hang on a moment while I get a drink. Can I top you up?'

'No, thanks, I'm fine.'

He went into the pub and emerged minutes later with a glass. 'You never told me you and Patrick were cousins,' he commented as he seated himself in Patrick's chair.

'I only discovered recently that you knew each other, and it just hasn't come up.'

'We were at school together.' He lifted his glass to her in a silent toast. 'So – how was your weekend?'

'Interesting!' Jess said. But she was not going to think about it now, nor about the bombshell Patrick had just dropped. What she craved was a normal, innocuous evening with no decisions to be made except where to go for supper.

'But it wouldn't be to you!' she added quickly. 'So tell me what you've been doing.'

And she leaned back with a sigh of relief, sipping her drink as he told her about the cricket match he'd been to with his brother.

Cassie had avoided being alone with her parents since the disclosure about her birth mother, and after Jess's return to Bristol had spent her time either in her room or, when she was around, with Verity. However, on the Monday evening she wandered into the kitchen as Fleur was preparing the meal.

'What time's dinner?' she asked.

'In about half an hour.' Fleur waved a floury hand towards the table. 'Sit down and keep me company.'

Cassie hesitated, then did as she suggested. 'What's the latest on Auntie Jen?' she asked, wondering belatedly how she should now refer to her.

'It seems she's in an induced coma, which I hadn't realized.'

Cassie frowned. 'Is that good or bad?'

'I think it's to give the brain time to recover after an injury. Still, Lynn says they were hoping to bring her out of it today.' Fleur turned to face her. 'Darling, I'm so sorry about all this. The timing of everything couldn't have been worse.'

'You don't really like her either, do you?'

Fleur sighed, turned back to put the dish she'd been filling in the oven, and came to sit opposite her.

'I'm not proud of that, especially if it's coloured how you think of her. As I told you, I was jealous and resentful from the outset, which God knows I shouldn't have been, but she really didn't help, especially in the early days. I've always felt she was crowding me, pushing in all the time.' She shrugged. 'We're just different kinds of people; we wouldn't have been friends even in the normal course of things.'

Cassie was quiet for a moment. Then she said diffidently, 'We're still going on holiday, aren't we?'

Fleur threw her a quick, anxious glance, but she was looking down. 'Well, yes. I mean, it's not as though she was—'

'A relative?' Cassie supplied, with a half-laugh.

Fleur said carefully, 'Would you like to go and see her? If she's allowed visitors, that is?'

'Do you think I should?'

'What I think is neither here nor there. As I told you, I'm hopelessly biased and always have been. But if the poor woman is dying, and conscious, and you feel you'd like to, then I'll take you.'

'Thank you,' Cassie said, which was no help. Then she looked up, determinedly meeting her mother's eyes. 'I have a confession to make, Mum. Well, not exactly a confession, but an admission.'

'That sounds very mysterious!' Fleur said lightly, relieved that the subject had apparently changed.

'I don't know if you remember, but a few weeks ago Gran asked me to look for a book of hers in one of the boxes she left in the loft.'

'Yes?'

'Well, I found it, but . . . a letter fell out of it. From you.'

'From me? Good Lord! I can't remember when I last wrote to her!'

'This was in October 2000.'

'Oct—' Fleur's eyes suddenly widened. 'That would have been about the time—'

'Yes.'

'God, darling,' she said shakily, 'you really are having a baptism of fire, aren't you? I don't know what I said in the letter, but I do know what it must have been about.'

'Me,' Cassie said baldly. 'When I read it I couldn't think what the problem was, since Jess had already been adopted, but last night in bed I suddenly remembered it and realized Gran couldn't have been happy about – about the surrogacy.'

'No,' Fleur acknowledged quietly, 'she wasn't. But you know Gran. For all her forward thinking, she can sometimes be very old fashioned.'

'Did she come round?' Cassie wasn't meeting her eyes.

'Oh, sweetheart, of course she did! One look at you and she adored you as much as the rest of us did!'

'But it's obvious she doesn't like Auntie Jen either!' Cassie said with a shaky smile.

The kitchen timer sounded behind them and Fleur stood up. 'That's to remind me to put the potatoes on.'

'Anything I can do?'

'You could lay the table, if you would. Cheese, not dessert, this evening.'

Cassie pushed back her chair. 'OK.'

The painful conversation had reached a natural end, and both of them were thankful.

When they were alone later that night, Fleur related it to Owen.

'Poor little thing!' she ended. 'She was besieged on all fronts!'

'Were you serious about going to see Jenny, if circumstances allow?'

'Lord knows we're pressed for time, but we could ask Lynn to sound out Ron, and if he okays it and she's conscious, it's the very least I can do.'

Owen just squeezed her hand. He would never forgive Rose Linscott for the way she'd behaved over the surrogacy. In fact, he laid the blame for Fleur's problems squarely on her shoulders. Though she'd deny it, Fleur had always been influenced to some extent by her mother and her initial reluctance towards the surrogacy had been magnified a hundredfold by Rose's reaction to it.

'It's like a prize bull having his seed implanted!' she had declared. Words which still burned in Owen's memory.

'Darling?'

'Um?'

'You don't think we ought to cancel the holiday, do you?'

'No, I do not,' Owen said firmly. 'Nor, I'm sure, would either Ron or Jenny want us to. With a bit of luck she'll have turned the corner by the end of the week and we can leave with a clear conscience. Then, if Cassie wants to, you can go and see her when we get back. And if she's no better, our being here or not being here will make no difference to her.'

And with that philosophical endorsement in her ears, Fleur thankfully slid into sleep.

FOURTEEN

It was the day of Rose's monthly lunch at the Rosemount and she was looking forward to it. It always took place on a Wednesday, a tacit distancing from Saturday's regular coffee morning, and the midweek slot fitted in well with her other engagements. Furthermore she enjoyed the fifteen-minute walk to the hotel, though she allowed Henry to run her home afterwards.

St Catherine's was a pleasant town to walk through; its streets were wide and tree-lined, offering shade in this hot summer, and the gardens she passed were colourful and well kept. Though admittedly a holiday destination, it had never succumbed to the tawdrier trappings associated with the seaside, offering instead prettily landscaped gardens along the promenade and good quality souvenir shops.

As she neared the beach she met the ever-present breeze head-on, welcoming its familiar salty smell. The hotel was one street in from the promenade and therefore protected in some measure from winter storms, though the sea could be glimpsed from its upper windows between the buildings opposite. Henry had found a good home for himself, she reflected, as had she and Malcolm before him. She had much to be thankful for.

Tables had been set out in the garden under large umbrellas, but most of the residents, while enjoying their pre-prandial drinks outside, had elected to have their meal in the cool of the dining room, a decision with which Rose and Henry concurred.

After enjoying Pimm's under their umbrella, they therefore retreated indoors and were shown to Henry's usual corner table. Rose had a moment's disquiet at the force of the air conditioning, but once she was seated she was no longer in its direct path and settled back comfortably to look at the menu, selecting cold watercress soup with a swirl of cream,

followed by chicken galantine with Caesar salad, and a rasp-
berry sorbet.

Having placed her order, she let her eyes wander over the
now-familiar diners, each at his or her usual table. Henry was
regaling her with an account of a game of bowls that he'd
won the previous day, and she made appropriate noises at
what she trusted were appropriate intervals, while allowing
her thoughts to wander.

She had hoped to be invited to Sunday's lunch at Sandstone,
the last before the family departed on their four-week holiday,
but no invitation had been forthcoming and the weekend had
passed. She'd therefore phoned Fleur the next day to wish
them a pleasant trip, and learned of the drama that had befallen
the Barlow woman. It was of course very unfortunate and
Rose wished her well, though she felt Fleur had been inordin-
ately upset, on the verge of tears as she recounted what had
happened. Rose suspected there was more behind the story
but, not wanting to add to her daughter's distress, had forborne
from enquiring further. Nonetheless, falling under a bus in
Bromley High Street struck her as a highly unlikely scenario.

'Pity they don't give cups!' Henry finished with a smile,
and she struggled to understand what he was referring to. 'It
would have looked good on my mantelpiece!'

After lunch they returned outside and, since the terrace was
now in the shade, settled there for their coffee. As expected,
two of the ladies soon approached, asking if they might join
them, and Henry gallantly brought over extra chairs from an
adjacent table.

'I hope the family are well, Mrs Linscott?' Miss Culpepper
enquired.

Remembering that she'd seen Fleur at the surgery, Rose
hastened to dispel any dire suspicions. 'Yes, indeed, thank
you,' she replied. 'In fact, they're about to go on holiday – to
South America, if you please! Very adventurous!'

'Not like it was in our day!' nodded Mrs Hill. 'When I
was young, it was a big adventure to go on a package holiday
to Spain!'

Rose, who had never been on a package holiday in her life,

smiled in reply. There was a pause while a waiter brought their coffee, setting out cups, saucers, milk and a silver coffee pot along with a small plate of petits fours.

As he moved away, Mrs Hill added, 'Daphne and her family went to Australia last year. As well as the usual places like Sydney and Melbourne, they visited Alice Springs and Ayers Rock, or whatever they call it nowadays. They had a wonderful time!'

'Talking of Australia,' Miss Culpepper remarked, stirring her coffee, 'they still don't seem to have discovered who killed that man on the beach, nor, for that matter, *where* he was killed. It's not very pleasant to think a murderer might be walking around!'

'My dear Miss Culpepper,' Henry said bracingly, 'whoever he is, he'll be miles away by now! He's not going to sit around waiting to be caught, now is he?'

Miss Culpepper gave a delicate shudder. 'I suppose not,' she said. 'I do hope you're right, Mr Parsons.'

'They say he was involved in some scandal back in Australia,' Mrs Hill said thoughtfully. 'Perhaps it caught up with him!'

'Then why was he killed here, in our country?' Miss Culpepper sounded quite aggrieved.

'I shouldn't worry about it,' Rose said comfortably. 'After all, he's no threat to anyone we know.' And she reached for another petit four.

Hilary let herself into the house and was met by a blast of hot air. Dropping her bag on the hall table, she hurriedly went round opening all available windows and pulling curtains across those through which the sun still streamed.

She'd been at her regular Wednesday bridge four, something she usually enjoyed, but it had failed to lift the vague feeling of depression that had been with her all day, added to which Sybil's sun-filled sitting room had brought on the headache that was still troubling her.

Standing at the kitchen sink, she swallowed a couple of paracetamols with a glass of deliciously cold water and faced her malaise head-on. Mainly, of course, it was due to the fact that today was Clive's birthday, which led to her missing him more than ever. Since it was a working day, they'd arranged that he would Skype during his lunch hour, eight p.m. for her – two hours from now. She must certainly put on a brighter face by then.

But she acknowledged that there was another cause for her depression, and that was guilt over her continuing affair with Justin. She'd not heard from him for over a week, and while telling herself that this was a relief, she was missing him acutely. Why oh why couldn't she be strong-willed enough to finish with him completely? It wasn't as if she'd not tried – several times, in fact, since that ill-fated lunch in Exeter – but he'd always managed to talk her round and her persistent longing for him continued to undermine her.

Sighing, she turned from the sink. After Sybil's Dundee cake she wasn't hungry, but eating something might help her headache. An omelette, then, and afterwards she'd lie down for half an hour, hoping to feel better by the time she faced her son across the miles.

'You're looking a bit peaky, Mum,' Clive remarked after the requisite birthday greetings. 'Sure you're OK?'

So much for her relaxation! 'Yes, yes, I'm fine, darling.'

'In need of a holiday, perhaps?'

She smiled noncommittally but he was going on, 'Which actually brings me to something I wanted to run by you. How about coming out here, not for two or three weeks like you did last time, but for three months or so? Make it really worthwhile?'

She gasped. 'Three *months*? Goodness, Clive, I couldn't do that!'

'Why not? Now poor old Pip's no longer with us you've no pets to worry about, so there's nothing to stop you, is there? And if you're thinking you'd be an imposition, or something equally daft, I've the perfect solution!'

'Which is?'

'I told you Patty and I are moving into our own place? Well, it turns out it has an ADU attached – an accessory dwelling unit. I don't know if you've heard of them, but they're separate buildings that can be either attached to a property or built in its garden – or backyard, as they say over here – which is where ours is. They're becoming really popular as house prices continue to rise, either to rent out for additional income or to use as a granny flat. Ours should suit you perfectly! You'd be quite independent to do your own thing, but able to see us as much or as little as you want!'

When she didn't immediately reply, he added persuasively, 'You know how you loved the life here when you and Dad were over two years ago. And, incredible as it seems, you've never met Patty! She's longing to see you! So what do you think?'

'It sounds wonderful,' she said slowly. 'I suppose I'd need a visa?'

'No, there's something called an ESTA that does away with the need for one, as long as you stay for less than ninety days. It's dead easy, you apply for it online without having to go to the US Consulate or anything; all you need is to have your passport handy.'

Three months in the States! she was thinking. And hard on that thought, three months away from Justin! This, she thought with rising excitement, could be the answer to her problem, and, even better, she'd be near Clive, able to share his life for a while and meet his new girlfriend.

'And if you really liked it,' he added with a laugh, 'we could make it permanent!'

'Whoa!' she protested. 'I'm still trying to get my head round a three-month holiday!'

'No pressure, just something to bear in mind. I'd certainly be much happier if you were nearer at hand.'

'Now I'm getting old and decrepit?' she challenged.

'That'll be the day! Look, Mum, I have to go; I'm due back at my desk in ten minutes. Thanks again for the voucher – I shall enjoy spending it! – and we'll talk at the weekend as usual. But in the meantime do give serious thought to the suggestion. Love you!' And the screen went blank.

Hilary continued to stare at it for a few moments, then a smile spread slowly over her face.

*   *   *

That evening Jess had a call from Rachel, and since several of the crowd were present she retreated to her bedroom to take it, closing the door behind her.

'How are things going?' Rachel enquired. 'There's been more about our friend in the press and on TV, but they don't seem any nearer to finding whodunnit, to coin a phrase.'

'Actually, they're nearer than you might think!' Jess said in a low voice. 'Major developments this week!'

'Really?' Rachel's voice quickened with interest. 'What's happened?'

'Nothing's actually *happened*, but we found out something that could be crucial.'

'"We?" You've confided in someone?'

'My cousin, yes.'

'Well, go on, then!'

'You know I told you Maggie and I were going to the theatre? Well, Patrick and his girlfriend were also there and we chatted to them beforehand. His girlfriend's Australian—'

A sound reached her that she identified as the loose board outside her door and she stiffened, straining to hear anything further, but there was silence.

'Yes?' Rachel prompted impatiently.

Jess moved over to her bed and, feeling like a spy in some third-rate film, draped the duvet over her. 'She recognized Maggie,' she went on from underneath it, 'or thought she did – and later remembered she'd seen her at a dinner in Sydney.' She paused for dramatic effect. 'With Bruce Marriott!'

'With *who* – or rather *whom*? I can hardly hear you!'

'Sorry. I thought I heard someone outside the door – probably imagination!' But she remained under the duvet. 'I said she was with *Bruce Marriott*!'

Rachel's gasp came down the line. 'No!'

'And another thing, though it's nothing like as important, is that Dad had a drink with him the day before he was killed!'

'You're joking!' Rachel exclaimed disbelievingly.

'No, really. He didn't know him, they were just sitting next to each other at a bar, but Dad recognized him later from the artist's impression in the paper.'

'He must have had a shock!'

'Not nearly such as shock as if he'd known my connection!'

'So what are you going to do? You'll *have* to go back to the police now!'

'Yes,' Jess said slowly, 'I think I will.'

Kathryn said quietly, 'The children know something, don't they?'

She was washing the dishes after dinner while Justin leaned against a counter checking emails on his phone. His head jerked up, but with her back to him he couldn't gauge her expression.

'Do they?' he countered.

'Why else are they being so attentive all of a sudden? And all these comments about us being strained with each other: as far as I know we've not behaved any differently, certainly not in front of them. It can't only be because you've moved to the guest room – we explained about that. Which leads me to assume they know something that I don't, and that isn't a very pleasant feeling.'

'I'm sure you're imagining things,' he said.

She picked up a tea towel and began to dry the glasses. 'Perhaps,' she said.

Justin was distinctly rattled as he left the room; had he just been given a yellow card? Bloody kids, stirring things! But kids or not, he was now on thin ice, because if any rumours reached the office the consequences didn't bear thinking about. It had to be faced: if he didn't end this obsession with Hilary, both his marriage and his career might be in jeopardy. To give Hilary her due, she'd been saying as much for weeks and he'd talked her out of it. How would she react if he suddenly U-turned and said it was over – hurt, or relieved? Or both?

At the mere thought of her a treacherous wave of heat washed over him and he put a hand to the door jamb for support. This, he told himself, biting down hard on his lip, was nothing short of addiction, and addictions had to be dealt with before they proved fatal.

On the other hand, continuing with the analogy, going cold turkey could also be dangerous. Perhaps he should let her down gradually, just the odd hint to begin with? That would give them a few more weeks together. His spirits began to lift. An influx of business had kept him in the office over the last ten days but now he was impatient to be with her. Yes, he knew it was dangerous and yes, he had to be extra careful, so he'd set himself a deadline: in four weeks' time he would end it, once and for all. In the meantime . . .

In her lunch hour the next day Jess, heart hammering, phoned the police station. DS Stuart had given her a card with his direct number, so she was expecting to hear his voice when his phone was lifted. But the man who answered had a Welsh accent.

'DS Stuart's phone.'

Jess hesitated. 'Could I speak to him, please?'

'Sorry, ma'am, DS Stuart's on annual leave.'

Jess's heart plummeted like the proverbial stone. 'Oh no!' she murmured involuntarily.

'DS Morgan here. Perhaps I can help?'

'No, no thank you, it has to be . . . When will he be back?'

'He'll be in again on Monday. Can I tell him who called?'

'No, it doesn't matter, thanks,' Jess said quickly. 'I'll call back then.' And she rang off.

The sense of anti-climax was overwhelming and she was close to tears. She'd lain awake half the night rehearsing what she'd say to him and how she'd apologize for not being frank at their last meeting. The prospect of finally handing over all responsibility was incredibly comforting. Now she'd another four days before that relief would come, and she was increasingly uncomfortable with Laurence. When she'd returned to the sitting room after speaking to Rachel he'd kept glancing at her, and she was as sure as she could be that it had been his footstep that she'd heard outside her door – pausing on the way to the bathroom, no doubt.

Even more worrying was what she'd been saying at that point – that Tasha was Australian, which might have rung dangerous bells. How long had he been standing there? Did he make the creak that betrayed him as he arrived, or as he was leaving?

On the other hand, of course, it could have been caused by someone innocently walking past, perhaps not even Laurence. She was letting her imagination run riot, and if she didn't rein it in she'd be a nervous wreck by the time she saw Stuart, which would detract from her account. Time to get a grip.

Jess had two phone calls that evening. The first, as she was walking back from work, was from Patrick, and he wasted no time on preliminaries.

'Jess, please tell me you've been in touch with the police?'

'I tried,' she answered, 'but the man I saw before is on holiday and I didn't want to have to go through it all again.' She heard him swear. 'He's back on Monday,' she added quickly, 'and I'll certainly speak to him then.' She didn't dare tell him of Laurence's possible eavesdropping.

'I suppose that will have to do. I might tell you you've been causing me sleepless nights lately.'

'Me too.'

'Well, just watch your step.' He paused. 'Are you seeing Connor later?'

'He'll probably be round, yes.'

'Then stick to him closely. You'll be OK with him.'

'Should I tell him?' Jess enquired, half-dreading his reply.

Patrick thought for a moment. 'Not much point at this stage, but if things suddenly hot up, then yes, he'd be good back-up; he's closer at hand than I am.'

'Now you're making me even more nervous!' she protested.

'Good!' he said grimly. 'Call me at once if there are any problems. Promise?'

'I promise,' she said.

The second call, from her mother, came soon after, as she was arriving at the flat. Since she was the first back, she'd no need to retreat to her room.

'Hope this isn't a bad time, darling,' Fleur began breathlessly, 'but I've not had a second all day and we're leaving tomorrow afternoon.'

'Tomorrow?' Jess echoed, a sudden hollow feeling in the pit of her stomach.

'Yes; it's an early flight on Saturday so we'll spend the night at a hotel near Heathrow. I can't believe that in about forty-eight hours we'll be in Lima!'

'Lucky you!'

'Not sure what the internet connections are like down there, but we'll send photos when and where possible.'

'Well, have a wonderful time, all of you!' A thought belatedly struck her. 'Any news of Auntie Jen?' she asked, guilty she'd not enquired before.

'Better, thank God. She's out of ICU.' Fleur paused, then added diffidently, 'Cassie and I will go and see her when we get back.'

Jess bit back her surprise. 'And Cassie's all right with that?'

'Of course.'

She didn't dare pursue it. 'Well, that's a relief; I'm so glad she's out of danger.' She heard a voice calling in the background.

'Sorry, darling, I have to go. Verity can't find her yellow fever certificate! Love you lots!'

'Bye, Mum,' Jess said, but Fleur had already ended the call.

She stood in the middle of the sitting room, feeling suddenly bereft. Useless now to regret not telling her father about the body in her flat when she'd had plenty of opportunities. He might have cancelled their holiday; she couldn't imagine him flying halfway across the world if he thought she was in danger. But what could he have done, other than what she was now, if belatedly, doing herself? And they'd all been looking forward to that holiday for months. Her sisters would certainly not have thanked her for causing its cancellation.

If she could just keep things together till Monday, she told herself encouragingly, it would be all right. And what, for heaven's sake, could either Maggie or Laurence actually do? She was letting her imagination run away with her.

Behind her the flat door opened and Maggie's cheerful voice said, 'Oh, you're back! Get out the gin, for God's sake! I've had the hell of a day!'

She'd read too many thrillers, Jess admonished herself; it was ridiculous to think she could be in any real danger.

'Gin coming up!' she said.

Kathryn stood at her sitting room window staring down the garden. The roses needed deadheading again, she noted, and the grass could do with cutting, though that was Justin's province.

Was she doing the right thing? She'd thought she could go on keeping her cool until he came to his senses, as she was sure he would, but she wasn't as strong as she'd thought, and after a couple of nights crying herself to sleep, she'd taken back control.

How much of it was her fault? She was willing to accept that she wasn't blameless; Justin was a passionate man whereas she was considerably more reserved, and at some level she'd been aware that this occasionally frustrated him. She loved him deeply but in her own less demonstrative way, and obviously that hadn't been enough. Perhaps, she thought, with a wry twist of her lips, she should have 'faked it', but such subterfuge had never occurred to her.

She'd known, some weeks before her children's intervention, that he was seeing someone, and not only because of the lipstick on the handkerchief. A couple of times she'd phoned his mobile to be met by voicemail and once, wanting his advice on something while she was in town, she'd called in at the office and been told apologetically that he'd been called out – unexpectedly, it seemed, since there were no appointments in his diary. When, that evening, she had enquired where he'd been, he'd obviously been caught off guard.

What did wives do in these no doubt very common circumstances? Write to an agony aunt? Run home to their mothers? Kathryn had no parents and the thought of confiding in some anonymous person was anathema to her. The fact remained, however, that she couldn't go on like this. She'd given him the chance the other evening to be honest with her, and he'd not taken it.

So she had reached her decision, and was about to put it

into effect. Though an only child, she had always been close to her cousin Anne, who, she'd sometimes thought, was better than a sister, since there was never cause for sibling rivalry.

She turned from the window to pour herself a strong gin and tonic. Then she seated herself in her favourite chair, picked up her mobile and, with slightly unsteady fingers, clicked on her number.

It had been a busy week at the office and there was a decided air of 'Thank God it's Friday!' among the staff as it drew to a close. Jess, however, had mixed feelings; without the daily routine of going to the office, more time would be spent with the group – a prospect filled at the moment with uncertainty. But Connor would be there, she reminded herself, and there was surely safety in numbers. Then, on Monday, she'd speak to DS Stuart.

On Friday evenings the garden centre remained open till six and Maggie took her turn in staying late. She'd reminded Jess at breakfast that that evening was one of those times, and asked her to make a start on preparing the meal.

'The boys are seeing to the booze as usual,' she'd said. 'Sarah's bringing trout pâté and Di has made her special lemon and honey chicken. I'll get the lettuce and tomatoes and some raspberries for dessert, but could you make a start on the potato salad? The spring onions are in the fridge drawer and I replenished the bottle of mayonnaise last week.'

Jess therefore arrived home with the prospect of peeling an inordinate number of potatoes, a pastime she didn't relish. The family would be at the Heathrow hotel by now, she thought, fervently wishing she was with them. Her own holiday, though ultimately enjoyable, had to some extent been overshadowed by the trauma of finding Bruce Marriott, a trauma that had still not been resolved.

Firmly closing her mind on that subject, she tuned the radio to a music channel, filled a bowl with potatoes and settled down to her task. But after only about twenty minutes there was a knock on the door. She frowned and glanced at her watch, confirming that it was far too early for any of the group to arrive. Pulling off her rubber gloves, she went to answer it and, with a sense of shock, saw Laurence Pope standing outside, a quizzical smile on his face.

'Maggie's not back yet,' she said quickly, seizing on all she could think of to prevent his entering.

'No, I know; she told me she'd assigned you the job of potato peeling, so I thought I'd come and give you a hand. It's one of my specialities.'

So he'd known she'd be alone. She forced herself to say lightly, 'Not necessary, really. You've time for a pint across the road – I'm sure you've earned it!'

But he was stepping past her into the flat and, with accelerated heartbeat, she closed the door and returned to her seat.

He extracted two bottles of wine from the carrier he was holding and placed them on the coffee table. 'I'll get the other peeler,' he said, reminding her that he knew the flat and its contents as well as she did. Oh God, Maggie wouldn't arrive for at least twenty minutes, depending on the traffic, Connor not for an hour at least. She wondered frantically if she could somehow contact him and beg him to come now.

Laurence returned with the peeler and another bowl, tipped some potatoes into it and seated himself opposite her, their knees almost touching. She was acutely aware of him, of his strength and of the danger she sensed in his handsome face and black eyes.

'I thought it would be a good opportunity to get to know you better,' he said lazily, as though aware of her inward panic. 'You're a quiet little thing, aren't you? Never volunteer much. So tell me, Jess Tempest, what makes you tick?'

She felt her face grow hot. 'I'm not sure I know what you mean,' she floundered.

'Oh, I think you do. I get the impression that the group's sometimes a bit too much for you and you'd prefer a quiet evening alone. Or perhaps,' he added with a sly look, 'with Connor!'

She held her voice steady. 'I admit there are times after a busy day at work that I'd like the chance to relax.'

'Then you chose the wrong flatmate! You and Maggie are chalk and cheese, aren't you? So, tell me about your other friends. The one who phoned you the other evening, for instance.'

Her eyes flew to his face. The banter had left it and his eyes now had a cruel, cat-playing-with-mouse expression.

'Rachel's one of my oldest friends,' she said, holding her voice steady. 'It was she who came to Italy with me.'

'Ah. I had the impression she's Australian?'

Jess's mouth went dry. After a moment, she forced herself to say, 'I don't know what gave you that idea.'

'Must have been something you said. Maggie used to live there; did you know that?'

'I knew she'd lived abroad. I don't think she mentioned Australia.' Jess glanced wildly at her watch. 'Connor should be here soon!' she added inanely.

His mouth twisted into an ironic smile. 'On his white charger? You're not a damsel in distress, are you, Jess Tempest, when we're having a friendly conversation?'

'No, I just meant—'

She was interrupted by the sound of the door opening and for a wild moment wondered if she'd somehow materialized him. Instead she heard Maggie's voice.

'Well, this is a cosy little domestic scene!'

Laurence looked up as she bent to kiss him. 'Greetings, my love. Just getting to know your little flatmate.'

Maggie glanced shrewdly from one to the other. 'Red Riding Hood and the wolf come to mind,' she said. 'Leave Jess to her spuds and come and help me unpack this lot.'

She went through into the kitchen and Laurence, placing his bowl on the table, rose slowly to his feet.

'Such a pity!' he murmured softly as he followed her.

FIFTEEN

Connor phoned while Jess was having breakfast. 'Happy Saturday!' he said. 'I was wondering if you'd like a trip out somewhere? Drive into the country, walk, pub lunch, that kind of thing?'

'Sounds lovely!' she said. Nothing would suit her better than to be away from the rest of the group, particularly Laurence.

'How about the Cotswolds, then? Bourton-on-the-Water, perhaps?'

'Great!'

'Right; I'll be in the underground car park in half an hour. OK?'

'See you there!'

Jess's heart lifted at the thought of a whole day with Connor and she couldn't help wondering if it would further their relationship in any way. They'd been out together a few times now – lunch, dinner, the cinema – but a light kiss goodnight as he dropped her back at the flat was as far as they'd progressed. And she admitted to herself that she wanted more, especially now when she was feeling so vulnerable.

The day was all she'd hoped it would be. The sun was high in the sky, the Cotswold countryside was at its best, and they drove with the car windows down, welcoming the refreshing breeze on their faces. Bourton was crowded, as they'd expected, but they managed to find a place to park and walked for some way alongside the river, stopping to look in shop windows and eating ice cream.

After lunch in a pub garden – a large helping each of moules and chips, washed down with spritzer – they returned to the car and drove farther into the countryside, delighting in the honey-coloured stone houses with their thatched roofs, ducks on a pond and even a game of cricket in progress on one of the village greens.

'Chocolate box scenery!' Connor remarked.

After a while they turned into a gateway on a country road, left the car and set off to walk to the top of a nearby hill. It was a steep climb and they'd little breath for conversation. By the time they returned to the car they were hot and tired and grateful for the bottles of water Connor had had the foresight to buy at the pub where they'd lunched.

Relaxed, sipping at her water, Jess mused, 'My family will be in Peru by now.'

'Well, that's a conversation stopper! How long have they gone for?'

'Four weeks in all, taking in Bolivia, Brazil and Argentina. The trip of a lifetime.'

'And you wish you were with them?' he asked, half-teasing.

She smiled. 'Not at this precise moment!'

'You were down there last weekend, weren't you?'

'Yes, it turned out to be quite traumatic.'

'Oh?'

She'd spoken without thinking; she'd no intention of telling him of the surrogacy or of her father's fleeting association with Bruce Marriott, but Jenny's accident was sufficient explanation and she related that. After a minute, she added, 'And I bumped into Roger while I was there.'

'Your ex?'

She nodded. 'I'd gone out for an early morning walk, and he was there on the beach exercising his dog.'

Connor was quiet for a while, then he asked diffidently, 'And how was it, seeing him again?'

'Odd,' Jess said simply. 'He was so exactly the same.'

'Any regrets?'

She shook her head. 'No, we've moved on.'

He gave a short laugh. 'That's a relief! I thought you were working up to dumping me!'

She turned her head to look at him. 'I wouldn't do that,' she said.

He reached out a hand and traced her face with one finger. 'That's good to know,' he said softly.

She wasn't sure which of them moved first, but suddenly she was in his arms and they were exchanging the kind of kisses she'd been hoping for. When they finally separated he said a little breathlessly, 'God, Jess, are you sure you're ready for this?'

'Why, aren't you?' she challenged.

'God, yes, but I've been holding back. I was pretty cut up by my last break-up, and determined not to lay myself open to such hurt again. So I vowed not to get seriously involved with anyone for a full year.' He smiled wryly. 'But then I met you! The trouble was I knew you'd also split recently after a long-term relationship. I was terrified of scaring you off!'

She smiled. 'Not much chance of that!'

He pulled her towards him again, burying his face in her hair. On the country road alongside them a tractor lumbered past, the driver leaning out with a ribald comment.

They laughed and waved back. 'Time we were going,' Connor said.

'I don't want today to end!'

'Oh, it won't!' he assured her. 'Not for some time, anyway! I suggest we go back to our respective abodes, wash and change, then go out for a slap-up meal somewhere to cele-brate. Saturday takeaway at the flat doesn't strike the right note somehow! Deal?'

'Deal!' she said happily.

By the time Hilary and Clive spoke again at the weekend they both had progress to report.

'I can't believe how smoothly it's gone!' Hilary said wonder-ingly. 'The ESTA was a doddle, like you said. And I spoke to Pauline next door and she's happy to keep an eye on the house while I'm away. I'll ask the post office to hold any mail, though there shouldn't be much, and I can put the lights on a time switch. When it gets darker in the autumn Pauline says she'll come in to draw the curtains and pull them back again in the morning.'

'That's great, Mum, you sound very organized! I've been

looking up direct flights to Denver, and though it's a fairly busy time there are plenty available, the earliest suitable one being the week after next.'

Hilary caught her breath. 'Goodness! As soon as that?'

'Well, there's no reason to delay, is there?'

No, there isn't, Hilary thought, but with secret reservations. She had still not seen Justin; he'd sent a text saying he'd be round on Thursday, but then had to cancel as some business appointment came up. At this rate she'd have left for America before she could even tell him she was going. Well, she told herself stoutly, that was his funeral.

'So how about we go for that, which would make it the tenth of August, and in the meantime I'll send you a link to a website showing the layout of the ADU.'

'That would be great!' she said.

Later that evening as she was getting into bed a text pinged on her mobile and she leaned over to read it.

Monday, two p.m. Promise! Justin xx.

Saved by the bell! she thought whimsically and, turning out the light, settled down to sleep.

As she walked to work on Monday morning, Jess, heart in mouth, again clicked on DS Stuart's number. And this time it was his brisk voice that answered.

'DS Stuart.'

'Oh, good morning. I'm Jess Tempest. I came to see you a few weeks ago, with some information on Bruce Marriott.'

'Yes?'

It was clear he didn't remember her. 'Well, I've just learned something and this time it really is urgent.' She bit her lip. That made it sound as though she'd been wasting his time on the last occasion.

'Then would you please leave a message with the Murder Room, madam. Their number is—'

'No – please!' She stopped dead on the pavement and someone cannoned into her, swearing fluently. 'I really must see you! You gave me your direct number and asked me to contact you if there was anything else. And now there really is, so please could I come and see you, preferably around lunchtime?'

If she went after work, questions would be asked about why she was late home, and she couldn't let that happen.

'I'm afraid that's out of the question; I'm just back from leave and haven't a spare minute all week. Really, the Murder Room are dealing with the case, they can—'

'But you gave me your *personal number*!' she pleaded, and he might have heard the tears in her voice, because his softened slightly.

'What was the name again?'

'Jess Tempest.'

He grunted; apparently that wasn't much help. 'Lunchtime, you said? Well, I certainly can't manage today, but if it's really urgent I suppose I could sacrifice my lunch tomorrow.'

'Oh, thank you so much! What time would suit you?'

'Somewhere between twelve and two, but I'll only be able to spare you a few minutes.'

'Thank you, I'll be there!' she said, and breathed a little prayer of thankfulness.

Another twenty-four hours to wait! With her nerves keyed to this pitch it wouldn't be easy, but at least he'd agreed to see her. She realized humbly that that was all she could expect.

Although no one could possibly see in, the bedroom curtains were drawn and the sun shining through them bathed the room in pink shadow.

Sex in the afternoon was thoroughly decadent, Hilary thought, lying back in post-coital languor. It had been wonderful, especially after the long gap, but, she reminded herself uncompromisingly, it was for the very last time. Three months was quite long enough to wean herself away from him and she'd no intention whatever of their affair resuming on her return – if, that is, she ever came back permanently. Clive's suggestion, repeated on Saturday, that she should consider moving over there was seeming ever more tempting.

Beside her Justin stirred, his hand trailing caressingly over her breast. 'God, I needed that!' he said. 'And so, it appeared, did you!'

She smiled. 'It was good,' she conceded, 'but it was for the last time.'

He moved impatiently. 'Oh Hills, don't start that again!' Time enough to tell her when he was ready. 'You know we've thrashed this out a dozen times. You really don't have to worry—'

'No,' she interrupted, 'this is different. I'm going to stay with my son in the States for three months.'

'What?' He raised himself on one elbow and stared down at her.

'I think you heard,' she replied steadily, though her heart was thumping.

'When was this arranged? You never told me!' Ironic indeed that he was being pre-empted!

'It's all happened very quickly – since I last saw you, in fact. And believe it or not, Justin, it has nothing to do with you! Clive suggested it because he thought I needed a long holiday and the new place he's moved into has a granny flat.'

'You're not a granny!' he said ridiculously.

'I don't think I'll have to prove my credentials!'

He leaned closer. 'You're not really set on going, are you? I mean, not yet? In another month, say?'

She shook her head. 'My flight's booked for the tenth.'

He fell back on the pillow. 'My God!'

'Look, I'm sorry, Justin, but you know I've been uneasy about this for some time, much as I enjoy being with you. This seemed to offer the perfect way of ending it with no hurt feelings on either side.'

He lay still, trying to absorb the sudden change in his life. He'd miss her like hell, but to be fair he knew it was time to put the brakes on. He'd been given a yellow card, after all.

He turned to face her. 'One more once?' he asked, mimicking Count Basie.

She nodded, tears in her eyes, and they made love again, more tenderly now the pent-up passion was spent.

'I'll miss you,' he said half an hour later, as he was doing up his shirt.

'Me too,' she acknowledged.

He looked down at her, then bent and kissed her. 'Thank you,' he said. 'For everything.' And, as she made a move to

get up, he waved her down. 'No, stay there. I'll let myself
out. Goodbye, Hilary. Be happy.'

'Goodbye,' she whispered, and as she heard the front door
close behind him, she buried her face in her pillow and wept.

Justin was in a sober mood as he drove back to the office
from his two o'clock 'appointment'. He'd granted himself four
weeks' grace before terminating the arrangement and this had
been snatched away from him without warning. In spite of
himself he felt a little resentful. However, since some gesture
seemed called for to mark this change in his fortunes he
decided to buy a large bouquet for Kathryn on the way
home – before remembering this was a well-recognized sign
of a guilty conscience.

A meal somewhere, then. He couldn't remember when he'd
last taken her out to dinner. Not this evening, of course; she
would as always have his meal ready when he arrived home.
Perhaps tomorrow, then, or at the weekend. And somewhere
really special.

Conscience slightly appeased, he parked the car and, having
checked in the rear-view mirror for telltale signs of his recent
activities, went into the office. As luck would have it, he met
Patrick on the stairs, and they passed each other with a brief
nod. His son would be pleased at the turn of events, Justin
thought sourly, and wondered how long it would take him to
become aware of it.

Jenny was propped up in bed when they arrived with their
various offerings. Her arm was still in a sling, her leg still raised
by a pulley; there were bruises under her eyes and a bandage
round her head, but her face lit up when she saw them.

'You're looking a bit better, Mum,' Gemma said as she bent
to kiss her. 'Are you in less pain now?'

'I'm fine. Doped to the eyeballs, so no pain!'

Ron conscientiously passed on messages from the neighbours, and Jenny nodded towards the stack of get well cards
on the bedside locker. 'Everyone's so kind,' she murmured.
'Lynn and Tony sent the most beautiful bouquet – we're
running out of places to put things!'

'Then I'd better take my grapes back again!' Freddie joked.

Jenny smiled, then her eyes fell. 'I suppose Dad told you Fleur phoned and asked if she can bring Cassie to see me when they get back from holiday?'

Gemma said awkwardly, 'That's great, Mum.'

'Which brings me to something I have to say, now that I have all three of you together. Two things, actually. The first is a heartfelt apology.'

Gemma reached quickly for her hand, which closed round hers.

'For almost twenty years,' Jenny went on, 'I've behaved in a thoroughly selfish and thoughtless way, and I want you to know I'm bitterly ashamed. I've thrown the whole family out of kilter and caused untold hurt, and I'm asking you, if you can, to forgive me.'

Ron moved awkwardly and started to speak but she shook her head at him. 'No, let me finish. Of course I'll always have feelings for Cassie – I carried her for nine months – but she was never mine and in my heart I knew that – I just wouldn't accept it. But most importantly I want you two to know I've always loved you both with all my heart, and I'm just sorry that when it mattered most I didn't show it.'

'Mum, it's all right!' Gemma whispered. 'You don't have to say any more. I behaved badly too and *I'm* sorry.'

Jenny squeezed her hand. 'You've nothing to apologize for.'

Ron cleared his throat. 'Right, love, you've said your piece and I'm sure the kids understand. So let's lighten the mood, eh?'

'Just one thing more. Last night I overheard something that absolutely appalled me.'

They exchanged startled glances.

'Everyone seems to think I stepped in front of that bus deliberately, and I'm telling you categorically *that isn't true*! Yes, for the last week or so I'd been very unhappy, but I would never, never be so desperate as to do anything like that. It was just that with my thoughts in such a jumble I wasn't looking where I was going. That is God's truth and I want you all to know it.'

She looked from one face to another, saw they all had tears of relief in their eyes. 'Right – end of sermon! Now, what did you do with that box of Milk Tray?'

*   *   *

Justin turned into his driveway full of good intentions. Kathryn had mentioned the lawn needed cutting, so he'd do it this evening. And he'd also fix that shelf in the bathroom that had been wonky for months.

He saw it as soon as he opened the front door, the single sheet of paper on the hall table, folded over to display his name. He came to a dead halt, a sudden coldness in the pit of his stomach. A Dear John letter? From *Kathryn*?

Heart in mouth, he snatched it up, opened it and read.

> *Dear Justin,*
> *After some thought, I've decided we need some time apart until things become clearer. I'm going to stay with Anne for a while, and I would ask you not to try to contact me. I shan't answer my phone, so please don't call. I'll be in touch in due course.*
> *Kathryn.*

In due course? What the hell did that mean? Oh God, this couldn't be happening! Two women dumping him in one day! The gods of chance must be laughing their bloody heads off!

Regardless of the message, he immediately took out his phone and called her number. The call was declined. This was *ridiculous*! She should at least allow him a chance either to explain or to defend himself! But wasn't that exactly what she had done, when she'd asked what the children knew? If he'd answered honestly then, he could possibly have forestalled this drastic action.

He looked about him, suddenly at a loss what to do. He wandered into the kitchen, to find another note waiting for him. This one read *Dinner in the fridge. Pre-heat oven to 150 degrees, cook for 30 mins.*

He opened the fridge door and saw a foil-covered dish containing shepherd's pie, doubtless made from yesterday's roast. When would he eat another home-cooked meal?

He straightened his shoulders. Well, he'd get nowhere by feeling sorry for himself, and he had to accept he deserved no sympathy. So he'd do what he'd originally intended: cut the grass and fix the bathroom shelf. Then he'd open a bottle of wine, heat up his meal and, contrary to normal practice, eat it on his knee in front of the television. And if he had enough wine it might help him to sleep tonight.

Tuesday at last. It took all Jess's concentration to keep her mind on her work that morning, but she was grateful for its distraction. With crossed fingers, she informed the office manager that she'd a dental appointment and might be a little late back from lunch, feeling guilty when it was accepted without question. So at twelve forty-five she set off for her second visit to the police station, praying that the detective would believe her story and provide the perfect solution.

This time, when she gave her name at the desk she was asked to take a seat, and minutes later the two detectives she'd met before came through the security door and approached her.

'Ms Tempest? DS Stuart and my colleague, DC Masters.'

Jess stood up nervously and nodded acknowledgment. 'Thank you so much for seeing me.'

'Would you like to come this way?'

He showed her into the same interview room, and as she seated herself murmured, 'Ah, now I remember you! The lady who didn't want to give her name!'

Jess flushed. 'Yes, and I'm afraid what I told you last time wasn't exactly true.'

He glanced at the notes he'd brought with him. 'I hope you're not saying you didn't see Marriott after all?'

'Oh, I saw him all right, but he was lying dead on the floor in my flat!'

The two men stared at her blankly.

'Oh, I didn't *kill* him,' she hurried on, 'I just found him there. But I thought if I told you, whoever *had* killed him would know it must have been me who reported it. Quite apart from the fact that they hadn't left a shred of evidence to back up my story.'

DS Stuart leaned back in his chair and regarded her for a moment in silence. Then he said slowly, 'I think you'd better start at the beginning.'

So she went through the whole episode again – the forgotten

paperback, the shock of finding Marriott, the approaching voices, hiding in the wardrobe and then, on emerging, the total absence of anything incriminating.

'I didn't think anyone would believe me,' she ended. 'I'd no idea who he was and there was nothing to show he'd been there at all! So I drove down to my sister's eighteenth and the next day went to Italy for two weeks.'

'And when you got back, you came to see us.'

'Yes. He'd been found and identified by then, so I had to do *something*. I thought if I said I'd seen him going into the block of flats you might be able to suss something out.'

'You have a touching faith in our abilities,' Stuart said drily. 'Have you discussed this with anyone else? Anyone at all?'

'My friend Rachel; I told her when we were on holiday. And my cousin Patrick, just in the last week or so.'

'No one local, who might know those you suspect?'

She shook her head. 'No.'

'Well, please don't repeat anything we discuss now with anybody. So, how many people are you sharing this flat with?'

'Only one, Maggie Haig, though she keeps open house so there's nearly always a crowd round. But it's Maggie I need to tell you about.' And she repeated Patrick's tale of Tasha seeing her in Sydney with Bruce Marriott.

Stuart whistled through his teeth.

'Is that enough to charge her?' Jess asked hopefully.

He shook his head. 'I'm not saying I don't believe you or your cousin's girlfriend, but it's all uncorroborated and we need evidence before we can make a move.'

Seeing her crestfallen face, he added, 'But at least it gives us a platform to start from. Now, you said there's a group of people who often visit the flat. I'll need names and addresses.'

Jess supplied what she could, though she didn't know where any of them lived. 'Laurence Pope is the most likely bet,' she added. 'He's Maggie's boyfriend and he made a point of letting me know he'd heard me mention Australia on the phone to my friend. He asked if I knew Maggie had lived there.' She gave a little shudder.

'Do you think you're in danger?' Stuart asked sharply.

She considered. 'Not really. I'm careful not to be alone with him.' Though she couldn't always prevent it, she remembered uneasily, as when she'd been peeling potatoes. She hesitated. 'If you've not enough to go on, suppose I call their bluff in some way?'

Stuart frowned. 'How do you mean?'

'Perhaps one evening, when everyone's there. Safety in numbers!' She gave a nervous laugh. 'I could say something that proved I knew what had happened. The police could be listening outside and rush in when they gave themselves away.'

Stuart sat back, pulling at his lip as he reviewed possibilities. 'We couldn't do that, but there's a possibility we could make use of that open house policy.'

Jess leaned forward eagerly. 'How?'

'We might be able to bring in an off-duty officer. Suppose he posed as a work colleague and you suggested inviting him round for the evening. Would that work?'

Her face lit up. 'Perfectly! Especially if I said he was new to the area and didn't know anyone!' She broke off. 'But what could he do, if he was off duty?'

'Oh, he could put himself straight back on if the need arose, don't worry on that account. In the meantime, you could start talking about this new colleague and how he seems to be at a loose end. Incidentally, where do you work? He'd need to gen up on it.'

'Steadman and Maybury.'

'The PR people?'

She nodded.

He thought for a moment, tapping his pen on the desk. 'When do you suggest would be the best time for this operation?'

'Oh, Saturday,' Jess said promptly. 'Some weekdays only a couple or so turn up, but on Saturday we have a takeaway and usually it's a full house.'

'What time does the evening start?'

'They begin to drift in round about half past seven and we sit and talk over drinks till eight thirty, when the food arrives. Then we go out to a pub or club.'

Stuart nodded, still tapping his pen. He turned to the DC. 'Bob, would you nip up to my office and check the duty roster?

See who's off on Saturday, and if any of them happen to be around, bring one down, would you?' He glanced at Jess. 'And pick the prettiest!' he added.

'Right, skip.' With a grin, Masters left the room, returning soon after with a fellow officer.

Not exactly pretty, Jess thought, amused, but then she hadn't seen the others! He was personable enough, though – mid-thirties at a guess, tall, blue eyes, mid-brown hair and a bump on his nose, probably broken at some time. He was introduced to her as DS Ben Ridley, and once again Jess related the circumstances that had brought her here.

'Looks as if this might wrap it up!' he commented, when it was explained to him what he was required to do.

'Let's certainly hope so. To recap: with it being the weekend you wouldn't have been in the office, so you won't need to meet till around seven thirty.' Stuart turned to Jess. 'Say he waits for you in the foyer and you go down to collect him?'

Ben Ridley looked doubtful. 'The trouble with that, Rob, is it wouldn't give us much time to finalize things – they'd be expecting us back almost immediately. Better perhaps to meet somewhere else and we could agree the finishing touches as we make our way to the flat?'

'Good point,' Stuart agreed.

'Outside the office, then?' Jess suggested. 'It's about a ten-minute walk – that should give us time.'

Both men nodded.

'Right,' Stuart said. 'Steadman and Maybury offices at seven thirty. And in the meantime, Ben, you can think up a new name for yourself.'

He leaned back in his chair. 'Taking all the timings into account, I reckon things should kick off about eight, when you're all settled and before the delivery of the takeaway at eight thirty. So I'll have back-up on standby around that time, in case you need them.' He checked the notes he'd made. 'At Flat Five, Sussex Court. Thanks, Ben.'

Ridley got to his feet and nodded to Jess. 'Till Saturday, then. And when we meet I'll be Dan Crowther.'

Jess nodded. 'Till Saturday,' she replied.

SIXTEEN

Around six weeks earlier

It had been a busy week and Maggie was glad she'd blocked out the afternoon in her calendar. At Laurence's suggestion, she'd also cancelled that evening's get-together. Jess would be on holiday so Connor mightn't have come anyway, and Dom and the girls could find somewhere else to hang out.

Laurence, however, *would* be coming, and she felt the warning tingle that always preceded meeting him. He'd a business lunch but should be free around four to four thirty, and had suggested she prepare a picnic supper and they drive out into the country. She decided to stop at Cribbs Causeway on the way home, have a bite of lunch, stock up with food for the picnic and perhaps take the chance of looking for some new shoes. So, having fulfilled all these intentions, it was almost three o'clock when she finally set off for home.

And, as often when she was alone, Laurence flooded into her mind and she slapped the steering wheel in frustration. Although it was now over four months since they'd met, she was still no nearer knowing him. All she did know was that there was something dangerous about him, something she couldn't put a name to but that occasionally raised the hairs on the back of her neck. He was a passionate lover, though, which added spice to her life, and for the moment she was prepared to settle for that.

Though she phrased it differently, even to herself, he had actually picked her up in a bar. She'd stopped off at a pub after a particularly difficult day, and after searching in her bag for her purse, she remembered, to her embarrassment, that she'd taken it out to pay for petrol, then slipped it into the glove compartment rather than her bag on the back seat. She was apologetically pushing the glass away from her when a voice behind her said, 'I'll get that!' and someone reached across her and put some coins on the counter.

He was tall, she noticed as he carried their glasses to a table, with a broad back and rugby-player's shoulders. Good looking, though not really her type. However, the least she could do in the circumstances was have a drink with him.

'Laurence Pope,' he said by way of introduction, reaching a large hand across the table.

'Maggie Haig,' she replied, taking it and feeling it almost crush her own. 'This is very kind of you,' she continued quickly, aware of his assessing black eyes.

'My pleasure.' He had an attractive speaking voice, which for some reason surprised her.

'I'm not usually so scatter-brained, but it's been one of those weeks!'

He smiled. 'Tell me about it! Office job?'

'No; well, not quite. I run a garden design business but with a garden centre attached, and that's what has run me off my feet this week.'

'Peak season, I suppose?'

'Yes.' Anxious to put an end to this small talk and get home, she finished her drink as quickly as politeness allowed and reached for her bag.

'So thank you again!' she said brightly, getting to her feet. 'Your good deed for the day!'

'I'd like to see you again, Maggie Haig,' he said.

And that was how it started. They went to bed the second time they met, and that was when she realized that, although enjoying a challenge, she was in danger of getting out of her depth. Accepting that she'd feel happier meeting him when other people were around, at least until she knew him better, she invited him to join the group that had gradually come together over the last year or so. Safety in numbers, she'd thought, without analysing the sentiment.

Back at the flat she parked in the basement car park, gathered her shopping together and went up in the lift. She wouldn't be much ahead of him, she realized; just time for a quick shower before putting the picnic together. The day had clouded over but there was little chance of rain.

Showered and changed but with her hair still wet, she was putting a chilled bottle of Saumur in the hamper when the doorbell rang. He'd made good time, she thought as she went to open it.

The man standing in front of her was the last one on earth she expected to see.

'Hello, Mel!' he said, and quickly put a hand on the door to prevent her instinctively closing it.

She moistened suddenly dry lips. 'Hello, Bruce.'

'Well, the least you can do after all this time is invite me in.'

'It's . . . not really convenient,' she began. 'I'm expecting someone and we're going straight out.'

He pushed her to one side and went ahead of her into the flat, where he stood looking about him.

'Done all right for yourself,' he commented. 'But then that was always your aim in life, wasn't it? Whoever else got hurt in the process.'

'Bruce, I really don't—'

'I thought you might be interested to hear how your vindictive little act of revenge played out. Incidentally, how much did they pay you for that package of spite?'

'They didn't, I just—' She broke off. 'How – how did you find me?'

He gave a harsh laugh. 'Don't flatter yourself that I've spent the last three years looking for you, because I haven't. I was over here on business and extended the trip to take in a couple of weeks' holiday. And lo and behold, who should I see being interviewed on TV but someone called Maggie Haig – same initials, that's clever – who, despite a change of hair colour, was all too horribly familiar. And since you apparently had a garden centre in Bristol, I thought I'd look you up to see what you had to say for yourself.'

'But – how did you find me *here*?'

'Followed you back, didn't I? Admittedly you led me quite a dance. I lost you a couple of times in the mall. Anyway, as I was saying, I thought you might be interested to hear the amount of havoc you caused. Vitriol in the press, clients leaving in droves, business on the brink of collapse and my marriage breaking down. That's just for starters.'

'Bruce, I'm sorry. I just—'

'Oh, you're sorry! That makes it all OK, then.'

Her temper rose to meet his. 'Well, it was all true, wasn't it? You brought it on yourself! As for your marriage, it's a wonder Sonia stayed with you as long as she did!'

His mouth tightened. 'Purely as a matter of interest, what straw broke the camel's back, so to speak?'

She bit her lip, remembering the hurt. 'Your giving Madeleine Connaught my bracelet.'

He raised his eyebrows mockingly. 'All that destruction over a trinket? And I certainly don't recall it being *your* bracelet.'

He knew perfectly well what she meant, and she wasn't going to argue with him.

'I'd like you to go now, please,' she said, steadying her voice.

'Oh, you would? Well, I've not finished with you yet, madam! I reckon you owe me several thousand dollars, at a conservative estimate—'

Her temper flared again. 'I owe you *nothing*! Your business trebled in value during the time I was with you! And after the way you treated me—'

'*I* treated *you*? That's rich! You betrayed something I told you in confidence, that no one else knew, and it almost destroyed me!'

'Then I hope you were more careful in your pillow talk with Madeleine!'

He seized her arm, pulling her towards him, his furious face inches from hers. 'You scheming little bitch! I—'

'What the *hell* is going on?' Laurence! she thought. Thank God! 'Get your hands off her, you bastard!'

'Be careful who you call a bastard, sonny!' Bruce flung over his shoulder.

'I said get your hands off her!'

'When I'm good and ready! And a word of warning, mate. If she's with you, you want to watch your step or she'll stick a knife in when you least expect it!'

'Talking of knives!'

They both glanced at him, and to her horror Maggie saw that he'd produced the pocket knife she'd often seen him use to slice apples, open letters, cut string.

'For God's sake, Laurence! Put it away!'

'"When I'm good and ready!"' he replied through gritted teeth. 'Wasn't that the phrase? Now, step away from her before I make you!'

Bruce gave a laugh, turning to face him. 'Are you threatening me, you arrogant Pommy bastard?'

It was over in seconds. Laurence lunged, Maggie screamed and Bruce, a look of surprise on his face, fell backwards to the floor. Maggie dropped to her knees beside him, feeling frantically for a pulse.

'Ring for an ambulance!' she cried. 'Quickly, Laurence, for God's sake.'

She turned, looking up at him urgently, saw he was breathing heavily, with an oddly triumphant look on his face. 'No point,' he said. 'He's a goner!'

'No, he can't be!' She began frantically to try to resuscitate him while Laurence stood impassively watching her until, realizing the futility of it, she sat back on her heels. 'Oh my God,' she said, 'what have we done?'

She began to shake. Laurence helped her to her feet, settled her in a chair and poured a glass of whisky for them both. She kept convulsively replaying the last few minutes in her head. This couldn't have happened! It just couldn't! It was an effort to keep her eyes averted from the still form on the carpet.

A random thought struck her. 'How did you get in?' she asked dully.

'One of you had left the door on the latch. Never mind that, though. Our first priority is to get him out of here.'

She looked at him blankly. 'We have to call the police. I'll explain—'

'No way! No police!'

'But Laurence, we have to! How else—'

'I said no police! Do you think I want to spend the next ten years or so behind bars?'

'But surely you wouldn't have to! You came to my rescue, as you saw it!'

'*They* wouldn't see it that way. Who the hell is he, anyway?'

'Someone I knew in Australia. But you didn't have to kill him!'

'See? If that's what you think, what do you imagine the police will make of it? Now shut up and listen: if I move my car right up against the lift, with luck we can tip him into it without anyone noticing.'

She looked at him in horror. 'We?'

'I know I'm pretty strong, but it would be a hell of a lot easier with help. Between us we can get him upright and walk him into the lift. If anyone sees us they'll assume he's either drunk or stoned.'

She stared at him speechlessly as he carried the two empty glasses back to the kitchen.

'I'll go and move it now, before the office crowd spill out. You can—'

She stood up quickly. 'I'm coming with you! I'm not staying here with . . . with him!'

'Right, come on then.'

They left the flat together. 'And this time,' Laurence said, 'I'll make sure the door's properly shut.'

It was a continuing nightmare. As the car park was private to residents of the flats it was relatively quiet and they'd been able to park Laurence's car right alongside the lift. Back in the flat Laurence managed after a struggle to heave Bruce first into a sitting position, then, with Maggie's reluctant help, to his feet.

'I think I'm going to be sick,' she whispered.

'Not now, you're not,' Laurence said grimly. 'Open the door quickly, while I balance him, and once we're through, pull it shut behind us and ring for the lift. And pray no one comes up in it.'

His unholy prayers were answered. The empty lift arrived and they staggered into it with Bruce between them. Their luck held in the car park. Only two cars had arrived in their absence, and they were at the far end. Laurence opened the boot and between them they managed to manoeuvre the body inside, bending Bruce's long legs to enable them to close it as Maggie again struggled with nausea.

'Get in!' Laurence ordered, opening the passenger door.

'Where are we going?'

'God knows, just away from here.'

He started the engine and they emerged from the basement car park into the heavy rush-hour traffic. Everything looked so unbelievably normal.

'You said you knew him in Oz; were you living together?'

'No, but we were an item.'

'So what did you do to make him react like this?'

She was silent for a moment. Then she said slowly, 'I informed the press about something he'd told me in private, which hit the headlines. It apparently had far-reaching effects.'

'What kind of something?'

'Something underhand he'd done at the start of his career, which helped him launch his business. It wasn't illegal, but it wasn't ethical either and it involved betraying the trust of a friend. So you could say he was hoist with his own petard.'

She wiped her eyes. 'I've regretted it since; it was an act of petty revenge because he was dumping me, but in the heat of the moment I'd not thought it through. I wanted to hurt him, but I hadn't meant it to ruin his life. I tried to apologize just now, but he wouldn't let me.'

'Will he be missed, do you suppose? I mean, does he live here nowadays?'

'No, he said he was over on business.'

'Good, that gives us a margin, then.'

Maggie had started to shake again. Pictures of herself and Bruce in happier days kept drifting into her head and she began to cry softly.

'For God's sake!' Laurence said impatiently. 'He was attacking you, wasn't he?'

'He still didn't deserve that!' she whispered.

'Well, he got it.'

It struck her how totally unrepentant he was, with no sign of regret for the unknown man whose life he'd snuffed out. On the contrary, he was enjoying the challenge of planning their next move.

They drove for about an hour.

Laurence broke a lengthy silence. 'Our best bet is to throw him into the sea. I know a place where there are steep cliffs and you can drive quite a way up. I'll check on my phone but I think high tide's around midnight. With luck the currents

will carry him a long way out and we'll never hear of him
again.'

Maggie shuddered. 'Someone might see us.'

'Not if we wait till dark. We'll park somewhere till it's safe
to go on and in the meantime you can show me how grateful
you are that I rescued you.'

'*No!*' she said convulsively.

'Oh, yes,' he contradicted, a smile in his voice.

And later, having parked in a layby in a country lane, they
climbed a gate into a field and, hating herself but unable to
resist, she perforce lay down with him in the grass.

The final part was the hardest. Bruce's limbs had begun to
stiffen and it was no easy task to disentangle his arms and
legs from the confines of the boot and stagger with him up
the rocky uneven hillside in the dark. Sweating and struggling,
they finally reached the top and with one last, muscle-straining
heave managed to tip him over the cliff edge. After what
seemed a lifetime, there was a loud splash from far below.

They barely spoke on the long drive home. Laurence put
the radio on and Maggie, emotionally exhausted, eventually
fell asleep. Which was as well, since it was the only sleep she
had that night. He dropped her outside the block of flats and,
unable to face the lift and the memories it held, she stumbled,
still half asleep, up the stairs and into the flat, just managing
to reach the bathroom before she was violently sick.

And that was the pattern for what remained of the night.
She'd lie shivering in her bed until another wave of sickness
claimed her and she'd stumble back to the bathroom. She lost
count of how many nocturnal trips she made, and in the
morning she was white-faced and shaky. Thank God it was
Saturday. She emailed the group, giving a stomach upset as
the reason for cancelling their meeting that night, and went
back to bed.

Monday evening. Maggie let herself into the flat, pushed the
door shut behind her and leaned against it, steeling herself not
to look at the floor where, she knew, that image would still
be imprinted. Or perhaps it was branded on her retinas and

would appear on whatever flooring she glanced at. This should never have happened; she still couldn't believe it had. How could things have gone so impossibly wrong?

She shuddered, pushed herself away from the door and went to pour a glass of whisky. Still nothing on the news. Suppose he was never found, that the strong tides had carried him far out to sea and he'd quite literally sunk without trace? If that could happen, she'd live like a saint for the rest of her life out of sheer gratitude. But even if he remained five fathoms deep, she reminded herself grimly, there was Laurence to contend with, and she'd not even begun to think about how to handle that.

It had been a totally nightmarish weekend; she'd cancelled all arrangements, pleading the ongoing stomach upset, but someone was sure to drop in this evening. For the first time she regretted her policy of open house. Suppose she broke down in front of them? It had taken all her control to behave normally at work and the effort had drained the last of her strength. Everywhere she went – at the centre, in the super-market, even in the street – she'd imagined people looking at her, as though they knew what had happened. That way, as she well knew, madness lay.

Restlessly, glass in hand, she walked through to her bedroom, glancing into Jess's as she passed and noting that she'd forgotten to take the book she'd been reading. Just as well she was away, Maggie reflected thankfully; she'd woken herself screaming last night, which would have taken a bit of explaining. Oh God, if only she could turn the clock back! But how far? Three days? Or six years? At what point had it all been set in motion?

She leaned forward to study her face in the mirror. Pale, but some blusher would help, and the darkness under her eyes could be camouflaged. Her hair at least needed no remedial treatment, falling sleek, brown and shiny to her shoulders. How long since she'd been blonde?

She straightened, shaking her head at herself. The past was past and must remain so – especially the most recent past. She had about an hour in which to disguise any signs of strain, and the sooner she made a start the better. Finishing her drink, she set to work.

SEVENTEEN

Patrick phoned that evening.

'How did it go? Did Tasha's statement do the trick?'

'Unfortunately not; with no evidence to back it up, it's just hearsay.'

He swore. 'God, you'd think they'd be grateful to her! They're doing damn all themselves!'

'Actually, they are doing something,' Jess told him.

'Oh? What?'

'They'll be making a move soon.'

'Did they tell you that? When?'

'I can't say any more, Patrick. Please don't ask me.'

'But damn it, Jess, you're in *danger*! They're not going to use you as a decoy or something bloody stupid, are they?'

'No, of course not,' she said, wondering whether in fact that was exactly what she'd be.

'Did you say anything to Connor?'

'No.'

He gave an impatient exclamation. 'So he won't be ready to help you if it backfires!'

Jess moistened her lips. She regretted now not having taken Connor into her confidence, particularly as they'd become closer at the weekend, but DS Stuart had been adamant. And now another deception lay ahead of her.

'Don't worry, Patrick,' she said quickly, 'I have to go now, but I'll keep in touch.' And she rang off.

Di and Dominic did not join them that evening, but the others met in one of their favourite restaurants.

'We've got someone new at the office this week,' Jess remarked casually, taking a poppadom from the communal plate on the table. 'He's a bit lost, not knowing anyone yet, and it's bound to be worse at the weekends. I wondered if perhaps I could invite him round on Saturday?'

'Well, it's open house, as you know,' Maggie replied. 'Bring him along by all means.'

'Hey, what is this?' Connor asked jokingly. 'Should I be jealous?'

'Of course not! I'm sorry for him, that's all.'

'Is he good looking?' Sarah enquired, spearing a bhaji.

Jess smiled. 'Reasonably, except for the bump on his nose!'

'Occasioned by a jealous husband, no doubt!' Laurence put in.

'What's his name?'

'Dan. Dan Crowther.'

'Time we had some new blood!' Maggie observed. 'No one's joined us since you came!'

Jess sat back with a small sigh of relief. The seed was sown.

Justin had spent the two most miserable days of his life. He must have been out of his mind for the last three months, behaving like a randy schoolboy instead of a respected member of the legal profession. Midlife crisis, he thought gloomily. He'd always looked forward to going home at the end of the day, but now the house was unbearably empty; it had simply ceased to be a home. His whole life had revolved round Kathryn, he acknowledged belatedly – her calm presence, the seamless efficiency with which she ran their home, the personal traits that made her so essentially herself – and now his greatest fear was not being able to entice her back.

God, what would he do without her? He'd been used to registering some interesting fact during the day and thinking, I must tell Kathryn that! Or a problem would arise which he'd look forward to discussing with her. Her quick, academic brain frequently solved a point that had been troubling him, and she in turn discussed her work with him. They'd often analyse a book they'd just read, or a television programme. Why in the name of heaven had he thrown all that away for a few romps in an illicit bed?

He'd tried several times to contact her over the last couple of days, but his calls were always declined. He'd even tried Anne's number, hoping to persuade her to plead on his behalf, but it had gone straight to voicemail.

He stood up restlessly and walked to the window, staring out at the summer afternoon, but the bright sunshine exacerbated rather than exorcized his depression. He returned to his chair and sat staring sightlessly at his computer.

There was a tap on the door and, without waiting for an invitation, Patrick came in, closing it behind him.

'What's the matter, Dad?' he asked quietly.

Justin felt a surge of gratitude; he'd been expecting a caustic comment, a smug *I told you so!* Instead, his son was concerned for him.

'I've been a bloody fool, Patrick.'

'I know.'

'I've no excuses. I went into it with my eyes open, fully aware my career would be jeopardized if it became common knowledge. How could I have been so insane?'

Patrick seated himself in front of the desk. 'Did you love her?' he asked.

Justin snorted. 'Of course not! I *liked* her, very much, and more dangerously I found her extremely attractive. Forbidden fruit, I suppose.'

Patrick was silent, remembering the unremarkable woman in the restaurant.

'And now?' he prompted after a minute.

'And now I've got my just desserts. Hilary's off to the States on an extended visit to her son and, far more importantly, your mother's gone to Kendal to stay with Anne.'

Patrick's eyes widened. 'Mum's left home?'

'In a manner of speaking. God, Patrick, what have I done?'

'When was this?'

'Monday. She wasn't there when I got home.'

'Have you spoken to her?'

'She's declining all calls. She left a note asking me not to contact her, said we needed time apart till things became clearer.'

'And you've just accepted that?'

Justin stared at him. 'What do you mean?'

'You're just going to sit here meekly at your desk until she allows you to speak to her?'

Justin frowned. 'I'm giving her what she asked for. It's the least I can do.'

Patrick shook his head despairingly. 'You don't know much about women, do you, Dad?'

This, Justin felt, was a reversal of the usual father and son talk. 'And what,' he asked a little aggressively, 'do you, with your infinite knowledge of them, suggest I should do?'

'Go after her, of course! Now!'

'But—'

'It can't be much more than a four-hour drive, and motorway all the way.'

'Patrick, I—' He broke off, then substituted, 'Suppose when I get there she refuses to see me?'

'At least she'll know you care enough to have tried!'

Justin flushed. 'I hadn't thought of that.'

'So collect your toothbrush from home, and go! I'll cover for you here.'

He hesitated a moment longer. Then, with a decisive movement, he pushed back his chair and stood up.

'You're right, Patrick. Thanks.' And with a pat on his son's back he hurried from the room.

The closer they came to the weekend, the more nervous Jess became. Suppose something went wrong? Suppose no one reacted guiltily when she related what she'd seen? Ben would be powerless to do anything, but Laurence would doubtless come after her later. Or suppose he did react, and attacked her before Ben could intervene? On the other hand, she might have been mistaken all along and neither Maggie nor Laurence had anything to do with the murder. In which case, who had?

The various scenarios circled endlessly in her head, interrupting her sleep and adding to her stress during the day. Several times she'd been on the point of pulling out and telling DS Stuart the police would have to manage without her. After all, they had her signed statement to act on.

Illogically, her family being thousands of miles away added to her vulnerability, though how their being at St Cat's would have made her any safer she couldn't explain. Even Patrick was fifty miles away.

Connor noticed her jitteriness when they met for lunch on Thursday. 'Anything wrong, Jess? You seem a bit jumpy!'

'No, I'm fine. A slight headache, that's all.'

'Have you taken something for it?'

'No, I'm OK, really.'

He didn't look convinced. 'You'd tell me if anything was wrong, wouldn't you?'

'Just give me a hug!' she said unsteadily, and as his arms came round her she reassured herself that at least he would be there at the confrontation. How the rest of the group would react she'd no idea.

DS Stuart had also been reviewing the situation. He knew he was taking a gamble, but despite extensive enquiries the last month had thrown up no leads; the top brass were getting restive and the press more and more strident. Although none of the names Jess had given him showed up on any database, her account certainly gave grounds for action, and the DI had okayed the plan. Ridley was a good officer and Stuart had every confidence in him keeping Jess safe. And if the worst came to the worst, back-up would be just round the corner. Nonetheless, he admitted to himself that he would be relieved when Saturday's encounter was over.

Anne Glover was three years older than Kathryn. She had married a farmer and their three sons, all of whom were married, worked with their father on the farm. Since they each had a house within its boundaries, the complex was like a miniature village. Patrick and Amy had loved holidays spent there when they were young.

His eyes on the M6 stretching ahead of him, Justin wondered what cover story Anne had given her family, sincerely hoping his transgressions weren't common knowledge. He'd spent most of the journey rehearsing his abject apology and was still not satisfied with it. However he phrased it, it seemed to imply that he wanted Kathryn back because he didn't like being alone in the house and having to fend for himself. He didn't, but that only accounted for a small percentage of the sense of loss he was experiencing.

And here was his exit. His heartbeat accelerating, he moved on to the slip road and within fifteen minutes the gates of Mulberry Farm came into view. He got out of the car, opened them, drove through and closed them again behind him. Then he slowly drove the remaining hundred and forty metres to the farmhouse itself, where he parked well to one side to avoid blocking access.

Aware that according to farm etiquette the back door was the main entrance, he made his way round the house and, steeling himself, knocked on it. A voice from inside called, 'What on earth are you knocking for? Come in, for heaven's sake, my hands are covered in flour!'

Even with his nerves jangling, Justin had to smile. He obediently opened the door and stepped into the large, stone-flagged kitchen. Anne, her hands in a bowl, turned towards the door – and went suddenly still.

'Justin!'

'Hello, Anne. I've come to see Kathryn.'

She flushed. 'I really don't think—'

'Look, I'm sorry you've been brought into this, but the only way we can settle it is face to face. Is she in?'

Anne still hesitated.

He sighed. 'I might as well tell you I shan't be leaving until I've spoken to her. Where is she?'

'In the sitting room, but perhaps I should—'

'Warn her? No need.'

And leaving her gazing after him he went quickly into the hall, stopping when he reached the door to the sitting room, which was ajar. With a silent prayer to whichever gods might be listening, he pushed it open.

She was standing by the fireplace flicking through the pages of a magazine, and looked up as he entered the room. Across it their eyes met and held. She'd been expecting her cousin with the promised cup of tea, and was totally unprepared both for the sight of her husband and for the wealth of emotion that swept over her on seeing him. She'd been missing him far more than she'd anticipated, and had tortured

herself by wondering whether she'd done the right thing.
Suppose he was relieved to find her gone and made no effort
to bring her back? Despite the pain and anger, the last month
or two had left her in no doubt as to how much she loved
him – perhaps that was why it had hurt so much.

And Justin, watching her standing there motionless, forgot
all the carefully chosen words he'd been rehearsing for the
last four and a half hours.

'Kathryn!' he said softly. 'Oh, Kathryn!'

He moved slowly towards her, their eyes still locked
together, and as he reached her she let the magazine drop
on to the coffee table and lifted both hands to cup his face.

'You came,' she said. And suddenly the pleasantly modu-
lated kisses that had characterized their marriage were no
longer enough. She pulled his face down to hers and started
to kiss him with an urgency that was altogether new to her,
feeling his arms crush her against him as he responded.

Five minutes later Anne appeared in the doorway with two
mugs of tea, glanced into the room and, after a moment, went
away again.

Jess had been wondering with increasing anxiety how she
could avoid spending Saturday with Connor, since he obviously couldn't be with her when she met Ben – or Dan, as
she must now think of him. But on Thursday evening, greatly
to her relief, he told her his mother had asked him to do a
few jobs for her at the weekend.

'So we'll have to postpone our planned walk till Sunday,
I'm afraid, but of course I'll be here in the evening. For one
thing, I'll need to keep an eye on this guy you're bringing
along!'

It gave Jess the perfect opening. 'In that case I'll take the
opportunity to go to St Cat's, check on the house while
the family's away and meet some friends for lunch, which I
didn't have time to do on my last few visits. And,' she added
teasingly, 'be back in time to introduce you to Dan!'

Then at last it was Saturday, and she was sick with apprehension. She'd barely slept the previous night, endlessly going

over possible outcomes, none of which seemed even remotely satisfactory.

Surely she couldn't be wrong? Maggie had known Bruce Marriott in Oz. He'd ended up dead on her carpet. How could that possibly be coincidence? Then again, how would the rest of them react? With the exception of Connor they were, after all, Maggie's friends rather than hers. Would they unite against her to defend Maggie? And what exactly could Ben Ridley do before back-up arrived, one man against the rest? It was as well she had the trip to St Cat's to take her mind off things.

And it did precisely that. It was only about a fifteen-minute train journey and she took a taxi from the station. The house felt strange with no one at home, even Minty, who was boarding at his cattery. There was a neat pile of mail on the hall table, dutifully collected by the neighbour who was officially keeping an eye on the house. Jess gathered that her grandmother had offered, but been told they didn't want to trouble her. She guessed her father had put his foot down, aware that Gran wouldn't be above sneaking the odd glance in a drawer or cupboard.

The usual Saturday crowd was at the tennis club – though not, Jess was relieved to note, Roger, who must be on call. She was able to catch up with a group of friends who were glad to see her and hear how she was enjoying life in Bristol – a question that today of all days needed a carefully edited reply. Several of them went on to lunch, a long-drawn-out affair that melded first into tea and then drinks in someone's garden, after which she was driven to the station to catch the train back to Bristol. Her brief escape was over and acute anxiety reclaimed her. At least, one way or another, it would soon be over.

As arranged, Ben was waiting for her outside the office and gave her a reassuring smile as she approached, his eyes raking her face.

'OK?'

'Not really!'

'Don't worry, it'll be fine. It's very good of you to help like this; it's the first glimmer of hope we've had since the beginning of the investigation.'

'Suppose I mess it up somehow? Say the wrong thing, or at the wrong time?'

'Would it help if I gave you a lead-in, to make the subject come up more naturally?'

She nodded gratefully. 'Yes, I think it would.' He was the police, she reminded herself, and he'd be with her throughout.

'Any suggestions?'

She tried to think as they waited on the kerb for the traffic lights to change but her mind had gone blank. This was the journey home she'd made every working day for the last few months, yet she felt strangely distanced, as though watching herself from a great height.

'You said you'd been about to go on holiday when it all blew up?' Ben prompted.

'Yes.' She moistened her lips, trying to focus.

'Where did you go?'

'Italy. Pisa.' How long ago it all seemed!

'Well, suppose I say I saw a postcard you'd sent the office pinned up on a notice board, and ask how you enjoyed it?'

'That would be great, thanks!'

'Look.' His voice was gentle. 'You must relax or they'll realize something's wrong.'

'Yes, I know. I'm sorry.'

'Don't be; you're being very brave.'

She gave him a tight smile. 'That's what's worrying me!' she said.

'So let's recap: I only arrived in Bristol this week, having transferred from the Oxford branch. I've checked out the firm, incidentally, so if anyone's interested enough to ask questions – which I doubt they will be – I can answer convincingly. I'm unmarried – not sure what my wife will make of that! – but have a girlfriend, Lois, who I hope will be able to join me here soon.'

Jess nodded distractedly.

'We don't know each other well, obviously, so it won't seem strange if either of us makes a mistake or doesn't know something about the other. But I do need a few facts about the flat. Is the front door the only way in or out?'

'Yes.'

'Apart from the fire escape, presumably?'

'Oh yes, I'd forgotten about that. I think you access it from Maggie's bedroom, but I've never seen it.'

She expected a reprimand on safety grounds, but he only asked, 'How many rooms are there?'

'Just the two bedrooms, the main sitting room and the kitchenette through an archway.'

'OK, now tell me what form this evening's likely to take. Until we throw a spanner in the works, that is.'

Jess tried to anchor her thoughts. 'Well, as I said they drift in in ones and twos any time between seven thirty and eight and we drink and chat until the takeaway arrives about eight thirty.'

'OK. Go through the group again for me.'

She did so.

'So it's Maggie and Laurence, and Dominic and Di, as couples. Which leaves Sarah and Connor unattached?'

Jess flushed. 'Actually, Connor and I have started seeing each other.'

'Ah! Sorry! And the others know?'

'Oh yes.' She stopped and drew a deep breath. 'And here we are: Sussex Court.' She could have wished their walk had been twice as long.

They went into the building and up in the lift and as they approached Flat 5 they could hear laughter coming from inside. Perfect timing, Jess thought. Please let Connor be there!

She put her key in the lock and gave Ben one last shaky smile. 'Good luck!' she said.

It all seemed so normal; apart from Ben's presence this scene had been replayed almost every Saturday for as long as she could remember. She'd been pleasantly surprised by the ease with which he fitted into the group – even Connor relaxed in his presence. He was an easy conversationalist and they'd accepted him without question. Jess even felt slightly guilty for having introduced a Trojan horse into their midst.

She'd been letting the various conversations wash over her when she suddenly became aware they were discussing holidays. And as she registered the fact with a jolt of apprehension she heard Ben say, 'You went to Italy this year, didn't you, Jess?'

Her fingernails dug into her palms and she forced herself to speak past the sudden lump in her throat. 'Yes; how did you know?'

'The postcard you sent the office is pinned up on the board. Pisa, wasn't it?' He smiled. 'Did it make you queasy, going up that tower?'

The rest of them, having heard about her holiday, continued to talk quietly among themselves.

Jess raised her voice slightly. 'Not nearly as queasy as I'd felt here.'

'How do you mean?'

'The day I left I came back after work to collect my paperback, and had a terrific shock.'

Conversation around her stopped as they registered the change in her voice.

'And?' Di asked, leaning forward to take a handful of peanuts.

Jess was pulsatingly aware of the whiteness of Maggie's knuckles as her grip tightened on her glass. She didn't dare look in Laurence's direction.

'Well?' Di again. 'Don't keep us in suspense! What "terrific shock"?'

This was it. The moment had arrived. Jess said clearly, 'There was a body lying here on the floor.'

There was complete silence. Then someone – Sarah, perhaps – gave a nervous laugh.

Connor said uncertainly, 'Jess?'

Laurence stood up suddenly and she tried not to flinch. 'Enough of this nonsense. Anyone for another drink before the food arrives?'

Jess said loudly, 'I didn't know who he was, but I do now.

It was the Australian who's been in all the papers – Bruce Marriott!'

Laurence's hand, reaching for his glass, briefly froze.

Dominic said mildly, 'If that's a joke, Jess, it's in pretty poor taste.'

They were all staring at her now. 'It's not a joke,' she said.

Connor said again, 'Jess?', anxiety strident in his voice.

Di's tone had changed. 'So what did you do?' she asked.

Jess moistened her lips. 'I hadn't time to do anything. I was still staring at him when I heard voices outside.'

'I said that's enough, Jess!' There was a new note in Laurence's voice too, one that raised the hairs on the back of her neck. 'I don't know what you think you're playing at, but it's gone beyond a joke.'

Before her courage failed, she abruptly changed tactics. 'You knew him in Australia, didn't you, Maggie?'

Someone gasped.

'Didn't you hear me?' Laurence grated. 'I said that's enough!'

But the damage had been done. Everyone's attention now switched to Maggie and Jess watched dispassionately as the colour drained from her face.

'*Did* you, Maggie?' Di again. 'Know him, I mean?'

'Look what you've done, you little devil!' Laurence hissed, his hand closing forcefully over Jess's.

Connor came to his feet. 'Let go of her!' he said sharply. 'Can't you see you're hurting her?'

Laurence ignored him and Dominic switched back to Jess's first bombshell. 'So what did you do, Jess? No' – as Laurence moved threateningly – 'let her go on, we can't leave it there! There were voices outside, you said. Did someone come into the flat?'

Jess, trying to blot out the pain in her hand, nodded dumbly. Ben must have slipped out of the room at some stage, because from the corner of her eye she saw him re-emerge from the corridor.

Everyone spoke at once. 'Who was it?'

Suddenly, viciously, Laurence jerked her to her feet. 'Get your bag, Maggie,' he said over his shoulder, 'and make sure your passport's in it. No time for anything else. Go!'

He thought she could identify them! Jess thought incoherently.

Maggie sat frozen in her chair, her wide eyes on the tableau unfolding before her.

'*Maggie!*'

'No,' she whispered. 'No, Laurence, I can't!'

'Do as I say! We've prepared for this eventuality – Plan B! Everyone else sit down and don't move, or Jess gets it!'

And suddenly, unbelievingly, she felt the point of a knife at her throat. Someone screamed and amid the sudden chaos Ben's voice rang out.

'Police! DS Ridley. Put the knife down! *Now!*'

'Not before I slit her throat!' Laurence said through clenched teeth.

Connor started forward and Laurence immediately increased the pressure so that a small bead of blood appeared on Jess's neck. Everyone was on their feet now, Di clutching Dominic's arm.

'I said *put your knife down!*'

But Ben's last word was lost as the door crashed back on its hinges and four men burst into the room. 'Armed police! Drop your weapon!'

Caught completely off guard, Laurence hesitated – and in the same moment a strong arm pulled Jess away from him. Connor reached for her and she buried her face in his shirt while two men wrestled Laurence to the ground, handcuffing his wrists behind him.

Maggie had started out of her chair and turned towards the passage but Ben stepped forward to block her path, nodding to one of the men, who seized her wrists and handcuffed them. Laurence was dragged to his feet, and in a sudden silence Ben stepped forward.

'Laurence Pope and Maggie Haig, I'm arresting you on suspicion of the murder of Bruce Marriott on or around the twenty-first of June. You do not have to say anything, but it may harm your defence if you do not mention when questioned something you later rely on in court. Anything you do say may be given in evidence.'

He nodded to the men, who escorted their still-resisting

prisoners out of the flat, then turned back to his erstwhile companions.

'Sorry about this, but I'm afraid I must ask you for contact details – names, addresses and phone numbers. We'll need to speak to you later.'

As they searched in their wallets for business cards he turned to Jess. 'You did brilliantly. Are you OK?'

Connor's arm still round her, she nodded – then jumped as the intercom buzzed.

Sarah spoke into it. 'Supper on the way up,' she told them.

'That's a point,' Connor said. 'How did your men get into the building?'

'Fortunately they arrived as someone was leaving, and I'd unlatched this door while you were all arguing.'

Dominic cleared his throat. 'What will happen to them now?'

'They'll be held in cells until they're brought before the magistrates on Monday.'

'They won't be released on bail?' Sarah asked, sudden fear in her voice.

'Not a chance of that.'

A knock on the door interrupted them, and Ben, who was nearest, opened it.

'Delivery for Haig,' said a voice.

Dominic came forward to take the carrier bags.

'Will you join us?' he asked Ben. 'We'll have two extra portions now!'

'That's good of you, but I'm still on duty and it's time I was getting back to the station.' He turned to Jess. 'I'll be in touch tomorrow. Thanks, everyone.' And he was gone.

Rather to their surprise, they found they were ravenously hungry. The usual selection of dishes had never tasted so good, and as they ate they plied Jess with questions, unable to take in the magnitude of what they'd just learned.

'How could you have gone through all that without telling me?' Connor demanded. 'I knew there was something wrong! I even asked if you were OK!'

'I know, I wanted to tell you, but by that stage I'd been told not to discuss it with anyone.'

'How did you find out about Maggie knowing that man?' Sarah asked, and Jess related the meeting with Tasha at the theatre.

'It was a pure fluke and Maggie's bad luck,' she ended. 'She must have recognized Tasha too – once seen she's not easily forgotten – but she managed to hide it very well.'

'I just can't believe it!' Di said for about the tenth time. 'Had she and this Marriott kept in touch? If not, how did he find her? And if they had, why did she kill him? Or do you think it was Laurence?'

'We'll probably never know,' Dominic said.

'I feel a bit guilty,' Jess confessed, 'first for having shopped Maggie, and second for breaking up the group. None of you will want to see me ever again, added to which I've no idea what's going to happen about the flat. I suppose it's up to the landlord.'

'Of course we'll all keep in touch,' Dominic said. 'I can't say I'd ever had much time for Laurence, but to give Maggie her due she helped us all over a rough patch and I for one am grateful. Stay on here if you can, Jess, and look for a new flatmate. Preferably one who isn't a murderer!'

Jess smiled, feeling Connor's hand tighten on hers. 'I'll do my best!' she said.